Postapocalyptic Fiction
and the Social Contract

Postapocalyptic Fiction and the Social Contract

"We'll Not Go Home Again"

Claire P. Curtis

LEXINGTON BOOKS
A division of
ROWMAN & LITTLEFIELD PUBLISHERS, INC.
Lanham • Boulder • New York • Toronto • Plymouth, UK

Published by Lexington Books
A division of Rowman & Littlefield Publishers, Inc.
A wholly owned subsidary of The Rowman & Littlefield Publishing Group, Inc.
4501 Forbes Boulevard, Suite 200, Lanham, Maryland 20706
http://www.lexingtonbooks.com

Estover Road, Plymouth PL6 7PY, United Kingdom

British Library Cataloguing in Publication Information Available

The hardback edition of this book was previously cataloged by the Library of Congress
as follows:

Library of Congress Cataloging-in-Publication Data

Curtis, Claire P., 1965–
    Postapocalyptic fiction and the social contract : "we'll not go home again" / Claire P.
Curtis.
        p. cm.
    Includes bibliographical references and index.
    1. Apocalypse in literature. 2. Science fiction, American--History and criticism.
3. Science fiction—History and criticism. 4. End of the world in literature.
5. Regression (Civilization) in literature. 6. Survival in literature. 7. Literature and
society—History—20th century. I. Title.
    PS374.A65C87 2010
    813'.087620938—dc22

                                                                                2010016279

ISBN 978-0-7391-4203-5 (cloth : alk. paper)
ISBN 978-0-7391-7648-1 (pbk. : alk. paper)
ISBN 978-0-7391-4205-9 (electronic)

∞™ The paper used in this publication meets the minimum requirements of
American National Standard for Information Sciences—Permanence of Paper for
Printed Library Materials, ANSI/NISO Z39.48-1992.

Printed in the United States of America

For Nina and Adam

~

Contents

~

Acknowledgments

The first draft of this book was written while on sabbatical from the College of Charleston. I received further grant support through the College to help with completing the manuscript. I thank the Department of Political Science and the College of Charleston for supporting my research. I received many helpful comments from the initial reader's review from Lexington Books. This book would never have come into being were it not for the dedication of my fellow writing group members, Alison Piepmeier and Conseula Francis. Their willingness to read multiple drafts of each chapter helped to focus my argument and made this project come to life. We have had many conversations about who is willing to head out on the road ahead of impending disaster and who is ready to walk towards the tidal wave. Those conversations sustained a project that at times seemed unwieldy. Mary Glenn Keadle worked tirelessly to assist in final proofing, and indexing. Both Erin Walpole and Alden Perkins of Lexington answered numerous emails assiduously, patiently, and with good humor. My husband, Larry Krasnoff, read many of these chapters, despite his own suspicions of the genre and his unwillingness to pack spices. Writing is a largely solitary task, and it requires a mental and physical space that depends on the willing work of others. I could not have written this book without a family ready to give me space to work, meals to eat, inspiring conversation and a willingness to ponder the what if questions.

~

Introduction
Thinking the End of the World

"Come and see
Come and see
The tides will come and go
Witnessed by no waking eye
The willows mark the wind
And all we know for sure
Amidst this fading light
We'll not go home again"[1]

Lying in bed, late at night in college in the mid 1980s, I would listen to the airplanes from the Brunswick Naval Air station take off and land. The sound of what seemed to be hundreds of planes flying off on some mission always made me wonder if this was it—were the bombs coming next? And if so was there anything to be done? The TV film *The Day After*[2] premiered my freshman year in college and as quaint as it seems now I remember warnings not to watch the film alone, televisions set up in common rooms for communal watching and counselors made available for consultation with students who might be traumatized.[3]

It seems as though most of my adult life has involved contemplating the possibility for a world ending event. Every place I have lived since college (Baltimore, Nashville, Portland OR, Charleston SC) has had its own potential for world ending event—could I ride my bike faster than a tidal wave? What would be the best route to escape to the hills? Is there a safe space to be found on the I-95 corridor? (I suspect the answer to that is no.)

As a political theorist, world ending events have another interest. The apocalyptic event creates the social contract thinker's state of nature. Such events by their very character are understood to destroy functional government, food distribution, organized medical care and the infrastructure on which we rely for most of what we do. If such an event creates a state of nature, then how might we think about coming together and creating a new social contract after such an event? Postapocalyptic fiction provides a window into that imaginative possibility. These novels focus on the very idea and possibility of starting over, with all of the potential hope and utopian imaginings that starting over implies.[4]

The novels addressed in this book express a modern outlook on the end of the world and its aftermath. The adherence to the tradition of the social contract reflects an understanding of both the individual and the nature and limits of the community in which she lives. I have briefly noted that not all postapocalyptic accounts reflect this modern outlook. Some, like the *Left Behind* series, present a pre-modern outlook, whereas others use the postapocalyptic setting for postmodern explorations.[5] Postapocalyptic accounts that reflect the modern view focus on the role of individuals in the recreation of community. The novels examined here take care to emphasize that these communities are based on consent and each of these novels reflects modern political philosophy's concern with legitimacy.

The modern character of these novels matters for the way in which the novels frame the political conditions of the account. Further these political conditions are the primary ground of the novels themselves. These are novels that take up the primary query of political philosophy: the deliberation over the conditions under which we would like to live. Now the modern reading of this question focuses on the deliberation over the desirability of the conditions; pre-modern and postmodern accounts shift their emphasis away from desirability to the immutability of the conditions (pre-modern) or the uncertainty of the deliberations (postmodern).

Postapocalyptic accounts have become increasingly popular. The television show *Jericho*, depicting life in a small Kansas town after multiple nuclear bombs have exploded in major cities across the United States, was snatched back from cancellation by legions of faithful fans. Multiple films of the last 50 years have presented the visual pyrotechnics of the end.[6] The possibility of a Biblical apocalyptic event has gripped the imagination of many Christian fundamentalists with the enormously popular *Left Behind* series. And as a genre this "survivalist" fiction seems to be attaining a few marks of respectability. In 2007 the Pulitzer Prize was won by Cormac McCarthy for the postapocalyptic *The Road* (analyzed in the next chapter). Geographer James Howard Kunstler has taken his warnings about peak oil production from *The Long Emergency* and speculated about life in a small community in the northeastern United States 10 years after the crash in oil production in *The World Made by Hand*. Beyond these fictional accounts, non-fiction authors are also fascinated. Scholarly analyses of bird flu, global warming, demographic winter, rogue nuclear attacks and even the musings of Alan Weisman's haunting *The World Without Us* and popular accounts of living off the grid or trends towards survivalism,[7] the contemporary version of the backyard bomb shelter, convince me that we live in an age where thinking about the end has fully suffused the popular culture.

My interest in apocalyptic events extends beyond the simple act of destruction. Part of wondering if there was anything to be done has meant years of thinking about the aftermath—what happens when the end becomes a new beginning?[8] What might this new beginning bring? How new would it really be? Can one start over in a world burned out by nuclear war? What if the event was a large meteor, or a plague, or environmental collapse? What would we bring to a state of nature and how might we think about the social contract? Theoretically the postapocalyptic fiction I examine here takes up the movement from the state of nature to civil society. In doing so the different accounts, like their traditional social contract forebears, emphasize the basic motivations of humans and the differing ways in which we seek to live together peacefully.

This book analyzes a selection of postapocalyptic novels that focus particularly on the idea of starting over. The book moves from those accounts where there is no point to starting over, to traditional social contract reasoning, to a re-imagination of what the social contract might look like. These novels provide an opportunity to think through two key foundations to the idea of the social contract: who is it that enters into such a contract and what is it that the social contract is supposed to produce? Thus the idea of human nature and the desires that motivate human behavior are on display in these novels. This book provides an overview of the social contract theorizing of Hobbes, Locke, Rousseau and Rawls. The last two chapters focus on Octavia Butler's *Parable* series, arguing that only Butler fully confronts the fiction of the social contract in all of its possibilities. Butler, who starts from what might look to be a highly Hobbesian understanding of fear, challenges the genre of postapocalyptic fiction, she disrupts our understanding of who is to be the hero of such an account and she complicates our understanding of security, the condition for flourishing central to all social contract thinkers.

Starting over produces a radically different mindset than the mindset focused on the cataclysmic ending. Starting over always has the hope of something better; and the blank slate, which is of course not so much blank as it is largely destroyed, of the postapocalypse can open myriad possibilities. Starting over can be the instigation for utopian imagining. The conditions from which the postapocalyptic account starts over is a kind of created state of nature from which and out of which we can think anew about where we are going if "we'll not go home again." Starting itself is the premise behind the social contract thinkers' imaginings about the state of nature. The "starting" of the state of nature theorists is always a backward looking justification for the present. Postapocalyptic fiction, on the other hand, can be a forward looking imagination of what might be (both as a warning and as a utopian impulse).

The state of nature musings of Hobbes, Locke and Rousseau, produced the idea of the social contract, the centerpiece of modern political philosophy, which still informs our political thinking today: a legitimate government is one based on the consent of the governed. Theoretically the state of nature musings of Hobbes, Locke and Rousseau are less than satisfying. Dependent as they are on inaccurate understandings of the indigenous peoples of the Americas, they are also short on the details of day to day life absent the edifice of government itself. The basic human motivations emerge, but the lives behind those motivations are absent. Postapocalyptic fiction provides a spatial and bodily context for the state of nature. This book argues that the space for twenty-first-century exploration of the state of nature is found in postapocalyptic fiction.

Postapocalyptic fiction provides flesh to the usual hypothetical imaginings of the state of nature and postapocalyptic fiction is written with an eye not to the academy but to the life of the ordinary reader. First, it works out the imaginative hypothetical of social contract thinkers in rich detail, although with little analysis. While fictional, postapocalyptic novels fill in the details of the state of nature scenario. Hobbes describes what the consequences of living in the state of nature are, but he does not fully describe who lives there or what the details are of their lives. Yes, we know that the inhabitants of the state of nature fear, but without characterization, that fear is simply asserted. In teaching Hobbes I often assign Octavia Butler's short story "Speech Sounds," where humans have lost the ability to communicate, precisely because it gives a brief slice of someone's life in a Hobbesian state of nature. This allows students to understand Hobbes better, and it provides them with the tools to potentially criticize the arguments he makes about human motivations.[9] The second advantage to using postapocalyptic fiction to think through the social contract is that it is written with an eye to the reader—the life of an ordinary person on the ground. Postapocalyptic fiction is not written for an academic audience assessing the character of the state of nature and the potential contract that might emerge from it. It is written for a variety of reasons, not least of which might well be to sell books, but as a particular niche of fiction postapocalyptic fiction is often grounded in the day to day.

I contend that postapocalyptic fiction speaks both to our deepest fears and to our desire to start over again. Postapocalyptic fiction describes our fears (of science and technology, of power and incompetence, of the random and uncontrollable, of extinction and, of course, death) and like the horror genre, the catharsis of seeing total destruction either relieves that fear or awakens a need to act to prevent it. Simultaneously postapocalyptic fiction offers the fantasy of starting over. I would argue that most readers of postapocalyptic fiction think of themselves as survivors of such accounts and they read this fiction as a kind of how-to manual.[10] In speaking to our fears postapocalyptic fiction can serve the didactic purpose of warning us away from particular behaviors. Postapocalyptic fiction, as with critical utopia and dystopia[11], criticizes where we are now and who and what we might wish to be. Postapocalyptic fiction reconfigures the conditions under which humans live and demands that humans rethink their premises for peaceful living together. Postapocalyptic fiction moves humans from the state of nature through the social contract and to a new civil society.

Postapocalyptic Fiction: A Genre?

I define postapocalyptic fiction as any account that takes up how humans start over after the end of life on earth as we understand it. The apocalyptic event or events cause a radical shift in the basic conditions of human life; it does not require the destruction of all humans or even the destruction of all potential conditions of human life. The end may occur either through natural or human made causes, but divinely sanctioned ends are not discussed here. The apocalypse is a term with both a popular and a technical meaning. I use the term in its popular meaning. I am focusing on what Warren Wagar has called "secular eschatology." Popularly "apocalypse" simply refers to a disastrous, violent and catastrophic end event. Technically "apocalypse," meaning revelation, refers within the Jewish and Christian context to divine prophecy concerning the end times and the final battle between good and evil (times which are understood differently in each tradition). The *Left Behind* series is an example of a fictional account of the technical, religious use of the term.[12]

James Berger's idea of the "utterly destabilizing disaster" (22) recognizes that we need not look to fiction to consider the idea of the postapocalypse. However, I look to fiction for both the imagining of what might come and how we might begin again. Fictional postapocalyptic accounts present the useful falsehood that there is a ground—a state of nature—from which we can come together and renegotiate our lives. Octavia Butler's postapocalyptic accounts challenge the usefulness of this lie and complicate what it means to start over.

Importantly this is a study of postapocalyptic fiction where the focus is on the starting over. This is the first of a few key distinctions in the genre. Apocalyptic fiction, whether it is secular or religious, tends to focus on the event itself. This trend is clear in films where the primary focus is surviving the event, not surviving the aftermath. I am interested in accounts where the event is the causal precursor to starting over. The novels I am analyzing do more than simply outline a twentieth-century version of the pioneer novel or earlier utopian accounts of island lands discovered elsewhere. What the postapocalyptic novel does is take the social criticism inherent in the apocalyptic text and the utopian impulse of the pioneer novel and outline an origin story ironically appropriate for our current time when the frontier is absent and the possibility of catastrophe seems imminent. There is a kind of fictional realism to the postapocalyptic account because it takes us from where we are now to a place where we can easily imagine being. It then uses that space to think about *how* it is we really want to live.

I distinguish between the potentially utopian postapocalyptic accounts analyzed here and the largely religious use of the "New Jerusalem" motif where the apocalypse brings about a new life for survivors, "the New Heaven on Earth in which the saved will live eternally with God."[13] The distinction I want to make is not simply one between the religious and the secular. Rather I want to look at accounts that understand the impossibility of the New Jerusalem while still trying to bring about a human made pocket utopia. James Howard Kunstler's *The World Made by Hand* reflects in its title (although not in the novel) the kind of postapocalyptic account in which I am interested: a human construct, which recognizes, like the modern political philosopher's insistence on the artificiality of the state, that communal living and the opportunity for human flourishing, depends on human effort (Kunstler's text is itself pre-modern, however).[14]

End of the world accounts serve multiple purposes. They are both didactic and cathartic. They provide both the voyeuristic satisfaction of terrible violence and the Robinson Crusoe excitement of starting over again. For political philosophy postapocalyptic fiction provides a window into a particular understanding of the social contract. The violence and destruction of the end creates a state of nature. All hierarchies, laws and systems for organizing people have been destroyed. People are seen stripped of the restraints society has imposed upon them and these novels reveal arguments about the potential for human savagery. Yet, in the chaos of the end comes the opportunity for a new beginning. This new beginning provides a space for exploration and examination of all that we have previously taken for granted: political arrangements, gender norms, social practices. Chapters 2, 3 and 4 analyze postapocalyptic accounts that simply reify these old arrangements. Chapters 5, 6 and 7 examine Octavia Butler's radical rethinking of our expectations and provide a critical space for rethinking what it is to be human.

Postapocalyptic fiction has taken up the "what if" question by imagining ends based on nuclear war (*On the Beach, A Canticle for Leibowitz, Malevil, WarDay, The Last Ship, The Road, The Pesthouse*), meteors (*Lucifer's Hammer*), earthquakes (*The Rift, Wrinkle in the Skin*), environmental degradation (*Nature's End*), plague (*The Postman, The White Plague, The Stand*), electromagnetic pulse (*One Second After*), some of each (*Where Late the Sweet Birds Sang, Gift Upon the Shore, Oryx and Crake, The Year of the Flood*) and more nameless abstract collapses (*Into the Forest, He, She, It, Parable of the Sower,* and *Parable of the Talents*). Postapocalyptic fiction exists at a genre crossroads between science fiction, horror and utopia/dystopia. Dystopian postapocalyptic accounts can be dystopian because there is no opportunity for starting over (as in *On the Beach* and *The Road*,[15] analyzed in the next chapter) or dystopian because the apocalyptic event is largely insoluble and the life that emerges from it illustrates a critical dystopia that warns us of where we might be heading.[16]

Utopian postapocalyptic fiction uses the destruction of one world to usher in a new and potentially better one. Many postapocalyptic accounts do "conveniently" remove from society those seen to be troublemakers in the world before the event. For example, Chapters 2 and 3 show how the erasure of non-whites and the positive description of female characters who accept patriarchal gender roles act as a kind of secular cleansing. Postapocalyptic fiction can do more than simply play at a reactionary response to twentieth-century social justice movements. These accounts can also analyze the very idea of the state of nature and the kind of contract that emerges from that state: what do we fear, what do we desire, how do we plan to allay those fears and realize those desires, how can human community help us to accomplish these ends.

There is a familiar trajectory to postapocalyptic fiction, a trajectory that Octavia Butler will disrupt in her own self conscious manipulation of the postapocalyptic genre. Traditionally, the main character (typically a white male) is introduced prior to the apocalyptic event with his problems, issues, loved ones, etc. There is a reason why he is out of town or out of the way or in a safe place the day of the event, so you rarely get to see the event through his or her eyes. Instead the event is witnessed from the perspective of some minor characters who will die dramatically mid-novel. The heroic survivor then goes through a familiar series of steps. First he must reconcile his immediate survival with his need to continue to survive given the water, hailstones, radiation, earthquakes, plague, etc. In the initial movements towards survival—finding food, finding or making shelter, the survivor stumbles upon a companion—usually someone weaker (a child, or a young woman) or sometimes an equal with useful know how (a gardener or a hunter). Once the small group has been established then mere survival starts to move into long term flourishing. They start to find food not simply for one meal, but for the next season. They seek to build a shelter beyond a one night avoid-the-elements contraption. Simultaneous with this move towards long term survival and the beginning of flourishing is the first sign of danger.

Inherent in all of these accounts is the necessary Other: the groups of people who do not react so well to the cataclysm. These people, who seem to band up far more quickly than our survivors, are bent on continued destruction (despite the total irrationality of this). So roving bands of cannibals terrorizing the countryside emerges as a threat from which our pair of survivors must find escape. Escape can only be found (Hegland's *Into the Forest* is an interesting exception here) in forming a larger community. Thus the typical postapocalyptic novel uses the threat to the safety of the small collection of survivors to cement their ties and to push those survivors into a more self consciously organized system. A community is formed, one that can actually fight back against the cannibals. Thus, such postapocalyptic accounts climax in the defeat of the cannibals and end on the note of hope as the small community learns of the existence of other like minded communities across the country from which the country and humanity will rise again.[17]

This book examines many of the novels that follow this trajectory. However, I am most interested in the challenges to that traditional script, challenges that complicate the seemingly simple move from the state of nature back to civil society. In Butler's reworking of the genre we find not only a young, black female protagonist. But we also find cannibals made human and little possibility of escape through a stirring end of the novel battle. Many postapocalyptic accounts follow Hobbesian lines: the state of nature produces a life that is "nasty, brutish and short" and the only way to make life better is to agree to put someone in charge. But postapocalyptic accounts also follow Lockean and Rousseauean scripts, emphasizing property or community over fear. Whether the following of these scripts is intentional or not, certain postapocalyptic accounts nicely fictionalize the theoretical arguments given by Hobbes, Locke and Rousseau on the social contract and the human invention of government.

Social Contract

Modern political philosophers famously constructed the idea of the state of nature in order to highlight that the legitimacy of the state rests on the consent of the governed. The only way to theorize legitimacy was to imagine a time and place where there was no government. Ancient and medieval political philosophers believed that the State was natural—that human beings' natural sociability, or the idea that "man is by nature a political animal" (Aristotle, *Politics*) meant that legitimacy had little import. If the State simply *is*, then whether it *should be* is not a question. One could question the skills or viability of a particular leader, but the idea of the State itself was simply extant. Modern political philosophers, who wanted to question the legitimacy of the State as an idea used the state of nature to claim that the State was a human construct and is not natural. Thus government was framed as an artificial construction based on the desire of the people living in the state of nature to leave that situation.

Carole Pateman, author of *The Sexual Contract*, criticizing the limitations of social contract theory, argues that: "The 'state of nature' and the 'original contract' are powerful political fictions, and their power derives from the fact that they have had purchase on and have helped create the modern world" (Mills and Pateman, 55). Martha Nussbaum (2006, 223) claims "Images of who we are and why we get together do have power in shaping our projects." The very idea of the social contract, which emerges from the deliberations of people living in a state of nature, is central to our current political life. Thomas Hobbes (1588-1679) argues that the state of nature is a place of justified fear, a "war of all against all" and that we seek to leave it in order to gain bodily security. John Locke (1632-1704) argues that the state of nature is a place where rational and free individuals can attain property through the labor of their bodies, but it is also an inconvenient place given the existence of the lazy and irrational few who steal the fruits of your labor. Jean Jacques Rousseau (1712-1778) claimed that the state of nature initially provided a pure experience for humans who lived peacefully, like animals, until competition drove humans to enslave themselves in the chains of custom and illegitimate government. For Rousseau we consent to enter into the social contract, not for protection of life and property, as with Hobbes and Locke, but rather to gain "civil freedom" and the true fulfillment of humanity.

All three of these theorists imagine the state of nature with varying degrees of detail and all three reference the indigenous peoples of the Americas as evidence for their particular points of view. These references are both historically inaccurate and colored by both their desire to make a particular point about the natural state of humanity and their racism towards anyone non-European. Anthropologically the story they tell about actual humans living without the institution of the state is unsatisfying at best and unbelievable at worst. If the fiction of the state of nature fails, however, the edifice of modern political philosophy fails as well. Consent is only a legitimate foundation for humans living together if we believe that there is no natural authority. Modern political philosophers reject the usual analogy between the state and the family because they understand that citizens cannot be understood to be permanent children. Hobbes, Locke and Rousseau are all trying to argue against the divine right of kings and in order to do so they must posit that there was once a time when there was no such authority. Thus the existence of political authority stems from an active decision by human beings to come together, give up some of the natural rights that follow from living in a wholly anarchic world and create a new kind of institution: government.

The state of nature exists for three reasons: it provides a counter argument to the claim that we are by nature political, thus making government a natural institution; it offers a mechanism for seeing humans as they really are, absent the conventions of an artificially constructed rule bound society; and it gives a moment for humans to consider what kind of government they would actually choose to live under. These reasons are crucial for justifying democracy, political equality, a fluid and changing system of rights and the understanding of justice that underscores most of contemporary political thought. However, the state of nature itself, the fiction on which these arguments are based, is not compelling. Postapocalyptic fiction, on the other hand, provides a compelling basis for rethinking the conditions of and thus the response to life in the state of nature. This kind of fiction provides a window into life absent central authority. And as fiction there is room for carefully analyzing the basic motivations of human beings and the impulses that might drive us together to live. As a means for justifying the legitimacy of political ties, these accounts have the advantage of emerging from a world destroyed: thus the characters know, in part, the thing they are trying to create (whereas Hobbes, Locke and Rousseau imagine their inhabitants of the state of nature embarking on something never thought before). But this knowledge does not necessarily ease the path back to a semblance of peaceful living. Thus postapocalyptic accounts are also useful because they illustrate the need both to think creatively when faced with impossible conditions and to avoid the desire to simply recreate what is now destroyed.

John Rawls' *Theory of Justice* (1973) shifted away from the literalism of the state of nature and solved the colonial impulse of Hobbes, Locke and Rousseau with the creation of an imaginary space, entirely hypothetical and abstract, the original position. In the original position we deliberate, behind a veil of ignorance that keeps us from knowing our race, gender, religion, class, to choose principles of justice—the framework of a social contract—to which we would consent. While the original position does not include any claims about the cannibalistic habits of indigenous peoples or any paeans of praise for their one-ness with nature, the original position is also not a place that any of us would recognize, except as an experiment in an episode of the *Twilight Zone* or some as of yet unwritten cyberpunk novel. The Rawlsian reader can *imagine* herself not knowing her gender, race, class or religion. But the experience of not knowing is, as critics have all noted, fully embedded in what one does know (it is easy for the white person to not "know" her race, for the man to not "know" his gender, for the wealthy person to not "know" his or her class).

One criticism of the way that social contract thinkers imagine the transition from the state of nature to civil society is particularly useful in highlighting the distinction between the accounts of the social contract in chapters 2-4 and those chapters addressing Octavia Butler. Charles Mills, author of *The Racial Contract* and co-author with Carole Pateman of *Contract and Domination*, distinguishes between contracts that embody ideal theory, what he calls "mainstream contracts," and those that confront the non-ideal, what he calls "Domination Contracts." Mills notes that, "For ideal theory, the project is, starting from ground zero, to map an ideally just society. For non-ideal theory, the project is, starting from an already-existent non-deal unjust society, to prescribe what ideally would be required in the way of rectificatory justice to make it more just" (Mills, 233). Postapocalyptic fiction can pretend to an ideal theory scenario by thinking of the event as creating a blank slate from which to work. But these novels never question the ways in which their recreations of civil society simply mirror more traditional forms of political and social order. Butler's *Parable* series, on the other hand, creates a new social world without imagining that the destruction of the old has solved all of the social, economic and political crises of the old.

The state of nature looks different when we recognize that it is inhabited by all of us—rich and poor, male and female, black and white. Octavia Butler recognizes that it is those at the top of the social and political hierarchies who tend to fall out of favor after the end of the world. But her accounts are not simply attempts at retribution for centuries of subordination. The end of the world is not an excuse to kill off powerful white men (in the way that the *Turner Diaries* uses the end of the world to kill off women, gays, blacks and Jews). The end of the world reveals the conditions under which we live. And political philosophy recognizes that it is from such conditions that we understand the nature of justice and how we desire to live. In this, postapocalyptic fiction is often a debate between the satisfaction of retribution and the difficult day to day work of starting over.

This book uses the transition from the state of nature to civil society as the lens through which to examine postapocalyptic fiction. This provides a new approach to postapocalyptic fiction, which in its secular form is already an under-theorized genre. Others who look at postapocalyptic fiction have done so to emphasize its didactic focus (Wagar, Mannix), its theoretical association with the postmodern (Berger, Rosen) and as a subtype of utopian/dystopian literature (Moylan). But there is no sustained analysis of postapocalyptic fiction from the perspective of political theory that focuses on those examples of the genre where starting over is the impetus of the story.

Overview

This book analyzes postapocalyptic fiction from the perspective of political theory. My goal is to think through the idea of the state of nature and the social contract and to reveal the ways in which this genre of fiction appeals to our fears and our desire to begin again. Chapter 1 begins with the impossibility of beginning again. Nevil Shute's *On the Beach* (1957) and Cormac McCarthy's *The Road* (2007) illustrate the conceptual backdrop to the project in that they each refuse any sustained analysis of starting over. Each provides an end that is, I argue, absolute. And so it is against the thought of such finality that the other accounts move forward. The way in which these two novels close off the possibility for human life reveals the underlying premise of postapocalyptic fiction: fear. Despite their obvious differences and the different times on which they reflect, Shute and McCarthy both explore the fear we have not simply of our own deaths, but the potential fear of extermination itself. Shute and McCarthy rule out the possibility of finding security—of creating a civil society that could somehow solve the problem of fear produced after an apocalyptic event. Fear informs the movement from the state of nature like setting of the postapocalypse to civil society. But fear should not simply be understood in Hobbesian terms. Rethinking the social contract means rethinking the idea of fear itself: what do we fear and what would security look like? Beginning with two books that refuse the reader the satisfaction of achieving security (although *On the Beach* does provide control over your death as a kind of security) illustrates how we think about the idea of a happy ending in a postapocalyptic novel. All of the novels after Chapter 1 have happy endings, yet those endings differ in how they understand the security that the characters all desire.

Chapters 2, 3 and 4 focus on classic social contract thinkers and their corresponding postapocalyptic fictional counterparts. Chapter 2 discusses Hobbes through *Lucifer's Hammer*, written by Larry Niven and Jerry Pournelle, published in 1977, which well represents the use of chaos and violence to justify recourse to traditional authority. Chapter 3 analyzes the Lockean social contract through Pat Frank's 1959 *Alas, Babylon*, a post-nuclear account of the survival of one small Florida town. Chapter 4 takes up the Rousseauean postapocalyptic accounts of Robert Merle's *Malevil*, published in France in 1972 as compared to the very different, yet still Rousseauean, *Into the Forest* by Jean Hegland, published in 1998. These three chapters outline a traditional move from the state of nature (produced by the apocalyptic event) to the communal re-organizing that culminates in the creation (or rejection) of a civil society. Each novel follows its social contract guide in how it understands human motivation, the role of fear and the impetus behind joining together to form a civil society.

After analyzing these fictional accounts that mirror traditional social contract theory I turn to John Rawls to consider his own rejection of the state of nature as the appropriate hypothetical space from which to imagine moving towards civil society. Rawls instead uses the Original Position, a thought experiment limiting the knowledge we have about ourselves that he argues helps produce a choice of just principles. In Chapter 5, I use an Octavia Butler short story that reflects the way in which John Rawls shifts the argument about the movement from the state of nature to civil society to a more abstract hypothetical imagining. Butler's story "The Book of Martha" (2005) provides a fictional accounting and critique of Rawls' understanding of the social contract, focusing on the idea of the hypothetical Original Position. This chapter makes the transition away from the traditional postapocalyptic accounts to Butler, the focus of Chapters 6 and 7 and this chapter begins the critique of traditional social contract thinking and the understanding of human nature that emerges from those accounts.

Chapters 6 and 7 analyze the *Parable* series, *Parable of the Sower* (1993) and *Parable of the Talents* (1998), focusing on vulnerability, the interplay between the desires for security and that of control, and the very idea of endings and new beginnings. The *Parable* series examines the context of the postapocalyptic landscape and moves from an argument about finding a physical space for security to finding a way of life that might bring about security. The *Parable* series analyzes security in a world where we recognize our own vulnerability and the vulnerability of those whom we love. Security is only possible when we recognize both the extent to which our security is wrapped up with the security of others whom we love and yet that security only follows our recognition that we cannot control others, even those whom we love. The *Parable* series then moves from an argument about striving for security to an argument for human flourishing. Butler's postapocalyptic account pays close attention to both the details of everyday life and to our desire for security. Butler re-imagines the social contract in a context of human vulnerability.

Notes

1. Meloy, Colin. "The Island: Come and See." Lyrics. The Decembrists. Three Stage Music, 2006.

2. Years later I saw the British TV movie, *Threads*, which was aired the same year. *Threads* takes the survivors of the nuclear war out one generation and is a far grimmer representation of the reality of nuclear war. *Threads* is hauntingly appalling about matters that *The Day After* never confronts.

3. I also remember the film as being bleak and fairly horrifying. Last year I showed it to a class of graduating seniors whose response to much of the film was laughter.

4. Robert Jacobs, "'There are No Civilians; We Are All At War': Nuclear War Shelter and Survival Narratives during the Early Cold War," *Journal of American Culture*, 30:4 (2007): 401-417. Jacobs discusses Shute's *On the Beach* and notes that "In popular culture narratives of survival, the individual was removed from society, isolated, while the grotesque surgery of nuclear warfare was performed" (402). This is the state of nature (one that Jacobs is essentially reading as Hobbesian).

5. Rosen's book includes chapters on Alan Moore's graphic novels, Kurt Vonnegut and Don DeLillo's *White Noise*; I would say that *A Canticle for Leibowitz* and P.C. Jersild's, *After the Flood* also fit this post-modern model.

6. A brief list: Post-nuclear (*Mad Max* and *Terminator* series), environmental (*Day After Tomorrow*), plague (*28 days Later*), meteors (*Deep Impact*).

7. Tom Junod, "The Organic Apocalypse," *Esquire*, February 2008; John Paul Flintoff, "Super Stud is Reborn as Mr Doom", *Sunday Times* (London), April 8, 2009; *The New York Times* "Escapes" section (Fridays) has often profiled kinds of homes or energy independence to facilitate living off the grid. Richard Mitchell's *Dancing At Armageddon* follows a number of survivalist groups and he uses the language of the social contract to analyze what these groups desire from the end of the world: "They want to express creativity, not achieve control. . . . It is the imaginative work of culture crafting not the artifacts of culture to which survivalists are attracted. Survival-

ists relish inventing new narratives, new primal means and fundamental meanings by which the world may be known. Survivalists seek to reinterpret the wisdom of science, not obedience to its laws. They want to reformulate the social contract, not the privileges of citizenship" (9-10).

8. Joseph Dewey would identify these as novels with a "millenialist spirit." Joseph Dewey, *In a Dark Time: The Apocalyptic Temper in the American Novel of the Nuclear Age* (West Lafayette, Indiana: Purdue University Press, 1990).

9. Rye, the protagonist, overcomes her fear and her focus on immediate survival in order to rescue the children who seem to still possess the capacity for speech. Butler hints at here what she further illustrates in the Parable series, that children provide an impetus to a different set of human motivations and a different understanding of security.

10. I have no way of proving this claim that readers of postapocalyptic fiction tend to think of themselves as surviving such accounts. However, in a Utopia/Dystopia class I did ask students whether or not they either read postapocalyptic fiction or thought about end like catastrophes and there I found that students who thought about it tended to then also think of themselves as surviving. Students who did not read those books or think about the end also presumed that they would die in such an event. James Wesley Rawles has written both a novelistic postapocalyptic account *Patriots* (2009). He followed this with the literal manual *How to Survive the End of the World as We Know It* later in 2009. I would distinguish here literal survivalists: those preparing for an end. And people who think of themselves as surviving an event. Not because they are preparing for it, but simply because they think of themselves as a survivor.

11. Tom Moylan, *Scraps of the Untainted Sky* (Boulder, Colorado: Westview Press, 2000), 187-194. Critical utopias and dystopias use the genre as a space from which to criticize the author's own world.

12. Tim LaHaye's *Left Behind* series provides a 13 volume postapocalyptic account where only believing Christians (alive and resurrected) are left to live out a millennial fantasy. The *Left Behind* series is a pre-modern fantasy. While it is surely as didactic and cathartic as any of the novels I do examine, its worldview is not one where the social contract has any relevant role to play. In political terms the *Left Behind* series is a medieval enactment, dressed up with airplanes and the internet, which is out to teach submission to divine authority. This is precisely what the social contract thinkers thought of themselves as arguing against. Their focus on the necessity for a social contract to provide a foundation of legitimacy for governmental authority was a response to the claim of authority from above—the divine right of kings.

13. Elizabeth Rosen, *Apocalyptic Transformations: Apocalypse and the Postmodern Imagination* (Lanham, Maryland: Lexington Books, 2008): xiv.

14. Kunstler's own account is wholly reactionary on gender and race and his imagining of a post oil world also includes turning much of the Hudson River valley into a pseudo medieval world of manors and free towns, buxom women and flagons of beer, and the seemingly ubiquitous need to discover new weapons of war. Kunstler's novel

owes more to the medieval imaginings of S.M. Stirling than to any serious rethinking of life after an apocalyptic event. Kunstler's future is, for him, desirable, and the nice part about it is that it is also inevitable. No action is required to change the course of our nation to avoid the consequences of a drop in oil production—because that drop in oil production will happen no matter what and if (IF) you situate yourself well, you can thrive from it—it will take the collapse of the economy, terrorist acts against cities and pandemic to teach you that "Light follows darkness." But his title is useful.

15. Or as in *Children of Men*, by PD James, or *Oryx and Crake*, by Margaret Atwood.

16. Margaret Atwood's *The Handmaid's Tale*, Philip K. Dick's *The Simulacra*, Walter Miller's *A Canticle for Leibowitz*, P.C. Jersild, *After the Flood*.

17. I am not taking up the sub-genre of postapocalyptic fiction: the zombie end. Max Brooks' *World War Z: An Oral History of the Zombie War* is only one such example of this ever increasing sub-genre. But I am not interested in the zombie end here.

~

CHAPTER ONE

Last One Out,
Please Turn Out the Lights
On the Beach *and* The Road

"There's no hope at all, is there? For any of us?"[1]

In the introduction, I argued that postapocalyptic fiction as a genre features certain characteristics: a small group of plucky survivors contend with the chaos that emerges after the end; they learn how to identify friend and foe; they band together and they defeat the new enemy in order to rise again in a new form of society illustrating the victory that emerges out of the ashes of the end. Just as watchers of horror movies know that it is never a good idea to go into the abandoned home so do readers of postapocalyptic fiction know that the unruly group coming over the hill with clubs are likely cannibals. In recognition of the rules of the genre writers of postapocalyptic fiction take care to explain the mechanisms of destruction. As any good science fiction writer will do, authors of postapocalyptic fiction describe plausible ends and in order to do so those ends must be detailed (often through the inclusion of the stock scientist as a main character).[2]

Postapocalyptic fiction, as a genre, is didactic: *this* is what we need to be careful of; *this* is how we survive such an event. These two teachings are in tension with one another as the real warning is to avoid the event itself. But in the description of people coming together to survive after the end we see the needed tools for our own flourishing *now* before the end. Whether the warning is about environmental degradation, nuclear weapons or plague, postapocalyptic fiction points out the caution zones we should realize now and how we should act in order to both keep this event from happening and improve our chances of survival if it does happen. This is why so many posta-pocalyptic accounts read like how-to manuals. This is not to say that such accounts must be devoid of literary content, but the advice is always there.

The premise of this book is that postapocalyptic fiction provides a terrain for thinking about the social contract. Postapocalyptic fiction is premised on a state of nature: the hypothetical fiction that is the driving force behind the social contract. The apocalyptic end destroys all semblance of organized political life, thus producing the conditions of the state of nature. But in order for the social contract to emerge from the postapocalypse there has to be some thought that life can go on. This is the underlying assumption (and tension) of postapocalyptic fiction. The texts present dangers facing our society and the texts argue about how humans interact with one another, what humans need for survival and what humans need for the development of a future society. These texts all explore what drives human behavior when stripped of the accessories of comfortable living.[3]

But what happens when a postapocalyptic account refuses to let humans come together for another try at civil society? How can we use postapoca-lyptic accounts that do not include a movement out of the state of nature of the end to further define what the conditions are for entering into civil society? The requirements for moving forward become clearer through analysis of those few postapocalyptic accounts where there is no life beyond the lingering deaths of the protagonists. I have chosen two postapocalyptic accounts that will both book-end this project and clarify the requirements for truly starting over. Nevil Shute's *On the Beach*, published in 1957[4] and Cormac McCarthy's *The Road*, published in 2007 both set the time period of the works that I examine in later chapters and provide a window into a form of postapocalyptic fiction that denies the possibility of a new social contract. These are still *postapocalyptic* works because they are set after the apocalyptic event. But they deny the social contract because there is no starting over that is possible after this event. Neither book focuses on the event itself; rather each explores the very meaning of the end of humanity (and in the case of McCarthy the end of all life on earth).

What is interesting about these two accounts is that they are outliers. In neither account is there any attempt to enter into the social contract or to recreate civil society. Further, even though each book is described as part of the postapocalyptic genre, neither fully embraces the framework of that genre (this is particularly true of McCarthy, as discussed below). *On the Beach* obviates this possibility of starting over by detailing the death of all human beings from radiation. *The Road* proves the impossibility of such a movement back to civil society by describing a postapocalyptic world entirely devoid of the conditions for a civil society. *The Road* describes not simply conditions of scarcity, essential for the potential workings of justice, rather *The Road* describes a world utterly dead—absent any life beyond the husks of humanity that wander searching for cans of food.

On the Beach and *The Road* defy expectations about the genre of postapocalyptic fiction.[5] In their refusal to follow the genre's framework they well illustrate how that framework shapes our thinking about the social contract. Neither account provides any possibility for the state of nature to drive us into civil society. In part because neither fully describes a state of nature: *On the Beach* is a civil society experiencing societal and human death; *The Road* goes beyond any understanding of the state of nature into the territory of nightmare. Beginning with these accounts provides an opportunity to illustrate a few key features of postapocalyptic fiction and the kind of postapocalyptic fiction that I think provides the means for rethinking the social contract.

Social contract thinkers tend to use states of nature that are either hypothetical or far fetched, but their premise is clear: describe humans without the usual accoutrements that civil society provides: safety, law enforcement, a system for deciding grievances, a framework that allows people to do what they choose (within limits). Postapocalyptic accounts strip away each of these and, as in the state of nature, humans have to rethink what is really necessary for survival and for flourishing. The point of the state of nature is to show us why it would be advantageous for us to band together. Part of my interest in beginning with *On the Beach* and *The Road* is that these accounts provide the possibility that there is no point, no potential mutual advantage, in banding together. What do accounts that detail the pointlessness of creating civil society tell us about the conditions necessary for entering into a social contract? These conditions are not limited to the possibility of human survival, although the meaning of human survival does matter. Why are we hoping to survive and what are we hoping to survive *as?* *The Road* cautions the reader of the difficulties of remaining human after the end—with cannibalism as the ultimate failure of humanity. *On the Beach,* on the other hand, describes fully human characters who are concerned primarily to go out with the right kind of attitude. Through analysis of the setting, the tone and the conclusions of *On the Beach* and *The Road* the requirements, material and human, for civil society are revealed.

On the Beach was published in 1957 and became a national bestseller in the United States.[6] Shute, a British author and aviation engineer, was living in Australia at the time of the publication and the novel is set in Southern Australia, on the outskirts of Melbourne. The novel describes the lives of a handful of Australians and one American as they await the drifting radiation that resulted from a cataclysmic war between Northern hemisphere states. The main character, Peter Holmes is with the Australian navy and he travels with the crew of the last American submarine unit back to the west coast of the United States to view the destruction and to discern whether there are any survivors (there are none). But the main focus of the novel is on the lives of those who know that their lives will be ending soon. There is no thought that anyone will survive this radiation and species death is the specter that underlies the novel. While reviewers responded positively to the book (and the movie, made two years later, directed by Stanley Kramer met with critical praise) the novel has been largely ignored by academics.

Cormac McCarthy's *The Road*, published in 2007, won the Pulitzer Prize for literature in the same year. Set in the Southeastern U.S., *The Road* follows the travels of an unnamed father and son who struggle to survive years after a presumed nuclear war that has wiped out every living thing other than a few scattered humans. *The Road* follows a trajectory of increasing nihilism in McCarthy's work and Shute's novel seems light-hearted in comparison.

Within the postapocalyptic genre each of these books is a misfit. *On the Beach* lacks the usual spirit of know-how that might drive the survivors to push their survival forward. The means to survive longer are certainly there: living in a submarine, scouring the earth for cleaner places or hunkering down underground for a few years[7]. Instead *On the Beach* wants to reader to face the end with dignity.[8] *The Road* lacks all of the potential motivations for moving forward. Here the death of everything but for a handful of humans forces the question of suicide (the dignified option in Shute) to the front of the mind. McCarthy refuses to condone suicide and Shute refuses to promote know-how. On that score it seems that McCarthy would somehow be more hopeful. His protagonist has the know-how to keep himself and his son alive years after the world ending event; yet their continued living is nothing beyond a day to day struggle.

The Setting of the Postapocalypse

The starkest and most immediate differences between these two books are the radically different worlds of the end. One might imagine that the differences in setting for the postapocalypse might simply be the difference, for example, between the aftermath of a nuclear war vs. the aftermath of a plague. Instead here are two novels that each deal with a world post-nuclear war, and yet each sees that world differently.

Lieutenant Commander Peter Holmes of the Royal Australian Navy woke soon after dawn. He lay drowsily for a while, lulled by the warm comfort of Mary sleeping beside him, watching the first light of Australian sun upon the cretonne curtains of their room. He knew from the sun's rays that it was about five o'clock; very soon the light would wake his baby daughter in her cot, and then they would have to get up and start doing things. No need to start before that happened; he could lie a little longer. (1)

These opening lines of On the Beach do not herald the pain and suffering of the end. Instead we see a character comforted by the presence of his family, awakened by a sunny day. There is no hint here that anything is amiss. There is no sense of urgency. There is no question about anyone's survival and no expression of any existential dread.

In the next paragraph we learn that Peter is sunburned from a sailing race, that Christmas has been celebrated with a barbecue with friends and that "He woke happy" not realizing exactly what he was happy about. By the end of the paragraph he remembers that he has an appointment with his Navy commander with the chance for future work. "It meant work anyway. The thought of it had made him happy when he went to sleep, and his happiness had lasted through the night" (2). So the weather is beautiful, the protagonist is surrounded by friends and family and has work that he loves, how exactly is this a postapocalyptic text? Where is the chaos, the breakdown of civil society? How can the skies be sunny? How can Christmas still be celebrated? This does not seem to be a description of the state of nature. There is clearly still order: order in the family, order in the acknowledgment of holidays, order in the existence of a functioning military. Particular characters (usually women) may react badly to the prospect of species death, but in general the novel portrays a functioning society where individuals move through predictable days.

This is not a novel set in the state of nature. People still go to restaurants and to the movies. There is planning for the future that is marred by uncertainty about the coming radiation, but it is not marred by the uncertainty of political collapse. When Moira and Dwight go to Melbourne for a night on the town they find that:

Most of the shops had plenty of good stock still in the windows but few were open. The restaurants and cafes were all full, doing a roaring trade; the bars were shut, but the streets were full of drunks. The general effect was one of boisterous and uninhibited lightheartedness, more in the style of 1890 than of 1963. There was no traffic in the wide streets but for the trams, and people swarmed all over the road. . . . As they passed the Regal cinema a man, staggering along in front

of them, fell down, paused for a moment upon hands and knees, and rolled
dead drunk into the gutter. Nobody paid much attention to him. A policeman,
strolling down the pavement, turned him over, examined him casually, and
strolled on. (61)

Even the presence of the drunken man fails to introduce chaos into this
scene. The stores have not been looted, police officers still show up on the
job and the one portrayed here is clearly unconcerned with inebriated citizens
if they are not harming anyone other than themselves. The description of the
crowd as possessing "lightheartedness" implies that the end of humanity has
finally given everyone the chance to pursue the life each has always wished
for (although that seems to include a lot of drunkenness). Moira comments
negatively on the presence of the intoxicated people after she and Dwight
leave the dance and see that "only the drunks remained, reeling down the
pavement aimlessly or lying down to sleep" (64). But her complaint "they
should do something about all this. . . . It was never like this before the war"
(64), illustrates first an expectation that there is a "they" that might well do
"something" and second that she sees no major shift between life before vs.
life after the war. If she uses life before the war as a guide to life now, then
she clearly does not expect chaos and terror around the corner.

Even when the submarine crew witnesses cities of the dead in their
travels to the Western coast of the United States, the settings are those of
sunny days "exactly as it would have looked on a Sunday or a holiday" (71).
These dead cities are described like movie sets prior to the entrance of any
actors. "Through the periscope they could see streets of shops shaded with
palm trees, a hospital, and trim villas of one storey raised on posts above the
ground; there were cars parked in the street and one or two flags flying" (71).
Everything looks normal, and beyond that pleasant, attractive, cute and
functioning. There may be no humans, but there is everything that humanity
has created, left neat and clean for someone to find and admire.

Likewise, in Edmonds, Washington, outside of Seattle one of the men,
who is from Edmonds, declares "It all looks just the same" (165). He jumps
ship and is last seen fishing in Puget Sound. While he does recount finding
his parents and his girlfriend dead, he reiterates "Apart from that, everything
is pretty much the way it always was" (178). This same "the way it always
was" attitude is maintained until the end when Moira drives south to watch
Dwight's submarine go out to sea to be sunk, "a bareheaded, white-faced
girl in a bright crimson costume, slightly intoxicated, driving a big car at
speed" (278). The scene is only marred by Moira's radiation sickness. But
it too is referred to obliquely: "Somewhere before Corrio a spasm shook her

suddenly, so that she had to stop and retire into the bushes; she came out a quarter of an hour later, white as a sheet, and took a long drink of brandy" (278). The reader knows Moira is sick, but little space is spent on describing hers (or anyone else's) radiation sickness beyond tiredness and trips to the bathroom.

At the end we have one suicide that can represent all the others—Moira, in her red pantsuit, drinking brandy, taking the cyanide pills prescribed to everyone so that their end would be as comfortable as possible. The only gesture towards the death of everyone is the overcast sky—the first not sunny day in the whole book. The end of humanity is set in sunny Australia where people go to the beach, sail boats, race cars, drink brandy (often to excess) and forthrightly face up to their imminent deaths. The death of humanity is organized and the fear that this story induces in the reader (discussed in greater detail in the following section) is only a fear of death.

The setting for *The Road* reminds the reader of the subject matter on every page. There is no chance that you might forget that the world has effectively ended through a description of a sunny day. Here the end of the world is associated with grey skies, ash, dead trees, cold rain and constant discomfort for its characters. Here the state of what I would call un-nature is in full bloom—there is no functioning government, no functioning economy, no functioning military. In fact there is seemingly nothing other than a few scattered humans, some of whom have been organized by bands of fanatic cannibals. Fear is everywhere: fear of starvation, of cold, of cannibals, of pain, of abandonment.

> When he woke in the woods in the dark and the cold of the night he'd reach out to touch the child sleeping beside him. Nights dark beyond darkness and the days more gray each one than what had gone before. Like the onset of some cold glaucoma dimming away the world. (3)

We see a man and a child. The man reminds himself, perhaps reassures himself, of the child's presence. The darkness is complete—there is no moon, no starlight, no reflected light from the city. And that darkness extends into the daytime with increasing grayness. Something is covering the world in a gray film, one that will obscure the world until its few inhabitants are blinded to it.

The Road opens in a dark, cold, unknown place. The man and the boy are cold, covered in "stinking robes and blankets." The man still dreams, but his dream of the boy leading him into a cave that houses some nameless, moaning beast of the deep is not a recollection of better days. There is no escape in dreams. "With the first gray light he rose and left the boy sleeping and walked out to the road and squatted and studied the country to the south. Barren, silent, godless. He thought the month was October but he wasn't sure. He hadn't kept a calendar for years. They were moving south. There'd be no surviving another winter here" (4). The man is uncertain of the date; he has not kept a calendar and clearly others around him are not reminding him of the month. His refusal to keep a calendar is not the idiosyncrasy of one choosing his own seasonal plan. Rather we realize that one cannot keep a calendar when survival is the issue. The man and the child are on the move, in search of a better place to be, not because they know of anything better in the south, but simply because there is no way to stay where they are and survive. This is not a world of Christmas and sailing and sunburns and the happy anticipation of a job needing to be done. This is an unknown dark world, one with "stinking robes" "soft ash" and "dead trees."

The man and the boy start out on the road, pushing a shopping cart and each wearing a knapsack "in case they had to abandon the cart and run for it" (5). The danger is in being seen and being caught. Every road must be observed for movement, for smoke, for footsteps. The countryside through which they move is largely dead. "Charred and limbless trunks of trees stretching away on every side. Ash moving over the road and the sagging hands of blind wire strung from the blackened lightpoles whining thinly in the wind" (7). The ash is everywhere from a nameless fire that must have consumed everything living in its path. But buildings are strangely present, burned perhaps, but usually intact. "Tall clapboard houses. Machinerolled metal roofs. A log barn in a field with an advertisement in faded ten-foot letters across the roofslope. See Rock City" (18). Whatever happened to this world it is living organisms that bore the brunt of its attack. Roads may be buckled and wires sagging, buildings partially burnt. But the weeds fall "to dust," the trees are lifeless burnt trunks, the skies are empty, the rivers "turned slowly in a gray foam" (25).

The artifacts of the world in which we live have little meaning for the boy who was born as the bombs fell. Buildings might mean food, but they are as likely to mean danger, potential ambush, the horror of "naked people, male and female, all trying to hide, shielding their faces with their hands. On the mattress lay a man with his legs gone to the hip and the stumps of them blackened and burnt. The smell was hideous" (93). This basement housing the prisoners of a group of cannibals clarifies that there is no safety to be had in the remnants of human artifice. Nor is there security in numbers. Those that work together do so to destroy the few humans left. "An army in tennis shoes, tramping. Carrying three-foot lengths of pipe with leather wrappings. Lanyards at the wrist. . . . They clanked past, marching with a swaying gait like wind-up toys. . . . Behind them came wagons drawn by slaves in harness and piled with goods of war and after that the women, perhaps a dozen in number, some of them pregnant, and lastly a supplementary consort of catamites illclothed against the cold and fitted in dog collars and yoked to each other" (77-78). These groups represent the consequences of working in concert—how can one trust in others when the only people working together do so to rape, enslave and eat their fellow survivors? That the boy should therefore mistrust all other humans surely makes sense. And that the boy still wants to help those that he finds (particularly the very young and the old) is a sign of his inherent goodness. But there is something terribly off in the above description. What can be the spoils of war that these bearded men have discovered? Is it really believable that when the world is utterly destroyed and the few survivors left after years of living in a wholly dead landscape would still continue to enslave and impregnate others? Frankly is it worth the effort to collect the vestiges of human artifice when death is imminent? This is one of the places where McCarthy's own tendency towards violence revealing the only meaning in the world rings false. Isn't the violence of the bombs enough? The violence of the landscape? Perhaps even the violence of the single cannibal?[9]

There is no potential safety in numbers, no potential hideout in the woods, no way to hide away in some valley far from prying eyes.[10] Security, which is essentially absent, can only be glimpsed in continuing to move down the road, in the luck of a found cache of food, or the discovery of a cistern of water untouched by the ever present ash. The landscape is still recognizable to the man, but for the reader and the boy it is a largely interchangeable description of "trunks that stood stripped and burntlooking" (83), a land that "was gullied and eroded and barren" (149), and the constant ash, rain and snow.

The Road is set in a dead world. It is largely empty, but still fraught with danger. It is burned out, yet filled with the remnants of supermarkets, highways, bridges and cars. On the Beach cannot really be describing a state of nature because its inhabitants clearly live in a fully functioning civil society. But neither is The Road a description of the state of nature, for there is no nature here. All that is left in The Road are the vestiges of what the protagonists of On the Beach enjoy: the clubs, the comfortable houses, the stores. It is not simply the case that government is absent from the world of The Road, the very idea of government is impossible. The boy knows nothing of a world where one could rely on something beyond the man to provide anything. Neither does the boy know a world where through one's individual effort one could carve out a space to live and a means to survive, not just to tomorrow, but to the next season. So here too the setting betrays any claims to the state of nature.

There is no nature here; there is no material from which one could build a functioning society. When social contract thinkers use the state of nature they are describing a setting from which one could move forward. But there is no future here. Even at the end of the novel when the boy goes with a group of friendly others who have been following him, awaiting the father's death, we get little sense that they will be able to do anything other than repeat the life the boy has had with the father, albeit perhaps more effectively.

The novel ends with a description of nature as it was: "Once there were brook trout in the streams in the mountains. . . . On their backs were vermiculate patterns that were maps of the world in its becoming. Maps and mazes. Of a thing which could not be put back. Not be made right again" (241). Nature has ended, humans remain; but they cannot live for long. The setting of The Road is as dead and grim as the setting of On the Beach is sunny and bright. Yet each tells the end of humanity and while their settings differ their tones parallel one another.

Tone

The Road has none of the "lighthearted" moments that feature so prominently in On the Beach. Yet each novel presents characters who try and get the proper attitude toward the end in order to get by, day to day. Each is trying to ask what it means to go on living when life has become physically pointless. The Road takes a metaphysical turn that On the Beach cannot match. But each is struggling to find some meaning for human existence. One way the novels exhibit this struggle is in the references to what has happened. How much does the reader learn early on? What kind of certainty does the reader get about what happened? And how do the characters themselves understand what the end of the world means?

Neither novel is presented as a subject matter surprise. The fly leaf of each identifies it clearly as postapocalyptic[11] (despite my own contention that neither fits the genre). So the introduction of the idea that something is terribly wrong is not going to come as a surprise to the reader. But how each introduces the wrongness reflects the tone that each novel takes on the end of the world. In the opening pages of On the Beach in between descriptions of Peter's sunburn and his happiness at getting another posting he considers that, "in the circumstance of the time he had almost given up hope of ever working again" (2). This is the first clue that something about the times is not quite right. What are these circumstances? They are clearly not simply particular to him, being "of the time"—so what kind of circumstances "of the time" would cause him to lose "hope of ever working again"?

On the Beach continues the juxtaposition of the normal and pleasant with the reminders that all is not right throughout the first chapter. By the end of the chapter you know what happened, although you do not yet know why or what this really means to the protagonists that are simply living their lives. The brief description of "the short, bewildering war" emerges in Peter's musings about why he does not move his car out of the garage and keep the bicycles, their only mode of transportation, under cover. "The little Morris was the first car he had ever owned, and he courted Mary in it. They had been married in 1961 six months before the war, before he sailed in HMAS Anzac for what they thought would be an indefinite separation. The short, bewildering war that followed, the war of which no history had been written or ever would be written now, that flared all round the Northern Hemisphere and had died away with the last seismic record of explosion on the thirty-seventh day" (3). So we learn there has been a war, one for which "no history . . . ever would be written." There is little passion in the description; Peter is not angry and he clearly is not identifying with sides. Something about this war makes it different from other wars and this is "bewildering" even to Peter who is in the Navy. We know, because no history of this war will ever be written, that something about this war has changed everything. A few pages later we hear the first of a refrain that becomes more constant as the novel develops "After all, from what they say on the wireless, there's not so long to go" (6). This comment is initially made by a farmer that Peter goes to for milk. But the question of what it is that there is "not long" to get to is still up in the air. But always coupled with the uncertainty is the commitment to living life as one always had.

If *On the Beach* is following the "how-to" guide tendency of postapocalyptic fiction then it is telling you how to face the end of humanity with dignity. There is a certain shame attached to those characters that are unable to handle the end of the world and we are to admire those who are able to both be matter of fact about what cannot be changed and yet still driven to be in the world. The admirable character both acknowledges the fact of the end and does not let that fact change too much how she lives her life now. John Osbourne, the scientist who travels with the American navy to observe the dead cities of North America, insists to Moira "you've got to face the facts of life someday." "One has to try and find out what has happened. It could be that it's all quite different to what we think. . . . Even if we don't discover anything good, it's still discovering things. I don't think we *shall* discover anything that's good, or very hopeful. But even so it's just fun finding out"

(59). Osbourne taps into the human drive to know about the world and even when humanity is in its last weeks, humans will continue to do what satisfies them most deeply.

Moira drinks her days away, drowning her sorrow about the end in talk of dances and parties. Mary, Peter's wife, even seems to admire her for this, but the male characters will never be described as being so weak facing the end, even the man drinking his way through the wine cellar at the club is celebrated for his commitment to a goal, not criticized for his drunkenness (a drunkenness that will maintain his body longer then most when the radiation arrives). The one moment when such weakness in a man is revealed, it is also met with distaste. Peter invites the Commander of the U.S. submarine, Dwight Towers, to his home for the weekend and Mary, Peter's wife, reacts with horror: "They're never all right. It's much too painful for them, coming into people's homes" (20). She recalls "the one who cried," a nameless man invited to such a party earlier. "He did not care to be reminded of that evening" Peter recalled (21). The embarrassment of facing a man's emotion over the death of his family is worse, somehow, than the end of the world. The end may be looming, but it is important to simply live life as one has always done. Failing to distract oneself or soldier on seems somehow to be in poor taste: if everyone around you is dying there is something rude about being upset about it. And so Commander Towers is kept busy during his visit so that he will not think too much about his assuredly dead family when faced with Peter's clearly living one. They plan a weekend of sailing, beach time and the entertainments of the above mentioned drunken Moira, "never a dull moment . . . in bed or out of it" Peter muses to his wife, who notes that Moira's wayward airs are "all on the surface" (22). Ultimately Dwight will teach Moira about how to live life in these last moths of humanity and will thus show his manliness and bring home the message of how one should die.

Both Moira and Mary learn to face the end through the interventions of men. Peter insists that Moira must be willing to see the end coming for her infant daughter, Jennifer. "It's the end of everything for all of us," he said. "We're going to lose most of the years of life that we've looked forward to, and Jennifer's going to lose all of them. But it doesn't have to be too painful for her. When things are hopeless, you can make it easy for her. It's going to take a bit of courage on your part, but you've got that" (141). This courage is something that Mary initially lacks; she cries and insists that speaking of death is Peter's way of trying to get her out of the way so that he can run off with another woman.[12] He replies in anger: "Don't be such a bloody fool. . . . If I'm here I'll have it [radiation sickness] myself. If I'm not here, if you've got to face things on your own, it'll be because I'm dead already. Just think of that and try and get it into your fat head. I'll be dead" (142). This is the only moment of anger in the novel, and it is important that it happens over Mary's refusal to do what is right for Jennifer. When the radiation comes Mary must be able to kill Jennifer because Jennifer might last longer through radiation sickness, dying of starvation, perhaps, rather than of the radiation. This is one of the few moments equivalent to *The Road* in the emotional reality of these postapocalyptic worlds. The desire to do right by one's child under impossible circumstances underscores the usual insistence that everyone face the end with the proverbial stiff upper lip. Mary clearly learns her lesson and is able to help teach Moira as they discuss Mary's plans for her garden, plans that Moira scoffs at knowing that Mary will not be around to enjoy them: "Well that's what I think. I mean I couldn't bear to—to just stop doing things and do nothing. You might as well die now and get it over" (181).

Both novels refuse the "get it over with" mentality. While all of the characters in *On the Beach* do eventually commit suicide, they do so as a way to take control over a death that is wholly inevitable. Rather than resign themselves to the oncoming radiation they will take matters into their own hands, but only after the initial symptoms of radiation sickness. Conversely, the one suicide discussed in *The Road* is presented as a failure of will and love. The mother of the boy, the wife of the man, has killed herself prior to the opening of the novel. She discusses with the man the futility of the lives they are living and the likelihood that they will be captured, raped and eaten by the roving bands of cannibals. She accuses the man of only living for the child and admits her own inability to do so.

> We're survivors he told her across the flame of the lamp.
> Survivors? she said.
> Yes.
> What in God's name are you talking about? We're not survivors. We're the walking dead in a horror film. (47)

If we understand the idea of a survivor to mean something beyond the fact of being alive, then the woman is making the point that many aficionados of postapocalyptic fiction might make. They have built no shelter, they have done nothing to guarantee a food supply (although they have rejected cannibalism), they are unable to do anything other than stumble from can of food to can of food, hoping that the cannibals do not find them first. In such a circumstance suicide seems not simply rational, but even, potentially, right.

He tries to counter her pessimism, "begging" her and claiming he will "do anything." But what can he possibly do? There is no plan that will provide them with any sort of security and he even admits to himself that his move-ment south with his son is not so much a plan for safety as it is simply the need to move somewhere. The woman counters even more strongly: "No, I'm speaking the truth. Sooner or later they will catch us and they will kill us. They will rape me. They'll rape him. They are going to rape us and kill us and eat us and you wont face it. You'd rather wait for it to happen. But I cant. I cant" (48). Everything that she says rings true. There has been no incident in the novel (nor is there one after she speaks) that challenges her understanding of the world in which they live: they will die and the only possible hope is that they will not be raped and eaten. And so for the woman suicide is the only legitimate response.

The man used to discuss with the woman the possibility of suicide. "The hundred nights they'd sat up debating the pros and cons of self destruction with the earnestness of philosophers chained to a madhouse wall" (49). But the man will no longer engage. "It's because it's here. There's nothing left to talk about" (48). To which he replies, oddly, "I wouldn't leave you." Here is where some authorial direction might help. Is he saying "*I* wouldn't leave you"? (Emphasis added). Chastising her because it seems that *she* is willing to leave? Or is he simply stating that he will not *leave*, a claim that is not true as he is clearly willing to leave her to figure out this death alone. There is no longer any space for earnest philosophical discussion; the reality in which they live is far from the comparative luxury of Plato's cave, for there is no way out, no route to the world outside. All they have are the chains of daily survival and the release of death. "I've taken a new lover. He can give me what you cannot" (48). Death provides both a release from the constant worry and an end to her physical suffering.

And yet the novel seems to be saying that there is something more—the relationship between the father and son is their reason for living. The novel implicitly argues that the woman fails in love because she cannot see beyond rape and starvation and being eaten. And yet how far can one admire the love the father has for the son? She is right—he cannot save them. And he will die leaving the son alone to face this dying world. That the son does not encounter cannibals but friends, others who "carry the fire" should not retroactively prove the father right.

But there is something strange about the relationship between the man and the child if we are to see it as the reason for persisting in this dead world. Neither the father nor the son is ever named. This works to imply a kind of universality of experience. But it does not always succeed. While the baby in *On the Beach* is named (Jennifer) she is usually referred to as "the baby." She is almost always only named by her mother—her father continues to refer to her as "the baby" and here we see the hint of what *The Road* brings home so forcefully: what does it mean to have a child in a world with no future? There are many reasons why the child in *The Road* may not be named (and of course the father is not named either). They stand in for any father and son. This can be a way of focusing the attention on the pair as the last vestiges of what we understand humanity to be. It is also an indication of the role that names play. There is no need for a name in a world that is ending. Names give particularity and meaning to human life.

Enough details about the child's birth are provided later in the book to identify the child as belonging to the man. This is not some truly nameless boy that the man came upon in the chaos of the days after the bombs fell. But knowing that the child really is the father's offspring does not relieve the sense that the father has little connection with this nameless and ageless child. The father's refusal to call his son by name belies his repeated claims that the father only lives for the son, "He knew only that the child was his warrant. He said: If he is not the word of God God never spoke" (4). If the child is his "warrant" then it is never certain what this warrant means—a guarantee that his own survival shall mean something? A reason to keep moving south in hopes of finding someplace warmer? A means for the father's own atonement? The woman recognizes (48) that the man can only live if he can live for the son. But what could this sacrifice possibly mean? He keeps his son alive so that he will know the love he has for the son. That is surely something the son will take with him. But is that sufficient meaning for what will be the short life the son lives?

On the Beach condones suicide; suicide is a form of love. It reflects the love the parent has for the child. Mary will assist in Jennifer's suicide and John Osbourne's mother commits suicide so that her own son does not have to worry too much about her at the end. She writes a note: "It's quite absurd that I should spoil the last days of your life by hanging on to mine, since it is such a burden to me now" (258). The idea that one should not become a burden to another runs throughout *On the Beach* and the reader is to admire John's mother just as they admire Moira for not pressuring Dwight to have an affair with her and to admire Mary for finally facing up to the end (although she continues to talk about how much they will enjoy the garden next summer). The characters are interconnected and each shares concerns with the others about the coming radiation and how people are doing. Yet no one ever really complains. When asked whether one is sick the usual response is to minimize one's pain.

This is a highly civilized depiction of the end of humanity, whereas *The Road* maintains only dregs of this civilized stance. The boy seems to have learned the conventions of familial love naturally and he strives to keep his father from knowing his pain. In many of their exchanges the boy speaks with more maturity and more awareness of the potential pain that he gives his father (the boy is speaking second).

> You dont believe me.
> I believe you.
> Okay.
> I always believe you.
> I dont think so.
> Yes I do. I have to. (156)

The boy's claim that he has to believe his father is both a gesture towards parental authority, this is part of what keeps the father going, that he is responsible for his son, but it is also a recognition by the boy that he lives through his father's fantasy that there might be others who do not eat people, that there might be a place where it is warmer, that there might be a place where there is more food.

> We're going to be okay, aren't we Papa?
> Yes. We are.
> And nothing bad is going to happen to us.
> That's right.
> Because we're carrying the fire.
> Yes. Because we're carrying the fire. (70)

The boy recognizes that his father might well lie to him (especially about dying, the father admits "Okay, I might" (86)). But both the boy and the man "has to" live by a certain fantasy of how they could live in this dead world.

> There's not any crows. Are there?
> No.
> Just in books?
> Yes. Just in books.
> I didnt think so. (133)

"Do you think there could be fish in the lake?" "No there is nothing in the lake" (17).

The boy lets his father decide the parameters of what the boy can know. And the boy's gift to his father is to accept, with little complaint, the father's version of the world in which they live.

But while the boy is willing to go along with his father it is not clear to me that the reader should be so willing. The woman is right. The man is living a fantasy and it is a dangerous one.

The final section outlines what message these novels are trying to impart to their readers. Each novel needs the postapocalyptic setting to impart their message. But the differing tones of the novel lead to two different messages to take from the end of the world.

Message

The impact of reading both books back to back is striking. Did Shute think that his subject matter was so appalling that he needed to reassure people that the sun would still shine and gardens would still bloom? Was McCarthy worried that we would not be sufficiently appalled and so he needed to describe a world wholly dead (one that produces a nagging suspicion in the reader—what could possibly have killed everything so completely? Isn't McCarthy giving human destructive capacity a little too much credit here?). On the other hand the worlds can be described as similar—each includes parents worried about the fate of their children in a world that is in many ways wholly unknowable.

If postapocalyptic fiction as a genre is didactic, then what kind of teaching emerges from tales of the end of all life as we know it? Yes, these accounts must surely be warnings, but a warning has little impact if there is not a clear sense of what we are being warned about. In both novels nuclear war brings on the end, but neither actually lectures on the dangers of nuclear proliferation (although *On the Beach* comes close). Each novel is careful to explore the idea of the end and the setting of the end and so perhaps the teaching is a more universal message of how one is to face up to the worst that we can imagine. But if that is the case then why choose an end of the world scenario? Surely there are already plenty of literal genocidal scenarios one could use to instruct readers on how to act when everything falls apart. So there should be reason, beyond death, that the postapocalyptic setting is chosen.

On the Beach counsels dignity; but it does so in a setting that makes such dignity easy to come by. *The Road* also counsels a kind of dignity; but this is one almost impossible to achieve. Dignity is connected to the world from which these humans will die. There is no difficulty the characters of *On the Beach* have to face (absent minor inconveniences, such as the shortage of gasoline) other than their impending deaths. The weather is wonderful, the food is plentiful, the fish are biting and the final grand prix car race offers the opportunity for true amateurs to race and win. Shute's novel is a strange postapocalyptic account in that it is both a description of the end of human life and a fantasy of a kind of playground for human pursuits in the final days before the end. "In Mary Holmes' garden the first narcissus bloomed on the first day of August, the day the radio announced, with studied objectivity, cases of radiation sickness in Adelaide and Sydney. The news did not trouble her particularly; all news was bad, like wage demands, strikes, or war, and the wise person paid no attention to it. What was important was that it was a bright, sunny day; her first narcissus was in bloom, and the daffodils behind them were already showing flower buds" (219). The bright sunny days will abound in the years and decades after this end. Thus one of the problems with the end is its utter pointlessness—if the world looks so good after the end then perhaps we can see how good it looks now and strive not to end it?

Sunny days are wholly absent in *The Road*. There is no moment where the lives of the father and son are anything other than difficult. Even when they find a cache of food the question of their safety from the roving bands of cannibals always looms. In such a world dignity has an entirely different meaning. In such a world the ethical refusal to eat human flesh becomes the fulcrum on which these survivors spin. "You dont eat people" "No. We dont eat people" (239). This exchange between the boy and the man he finds after his father dies establishes the only lines that need to be known. But there is no hope here that the boy has fallen in with a community of people who can begin again. He is with a group of people who will try and survive without eating other people. But they will all die, some likely at the hands of the cannibals who will certainly live longer. But human beings will die out. Under such conditions the father and son will only try to live another day—each for the other. But the son will have no son to follow him. And the world will, it seems, shrivel up on itself and disappear. If Shute's readers are struck by the pointlessness of endless sunny days with no humans or dogs or rabbits or cows to enjoy them, then McCarthy's readers are to see only an ever darkening globe, lifeless and bleak.

Both *The Road* and *On the Beach* share an odd hubris about the end of the world. While each is potentially arguing against the hubris of humans thinking that they cannot bring about an end both authors have produced novels that presume that humanity is the key to life on earth. It is strange that in both accounts all animal life dies even though there is good evidence (e.g. in the ruins of Chernobyl) that many animal species will bounce back after nuclear war. Even the ubiquitous cockroach of post-nuclear scares are absent in both of these books. McCarthy describes a world wholly dead—unrealistically dead—and Shute assures the reader that all life will die out. It is as if each is saying that the one thing you can use to comfort yourself at the end is that at least everything else died out as well. But what a strange message. Life has little pull for either novel.

"They'll all go in the end of course. There will be nothing left alive here by the end of next year" (226, *On The Beach*). "The man watched him. I dont know how many people there are, he said. I dont think there are very many" (205, *The Road*). What is it that has killed all of the living creatures on earth? Shute's novel clearly describes a post-nuclear world. McCarthy's novel gives few answers other than the man watching "distant cities burn" and this one paragraph:

> The clocks stopped at 1:17. A long shear of light and then a series of low concussions. He got up and went to the window. What is it? She said. He didnt answer. He went into the bathroom and threw the lightswitch but the power was already gone. A dull rose glow in the windowglass. he dropped to one knee and raised the lever to stop the tub and then turned on both taps as far as they would go. She was standing in the doorway in her nightwear, clutching the jamb, cradling her belly in one hand. What is it? she said. What is happening?
> I dont know.
> Why are you taking a bath?
> I'm not (45)

The "long shear of light" implies a nuclear blast and the details that emerge, the father's cough, the people immolated, Pompeii-like, the death of the birds all are clues to a potential nuclear blast. But this must have been more than one such blast. There is no indication of who set off the bombs, but there is clearly no space that is not burnt and dead. There is no evidence that anyone else exists, that there is anyplace else to be. But there is also no explanation for what kind of nuclear exchange could have created the extent of this wasted landscape. There is something supernatural about the overwhelming death. Just as there is something maddening in the man's refusal to respond to the light or share with his wife what must have been the utter terror of seeing the end.

Neither *On the Beach* nor *The Road* is interested in the immediate circumstances of the apocalyptic event itself. There are few descriptions of bombs falling or of the immediate circumstances that the bombs produced: the fear, chaos, violence and death. Instead each gives the aftermath of the end, and yet each views that aftermath radically differently. *On the Beach* portrays a world always sunny with an excess of food and drink. Survival both is and is not the primary problem. There is no question about their immediate survival—there is no threat to them, they live in a land of plenty and the beauty of the surroundings is present in almost every page that describes life outside of Melbourne. But survival is always a question as their death is imminent and everyone knows it. *The Road* inverts this survival issue: immediate survival is always a problem; the man and the boy are always hungry and never safe. They can never fully rest and never completely relax. But their long term survival (or at least the boy's) is taken for granted if they can solve the immediate needs. To the reader this is almost nonsensical. There is no chance of long term survival in a world where a handful of humans are the only living entities. There is no chance for living in a world devoid of plants, fish, birds (even their discovery of mushrooms seem to be desiccated mushrooms left from the world before its death). There is no mention of any group working to reseed the soil, or if that is even a possibility. In this *The Road* is a most confusing combination of pretended hope in the continued language about God, and utter hopelessness in the starkness of the reality that they live.

On the Beach does include a description of the war that produced the clouds of radiation. The actual account of the war that precedes the opening of the novel is only explained once, briefly, about a third of the way into the book. A war between Russia and China over Russia's purported desire to take Shanghai as a warm water port begins the war. But the nuclear exchange is described as beginning with a bomb being dropped on Naples, Italy, "by the Albanians" and then the bombing of Tel Aviv. After that Egypt seems to have bombed the United States and England, and then the U.S bombed Russia (thinking Russia had initially bombed the U.S.) and China is described as taking advantage of the use of nuclear bombs to target Russia. This exchange of bombs is discussed by members of the Australian navy, the U.S. navy and a scientist in strikingly dispassionate terms. While the "mistaken" nature of the eventual exchange seems to give them pause, their analysis of what happened is simply that "it's mighty difficult to stop a war when all the statesmen have been killed" (78). The only explanation for underlying causes is given by the scientist who decries the availability of nuclear materials: "The trouble is, the damn things got too cheap. The original uranium bomb only cost about fifty thousand quid towards the end. Every little pipsqueak country like Albania could have a stockpile of them, and every little country that had that, thought it could defeat the major countries in a surprise attack" (78). War is clearly futile, minor countries are described as irresponsible and the power of the "statesman" to keep things in equilibrium is easily upset once those statesmen are dead. But what kind of warning is this to the reader? Beware the random mistake by the military? Beware cheap uranium?

Even a facile discussion of the war's origins is absent in *The Road*. Other than the one description of the day of the bombs there is no mention of what kind of bombs fell, who dropped them or why. This might produce greater unease in the reader, but I think it reveals McCarthy's lack of interest in detailing the world into which the father was born. His memories of that world are all wholly personal—there is no attempt to place the political situation that produced this war. *The Road*'s didactic message is less political than that of *On the Beach*; it is also less political than most postapocalyptic fiction, a genre that tends towards the warnings of either the personality traits or the political conditions that produce or exacerbate apocalyptic events. On the other hand, *The Road* uses a fear of this desolation to perhaps awaken in the reader a desire to work against whatever forces might be out to produce it. As an open-ended warning McCarthy may leave more space for human agency to act against such an end. Shute leaves little room for an ordinary reader (one not connected to people in power) to do anything. There is the claim that leaders matter and so we should strive to elect the best leaders we can, but there is also the recognition that once those leaders are out of the way the military wheel will be set in motion and unable to stop. In this sense both are fairly hopeless novels.

That lack of hope works against one of the common themes of postapocalyptic fiction, which, are often hopeful celebrations of human ingenuity in their detailing of how people start over again. What the postapocalypse creates in each novel is something unique: *On the Beach* details a fully functioning civil society that happens to be coming to a quiet end. Shute prefaces the novel with the famous lines from T.S. Eliot: "This is the way the world ends. . . . not with a bang but a whimper." Yet Shute's novel ends not so much with a whimper as with an imagined Titanic-like soundtrack of "Nearer My God to Thee." "Whimper" implies the kind of sadness that the characters here do not express. Everyone follows the rules, they all take their suicide pills, and they all die quietly in their own beds or cars. *The Road*, on the other hand, outlines a wholly broken and dead world. There are not only no rules (something common to postapocalyptic fiction) there is also no nature. There is no material with which one could create a life. No fields to plant, no apples to pick, no shelters to build. The final lines, which recall the beauty of the trout swimming through the water reminds the reader that there are no trout to fish; the conditions for human sustenance are entirely absent.

These two novels then show through their absence what conditions are needed for a social contract to emerge. A social contract cannot emerge in a functioning society;[13] and a social contract cannot emerge from a dead world. When social contract thinkers discuss the state of nature they are describing

a set of conditions under which humans will act unencumbered by the restraints and rules of interaction under civil society. Whether through a fear
of punishment (Hobbes) or a desire to be seen as the kind of person who
obeys the law (Rousseau) we are described as beings that alter our behavior
when restricted by rules that we understand to be largely person made. Part
of why postapocalyptic fiction is seen to embody the state of nature is this
unencumbered quality—the world postapocalypse strips our behavior bare:
what would people do if they were not restrained? Clearly the characters of
On the Beach are restrained, if not by the law (although it is clear that the
law holds sway) then by the customs of "civilized" life. The Director of State
Fisheries makes a radio announcement moving the start of the trout season
(205), indicating both a fully functioning Department of Fisheries and a
people willing to obey such rules. Even the distribution of the suicide pills,
neatly packaged in red boxes and available at the corner pharmacy, illustrates
a society fully organized.

It would seem then that The Road shows humans without restraint. And
yet here too we see two kinds of humans: the man and boy who are living
by some unelucidated code to "carry the fire" and avoid cannibalism and the
clearly organized bands of cannibals. The cannibals wear a kind of uniform
(red scarves) and march in fairly orderly fashion, followed by "the phalanx
following carried spears or lances tasseled with ribbons, the long blades ham-
mered out of trucksprings in some crude forge upcountry. . . . Behind them
came wagons drawn by slaves in harness . . . and after that the women, perhaps a dozen in number, some of them pregnant, and lastly a supplementary
number of catamites ill clothed against the cold and fitted with dog collars
and yoked to each other" (78). This horrific scene, discussed earlier, depicts
an organized group. This group has acquired a steady food supply, and has
designated societal roles (warrior, slave, and prostitute). Presumably there is
a system by which one enters these communities (and the next chapter will
discuss such rituals in Lucifer's Hammer). So here too the parameters of the
state of nature are absent.

Hobbes' description of the state of nature describes neither the world of
On the Beach nor that of The Road:

> In such condition there is no place for industry, because the fruit thereof is
> uncertain: and consequently no culture of the earth; no navigation, nor use
> of the commodities that may be imported by sea; no commodious building;
> no instruments of moving and removing such things as require much force;
> no knowledge of the face of the earth; no account of time; no arts; no letters;
> no society; and which is worst of all, continual fear, and danger of violent

death; and the life of man, solitary, poor, nasty, brutish, and short. (*Leviathan*, ch. XIII)

While "continual fear" may well capture the daily life of the man and boy in *The Road* it does not reflect the leaders of the band of cannibals. But even here the description of the bearded band of cannibals hardly expresses all of what Hobbes expects us to get out of civil society: "knowledge of the face of the earth," "art," "letters" and "an account of time." So the cannibals are both organized and led, but they also are unable to do what humans do: build, improve, learn. More importantly the world of *The Road* lacks the material to make "commodities . . . imported by sea." Hobbes' description above is one of what human hands make. But in *The Road* all the survivors can do is to recycle the remnants of human industry. Swords made from trucksprings do not reflect the meaning Hobbes gives to human industry, which involves mastering the natural world. It is clear that Hobbes simply takes for granted the literal fruits of the world as something that must exist for human life to exist.

Locke and Rousseau make this point even more clearly. Locke describes the abundance of the earth:

> God, who hath given the world to men in common, hath also given them reason to make use of it to the best advantage of life, and convenience. The earth, and all that is therein, is given to men for the support and comfort of their being. And tho' all the fruits it naturally produces, and beasts it feeds, belong to mankind in common, as they are produced by the spontaneous hand of nature; . . . The fruit, or venison, which nourishes the wild Indian, who knows no enclosure, and is still a tenant in common, must be his, and so his, i.e. a part of him, that another can no longer have any right to it, before it can do him any good for the support of his life. (V, 26, 18)

Whatever happened the night those bombs fell and destroyed this world, there are no beasts, no fruit, no venison, no means by which to ensure "support" for one's life. There is no work to be done and thus nothing to own. Locke's expectation is that humans labor with the world to produce property, but is finding a hidden cache of canned food really labor? There is nothing that the inhabitants of *The Road* can do to improve the world.

Rousseau's description of nature argues even more strongly for the abundant riches that our surroundings offer for our pleasure and improvement.

> While the earth was left to its natural fertility and covered with immense forests, whose trees were never mutilated by the axe, it would present on every

side both sustenance and shelter for every species of animal. Men, dispersed up and down among the rest, would observe and imitate their industry, and thus attain even to the instinct of the beasts, with the advantage that, whereas every species of brutes was confined to one particular instinct, man, who perhaps has not any one peculiar to himself, would appropriate them all, and live upon most of those different foods which other animals shared among themselves; and thus would find his subsistence much more easily than any of the rest. (*Discourse on Origin of Inequality*, I: 47-48)

The beasts, the forests, the foods, *The Road* has destroyed this abundant earth and presented a fragile and broken world where humans can only fight over the last dredges of what civilization made.

So clearly the conditions of the state of nature include a natural world that provides the means for sustaining human life. The material out of which a functioning society can be created includes a natural world that can be enjoyed, if not mastered. That material includes human life that can be sustained and that can see a future for itself. Hobbes describes the "equality of hope in the attaining of our ends" (ch. XIII) as one of the reasons why we quarrel, but we should recognize that before the quarrel we *have* such hope. How can there be any hope (equal or not) of achieving what you desire in a wholly dead world? Even the characters in *On the Beach* are able to achieve a number of their ends—plant a garden, build a dam, race a car. Their lives may be ending, but they can live those last weeks as humans with plans for a future. But there is no possibility for a "rational life plan" (Rawls) in McCarthy's world[14] and without such a potential plan there is no reason to enter into a social contract to build a just society.

And so these two postapocalyptic accounts[15] defy the expectations of postapocalyptic fiction and reveal the conditions necessary for a new state of nature from which we can see civil society emerge. These two novels do not depict states of nature, they do not outline how we survive the end, and instead they detail how to endure the end and how to die with grace. The following chapters outline the ways in which other, more traditional, postapocalyptic accounts reflect either classic social contract thinker (via Hobbes, Locke, Rousseau, Rawls) or set out new ways of thinking about the state of nature and about the contract that emerges from it.

Notes

1. Nevil Shute, *On the Beach*, (New York: Ballantine Books, 1957), 271.
2. *Lucifer's Hammer* has the amateur astronomer and a scientist who buries the encyclopedia and medical texts for life after the end; *Malevil* needs no scientists and

instead has the Renaissance man who can farm and organize society; even Lauren Oya Olamina of the *Parable* series has a keen observant eye.

3. This raises a particularly difficult issue for the utopian accounts that emerge from postapocalyptic events. Is the event itself to be rationalized because the society that emerged from it is clearly better than what was destroyed? Some environmental postapocalyptic works seem quite comfortable simply answering yes. Ernest Callenbach's *Ecotopia* (New York: Bantam Doubleday, 1977) is one example. Other accounts, e.g. Marge Piercy and Octavia Butler, wrestle with the desire to both warn and entice. But the enticements of the better society are not dependent on the destruction of all that we now know (unlike *Left Behind* that not only rationalizes, but wholly defends, the destruction of all we have known).

4. The novel was serialized in both the *LA Times* and the *Washington Post*. In the review in the *Washington Post*, *On the Beach* was named "the most important and dramatic novel of the atomic age" qtd. in Peter J. Kuznick, "Prophets of Doom or Voices of Sanity? The Evolving Discourse of Annihilation in the First Decade and a Half of the Nuclear Age," *Journal of Genocide Research* (September, 2007): 433.

5. *The Road* was reviewed extensively, particularly after winning the Pulitzer Prize and being chosen as a book club selection on *Oprah*. Two reviews also mention *On the Beach*: Stefan Beck, "A Trackless Waste," *New Criterion* 25, (October, 2006), and John Breslin, "From These Ashes," *America* 196, (January 29, 2007). Other reviews of *The Road* include: Philip Connors, "Crenellated Heat," *London Review of Books*, (January 25, 2007); James Wood, "Getting to the End," *New Republic*, (May 21, 2007); Michael Chabon "After the Apocalypse," *New York Review of Books* 54, (February 15, 2007); Shawn Macomber, "Life after Death, Cormac McCarthy's Postapocalypse Western," *Weekly Standard* 12, (February 5, 2007).

6. The film of *On the Beach* got far more press than the novel. But the novel was reviewed in *Time* : "World's End," (August 19, 1957), *The New Republic* (Robert Estabrook, "After Armageddon" (August 12, 1957)) and *Maclean's*.

7. William Brinkley's *The Last Ship* recounts a US naval ship and a soviet submarine that travel the oceans in search of an island absent dangerous radiation.

8. Philip Beidler, "Remembering *On the Beach*," *War, Literature and the Arts, an International Journal of the Humanities* 21 (2009), 370-382. Beidler notes that in both the novel and the film, "one is finally struck by the end at how well the people die both as individuals and as people." (377).

9. Compare McCarthy's horror movie description of the victims of the cannibal to Octavia Butler's description of the children who have resorted to cannibalism on the road in *Parable of the Sower*. Which is more horrifying? The very excess of McCarthy's description pushes it beyond the believable to the merely pornographic while Butler's spare description chills. This passage is discussed in chapter 6.

10. This is one of the places where the novel does not ring true—the cannibals are also on foot and it seems strange that one could not just walk out of their territory. Or hide away more effectively—the cannibals are not using technological devices to chase people down, and yet they are always present.

11. *On the Beach* uses the phrase "the world after nuclear war," where *The Road* uses "postapocalyptic."

12. Shute shares with McCarthy an insistence that women cannot handle the end of the world and a persistent belief that they will exhibit only shallowness at the worst of times.

13. Or at least not without a revolution.

14. It may well be that the "rational life plan" is absent in most of McCarthy's fiction, not just in this postapocalyptic world.

15. There are other accounts that share this totality of an end, Margaret Atwood's *Oryx and Crake* and P.D James' *Children of Men.*

CHAPTER TWO

~

"... solitary, poor, nasty, brutish and short"

Hobbes and Lucifer's Hammer, the Classic Postapocalyptic Text

Hobbes is the classic state of nature theorist. His description of life in the state of nature as "nasty, brutish and short" captures the political realist's assumptions about human nature. Political realism argues that human beings are covetous and quarrelsome and only through the intervention of rules established by a chosen authority figure can peace be ensured. The Hobbesian state of nature defined by "the war of all against all" is a staple in postapocalyptic fiction. The apocalyptic event, through its destruction of official manifestations of authority (politicians, police, military), reveals humans fighting against one another for their survival. There is little chance for any survivor to relax after the event when there is "no mine and thine." This world demands eternal vigilance. Out of this violence and tension comes the desire for peace, the recognition that the desire for peace is mutual, and the choosing of an authority figure that we endow with the right to create rules and punish transgressors.

Many postapocalyptic accounts[1] set themselves up as Hobbesian, either through reference to the "nasty, brutish and short" descriptions of the state of nature or through a celebration of the violence that societal breakdown has produced. But to really be a Hobbesian account the novel must recognize the foundation from which Hobbes sets out his ideas on the state of nature: humans are equal, no one person has the strength (mental or physical) to legitimately hold sway over another, the social contract creates the sovereign, political authority is thus created by humans (it is artificial) and is not natural (bestowed by either God or by natural talents). A Hobbesian postapocalyptic account is not simply violent. These accounts argue for this political realist worldview: without rules, violence is inevitable and only a political authority, created and chosen by people, can produce security.

This chapter analyzes *Lucifer's Hammer* by Larry Niven and Jerry Pournelle as one such Hobbesian postapocalyptic account. In its discussion of the world after the event (which is a comet strike), the way in which survivors come together and the description of human nature that informs the motivations of the characters, *Lucifer's Hammer* captures well a Hobbesian worldview. It is not always wholly accurate (as with most postapocalyptic authors these wrestle with the idea of human equality); but it does reveal both what happens to humans when they are deprived of all that they have taken for granted and how and why such creatures would come together and establish a political authority.

Larry Niven is a prolific and award winning[2] science fiction writer with a clear interest in challenging humans through interactions with aliens, space travel and end of the world scenarios. He is generally known for his careful use of science and his novels and the worlds they create are thought experiments designed to question the reader's assumptions about human life. *Lucifer's Hammer*[3] reveals more knowledge about the science of meteors than it does knowledge about Hobbes, but the novel spends enough time on the aftermath of the comet to illustrate a concern with how humans interact in state of nature like scenarios. *Lucifer's Hammer* also shows how hard equality is to imagine in that the novel reiterates sexual and racial hierarchies.[4] The contract that emerges in the course of the novel is one built on racial genocide and patriarchal politics.

Hobbes: State of Nature and the Social Contract

Thomas Hobbes (1588-1679) is the first modern social contract thinker. He argued that humans once lived in a "state of nature," that we once lived without government, without laws, without authority. The violence of this state of nature convinced the humans inhabiting it that it would be better to choose an authority figure who would provide peace and protection. Hobbes (via Thucydides) outlines politically realist assumptions about human motivation: we are primarily motivated by fear, self interest and pride.

The state of nature is identified by a series of absences: no government, no order, no rules, and the subsequent consequences of that lack of order:

> In such condition there is no place for industry, because the fruit thereof is uncertain: and consequently no culture of the earth; no navigation, nor use of

the commodities that may be imported by sea; no commodious building; no instruments of moving and removing such things as require much force; no knowledge of the face of the earth; no account of time; no arts; no letters; no society; and which is worst of all, continual fear, and danger of violent death; and the life of man, solitary, poor, nasty, brutish, and short. (Ch. XIII: 9)

The state of nature produces conditions that make it impossible for humans to flourish. They might be able to survive, but they cannot progress. They cannot produce the hallmarks of human society: agriculture, transportation, trade, architecture, invention, learning, art and the delights of communal living. Not only is one unable to enjoy the usual fruits of human industry, but one also has to endure "continual fear, and the danger of violent death." Thus life will be lived alone (because you cannot sufficiently trust others to live with you), it will be lived hand to mouth (for you have no assurance that any food you secure will not be stolen), it will be potentially violent, it will not feel like a human life and you will not likely live long. Unlike McCarthy's postapocalyptic world in *The Road*, Hobbes does presume that there are the material conditions to live an industrious and pleasurable life. The social contract improves one's life, not because it produces an abundant natural landscape, but because it provides the framework within which one can enjoy and improve upon such a landscape.

Hobbes describes a state of nature from which we can escape by recognizing the mutual advantage of coming together and choosing a lawgiver and enforcer. There are three interrelated features of the framework of the social contract: a state of nature, a social contract and a description of human nature to explain how we move from the state of nature to civil society. In order to identify a fictional postapocalyptic account as Hobbesian the account needs to follow Hobbes in the setting of the aftermath, the willingness to come together and the recognition of who we are. First, of course, is the description of the aftermath as violent and chaotic. Second, is the recognition that this violence will only be solved by mutual agreement of the survivors to give up their natural right to anything and everything they desire. This includes realizing that no one person or group of people is so naturally superior to be able to naturally rule over us. Finally these survivors think of themselves as the kinds of beings who would make such a rational calculation.

Hobbes argues that human beings in the state of nature have the right to anything to survive. And while humans might kill another or take food that another had procured (but does not own, and so one cannot steal) the motivation to survive does not reveal any inherent evil in human nature.

> Nature hath made men so equal in the faculties of body and mind as that, though there be found one man sometimes manifestly stronger in body or of quicker mind than another, yet when all is reckoned together the difference between man and man is not so considerable as that one man can thereupon claim to himself any benefit to which another may not pretend as well as he. For as to the strength of body, the weakest has strength enough to kill the strongest, either by secret machination or by confederacy with others that are in the same danger with himself. (Ch. XIII:1)

Human equality is the foundation on which the conditions of the state of nature are built. The state of nature is violent because humans are naturally equal: if some were naturally superior over others then the very idea of political organization would arise naturally and there would be no chaos. Humans are equal because each can, using either their bodily strength or their wits, kill another. Thus each of us feels vulnerable at the presence of another human—each of us can die as easily as another and each of us has the ability to kill another.

This does not mean that we have some inherent desire to kill others; in fact it is quite the opposite, we have an inherent desire for peace, for relief from the constant tension of living with the threat of imminent death. We may be naturally mistrustful of others, something that Hobbes proves by noting our tendency to lock our doors even when we do live in civil society. Yet there is still, as Hobbes says, "no sin" in this mistrust:

> Let him therefore consider with himself: when taking a journey, he arms himself and seeks to go well accompanied; when going to sleep, he locks his doors; when even in his house he locks his chests; and this when he knows there be laws and public officers, armed, to revenge all injuries shall be done him; what opinion he has of his fellow subjects, when he rides armed; of his fellow citizens, when he locks his doors; and of his children, and servants, when he locks his chests. Does he not there as much accuse mankind by his actions as I do by my words? But neither of us accuse man's nature in it. The desires, and other passions of man, are in themselves no sin. No more are the actions that proceed from those passions till they know a law that forbids them; which till laws be made they cannot know, nor can any law be made till they have agreed upon the person that shall make it. (Ch. XIII: 10)

Hobbes is making two points here. One, if people accuse Hobbes of describing humans as inherently evil, then he wants to know why people in civil society act with mistrust. In other words if Hobbes is being taken to task for being overly harsh in his description of human life absent the rules of civil society then he wants to know why the harshness of human behavior in civil society is not an indictment of human behavior? But his more important point is that there is nothing inherently wrong with the mistrust that motivates human behavior. The very idea of good and evil, right and wrong are dependent on the conventions of civil society. This is not to say that the behavior really *is* wrong (objectively), but that the humans have no vocabulary for that wrongness. Rather Hobbes is making a deeper point.

Evil is a term that requires a civil society to produce an agreed upon meaning. However the people in the state of nature certainly recognize that life in the state of nature is not desirable. They seek to alleviate some of their constant fear; they do not somehow yearn for the violence. Finally, there truly is nothing "sinful" in doing what one must to survive.

> And therefore so long as a man is in the condition of mere nature, which is a condition of war, private appetite is the measure of good and evil: and consequently all men agree on this, that peace is good, and therefore also the way or means of peace, which (as I have shown before) are justice, gratitude, modesty, equity, mercy, and the rest of the laws of nature, are good; that is to say, moral virtues; and their contrary vices, evil. (Ch. XV: 40)

Individuals recognize what they desire (and thus call good) and what they detest (and thus call evil). But there is nothing communally recognized as good and evil as such, because there is no community as such. Peace is possible because each individual desires it and is consequently also averse to violence. Humans are thus not naturally violent; rather humans are willing to use violence when their well-being is threatened.

So humans individually desire peace. Individuals also recognize a kind of affinity with other individuals. We know that we each desire similar sort of things because of the tension that arises out of mutual desire for items that cannot be equitably shared ("if any two men desire the same thing, which nevertheless they cannot both enjoy, they become enemies"). The violence of the state of nature is due to our equality and our similarity. Yet the same equality and similarity help us recognize that we see that all desire peace, which can be shared. But peace cannot exist until we give up our rights to do anything we must to survive in the state of nature. "The passions that incline men to peace are: fear of death; desire of such things as are necessary to commodious living; and a hope by their industry to obtain them" (Ch. XIII:14). The hope that we might be able to accomplish something lasting through our "industry" is not misplaced. And it is this hope that underlies our willingness to create a sovereign entity to create and enforce the law.

"[T]he motive and end for which this renouncing and transferring of right is introduced is nothing else but the security of a man's person, in his life, and in the means of so preserving life as not to be weary of it" (Ch. XIV:8). We are moved to associate with others like us, creatures whom we mistrust, because we recognize that we all desire peace so that we might work to improve the conditions of our lives.

Once we come together we create ("authorize," literally understood) a sovereign, either in one or many persons (i.e. we create government by choosing a form of government), and we then give our right to do anything to this sovereign. The only right that we retain is the right to self defense (given that the only reason that we entered into the contract in the first place was to attain peace). Thus we exchange the right to do whatever we want ("the right of nature") for peace.

> Whensoever a man transferreth his right, or renounceth it, it is either in consideration of some right reciprocally transferred to himself, or for some other good he hopeth for thereby. For it is a voluntary act: and of the voluntary acts of every man, the object is some good to himself. (Ch. XIV: 8)

Again, Hobbes does not intend for the reader to understand this definition of a voluntary act as evidence of a selfishness that needs to be rooted out of human behavior. Rather, Hobbes is indicating, with optimism, that the very fact that we are motivated to act in ways to improve our own situation is a sign that peace is possible, that a social contract will work and that civil society can flourish.

> This is more than consent, or concord; it is a real unity of them all in one and the same person, made by covenant of every man with every man, in such manner as if every man should say to every man: I authorise and give up my right of governing myself to this man, or to this assembly of men, on this condition; that thou give up, thy right to him, and authorise all his actions in like manner. (Ch. XVII: 13)

We are thus tied together because of the mutuality of the exchange of promises, promises which are backed up by a sovereign entity. We will protect what is ours, and we understand that protection is more likely to be found if we enter into a social contract with one another. Hobbes outlines the state of nature in order to explain how and why it is that we live in civil society now. To channel a Hobbesian world view as a postapocalyptic fiction writer is to understand that the state of nature like setting of the world after the end is itself only a means for coming together and creating a civil society.

From this brief outline of Hobbes' view on the state of nature, the humans who inhabit it and the social contract, the pieces of the Hobbesian post-apocalyptic account are apparent. It cannot simply be a violence-fest, rather it needs to reflect human equality, the mutuality of desire and the potential for human flourishing in civil society.

Lucifer's Hammer

Written in 1977, *Lucifer's Hammer* was a bestseller that noted its end of the world scenario on the front cover. The event is based on a comet strike and the first half of the novel outlines the discovery of the comet, questions about whether it would strike the earth, and the introduction of the various characters who will survive the impact. But, unlike many "comet near miss" novels and films, the real impact of *Lucifer's Hammer* happens after the comet (or parts of it) does strike and the aftermath of the flooded and radically changed California coast and inland valleys. It is a large novel that spends its first half introducing myriad characters and the second half bringing those characters together in the valleys of the foothills of the Sierra mountains.

The main characters are fully introduced in their pre-comet lives so that the reader can evaluate the strengths and weaknesses these characters might exhibit in the world post-comet. The protagonists are: Tim Hamner, the heir of a soap company fortune whose interest in and support of astronomy results in his discovery of the comet and its being named after him; Senator Jellison, who owns the all important ranch in the foothills of California's Sierra mountains and his daughter Maureen who meet Tim Hamner at a cocktail party opening the novel; and Harvey Randall, documentary film maker and his wife Loretta about whom we learn "the one attempt to take her on a hike with their son had been a disaster" (12), clearly indicating who will live and who will die when the comet strikes. All of these characters are powerful people, wealthy, connected and at the top of their game. But we also get clues from the very opening that these characters have traits and capacities that will serve them well after the comet falls.

The physical descriptions of Senator Jellison, Harvey Randall and Tim Hamner each capture men who might have "a bit of a paunch" or drink a little too much, but are physically capable: "tall" "muscular" and in Randall's case, with camping experience. Maureen Jellison is primarily described as physically beautiful, although also intelligent and working for her father and so connected to power.[5] The opening party sets up a portrait of beautiful, strong people who are surrounded by conversations typical of any cocktail party among the rich and powerful; who looks like what, who would like to be sleeping with whom, who is involved in crazy, expensive pastimes (Tim Hamner). From a Hobbesian standpoint what we want to see are the advantages that these characters have given the fully functioning society in which they live. Hobbes, who believes that humans are naturally equal, recognizes that civil society confers inequalities upon people—through wealth, fame and the conventions supported by that society. In these opening pages we encounter those who might think of themselves as being naturally superior. These characters are all successful in their jobs, but their jobs—Senator, soap manufacturer (and amateur astronomer) and documentary filmmaker—are wholly of civil society. If these characters possess skills that would be useful to the state of nature their jobs do not reveal those talents.

Lucifer's Hammer plays with the claims of Hobbesian natural equality. On the one hand it seems to wrestle with the fact of that equality. Can it really be the case that humans are naturally equal? Surely the know how and physical prowess of Senator Jellison, for example, will produce in others a recognition of natural superiority? On the other hand it reminds the reader of the foundation of Hobbesian equality: equal vulnerability in the face of death and equal capacity to kill another using wits or strength or group power. The novel illustrates well how this natural equality works in a world absent the rules of civil society.

The world prior to the comet's impact matters little to the Hobbesian analysis here. It obviously matters to the novel and the introduction to characters in their home setting—their artificial setting—helps to clarify what these people might be able to accomplish in the state of nature. Niven and Pournelle do not only focus on people in conventional positions of societal power. They also introduce Alim Nassor, who "could still walk into City Hall and get in to see people. He'd been able to do that ever since he broke up a riot with his switchblade and the razor blades in his shoes and the chain he carried around his waist" (72). Nassor exhibits a kind of raw power: a willingness to use violence outside of the sanctioned violence of civil society that could give him a potential advantage in the state of nature. Nassor, in fact, is living in civil society as if he were in the state of nature; having opted out of the rule bound conventions of that society. He is described as "a natural leader." And yet the naturalness of his leadership is built on Nassor's contrasting style of leadership to that of the political authorities. So this natural leadership is actually a constructed style of leadership in a world of white political authority. Niven and Pournelle are setting Nassor up for failure in the "real" state of nature.[6]

The transition from civil society to the state of nature might seem to be marred by one non-Hobbesian circumstance: some (Jellison, Hamner, and an astrophysicist, Forrester who has the most far reaching plans for moving beyond the end of the world) recognize that the comet is likely to hit earth (the government is playing down this possibility, so few are preparing). These characters are able to prepare for the end. In some cases this preparation is simply the preparation for a long camping trip (four-wheel drive vehicles, razor blades, sleeping bags). Hamner has a list of desired items (dog food, sunscreen, other first aid equipment) and he goes through the trouble of making beef jerky and pemmican (and he packs spices). In the case of Forrester the packing included sealing books in plastic bags protected with insect spray and mothballs and burying them in his septic tank. On the day of the comet Forrester leaves his house with his insulin (and extra stashed away) and "one really valuable item," "Volume Two of *The Way Things Work*. Volume One was in the septic tank" (276). These preparations are not wholly for naught; but the novel does illustrate well that preparing for this kind of postapocalyptic event means doing more than just setting down a supply of food for a few weeks or months. The preparations that people make are often defeated by chance or thieves (who, according to the conditions of the state of nature, are acting fully within their rights). People who were moderately prepared (with a supply of food, a vehicle and maybe a weapon) do have the advantage of potentially living through the first week. But such preparations do not challenge the basic equality of the survivors of the comet. The best preparation is ultimately the recognition of the impact of what has happened.[7]

Chaos

Hobbes argues that the conditions of the state of nature result from the absence of a common power to "keep us in awe." The reason life in the state of nature is "solitary, poor, nasty, brutish and short" is that civil authority is absent. Without established laws and a system for the enforcement of those laws, humans have the right to do whatever they need to do to survive. One clear contrast between Hobbes' argument and the conditions apparent in the postapocalyptic accounts discussed in the previous chapter was that neither in *On the Beach* nor in *The Road* did we see Hobbesian conditions. *On the Beach* describes a world dying, but with a fully functioning civil authority. *The Road* is a world absent civil authority, but also so extreme that there is little one can do to survive (so yes, it is Hobbesian in that one has the right to do what one can to survive, probably including cannibalism, but no, it is not Hobbesian because Hobbes presumes that there are the means for survival). The question for Hobbesian postapocalyptic accounts is then whether the event of the postapocalypse destroys, as we saw in *The Road*, these means for survival. If *The Road* fails as a Hobbesian account, in part, because nature is dead, then does it fail here in *Lucifer's Hammer* where survival (particularly in the days immediately following the event) is so difficult?

The chaos of the event itself has to be separated from the chaos of the aftermath. A Hobbesian state of nature, while a "war of all against all" is not chaotic because of tidal waves, earthquakes, hurricanes or volcanoes. Rather a Hobbesian state of nature can emerge from the aftermath of such incidents when those incidents destroy the authoritative infrastructure of civil society. So the chaos that titles this section is not the chaos of the comet's strike, but rather the chaos that emerges when people realize what that comet strike means. Preparation and luck will help (but not guarantee) that you survive the impact of a calved comet (or it won't), but the event is not the point.[8] Niven and Pournelle devote about 60 pages to the experience of the comet fall itself through the various characters to whom we have been introduced and some new characters brought in simply for their spectacular deaths (the 17 year old who surfs the tidal wave into Santa Monica until he crashes into a 30 story apartment building). What the violence of the event does do is instill knowledge, knowledge that people in Hobbes' state of nature would have from birth.

In order for a true Hobbesian state of nature to exist the inhabitants of that state need to know its conditions. From Hobbes' perspective knowledge of the conditions of the state of nature, "the war of all against all," is possessed by the inhabitants of the state of nature. He does not explain in the *Leviathan* how people learn that life is difficult in the state of nature. People live that difficulty every day and it is because that difficulty is so obvious to them that they are willing to enter into the social contract and give up their right to everything. The people Hobbes imagines living in the state of nature do not need to be taught that they live in violence because they experience that violence daily. But we who have become accustomed to the advantages of civil society must learn the consequences of a life without both laws and those willing to defend us against violators of those laws. The advantage that we have, the advantage of the postapocalyptic account in creating civil society again is that we do know about civil society and what it can offer us.[9]

And so *Lucifer's Hammer* uses the comet fall not only to entertain through pyrotechnics, but also to show the death of the rule of law. The novel emphasizes the proximity we have to a Hobbesian world when the comet instigates a massive exchange of nuclear bombs between China and the USSR (witnessed by the last surviving astronauts, two Soviet and two American, who witness both the comet strike and the nuclear exchange). This insult added to injury reveals a Hobbesian understanding that political states are always in a state of nature with one another (because there is no common sovereign ruling over the world). The rule of law dies not simply through the comet, but also through instruments of war. But the event, comet and/or nuclear bomb, is not the focus; rather it is the aftermath that drives the novel's climax. The aftermath illustrates the state of nature at work. In the aftermath the characters must learn that most of which they had known and relied upon is gone. This is played out in *Lucifer's Hammer* with multiple characters.

Eileen (who will pair up with Tim Hamner) lives through the initial earthquakes and sees that her boss has been killed by falling glass. She does what anyone would do in such an event. Having realized that the phones are down she goes out to the street to look for the police: "There were police outside, and one was Eric Larsen. She started to call him, then she saw what was happening and she stood quietly in the ruined doorway" (230). She soon understands "that the police . . . weren't police anymore" (233). Eric Larsen, who represents civil authority, is the first person who must learn what it means to no longer live in a rule bound world. In the immediate aftermath of the earthquake he encounters some men in a car with a "support your local police bumper sticker" who ignore his calls to put down their guns that they are using to kill the remaining members of the religious group that impeded their escape. "It's over! That was the end of civilization you just saw, don't you understand?" (231), Larsen is told by one of the men. "And suddenly Eric did understand. There weren't going to be any ambulances to take the injured to the hospitals." Eric responds with an action that reflects he is "still a civilized man." Eric returns to the city jail to free the inhabitants ("no one deserved to drown like a rat in a cage") (240).

Tim Hamner, who has been caught in the earthquake outside of Eileen's store (and he has also been casually dating Eileen) uses the last vestiges of people's societal expectations by pretending to be a reporter covering the earthquake. In this he both escapes notice as the man who first saw the comet and he escapes becoming the target of the violent stampede of people to safe ground. He plays on people's instinctive responses, responses that are now wholly out of tune with the conditions under which they live. Eileen recognizes the game Tim is playing and joins in: "Okay, Chief, I'm here. . . . Bit of trouble back there" (237). "'Rioters are publicity-shy,' Tim said. 'Glad to see you. I'd forgotten you work around here'" (237). And so Tim and Eileen go off together to find high ground as the rain that has started falling since the earthquake is salt rain—the mist from the oncoming tidal wave.

Eileen, who describes herself as "*damned* good" behind the wheel of a car, drives them (in a car they find with the keys dangling) and she adjusts herself quickly to these new conditions. They call warnings to people along the side of the road (but they do not stop to pick people up) and they see a woman running from a burning building toward them with a "bundled blanket" that she "thrust[s] . . . in the window. 'His name is John!' she screamed. 'Take care of him!'" John, the baby wrapped in the blanket, is dead and Eileen flatly orders Tim "Throw him out."

> "We aren't going to eat him. We won't be that hungry." It shocked Tim, so much that he thrust the baby out the window and let go. "I—felt like I was letting some of my life drop onto that pavement," he said. "Do you think I like it?" Eileen's voice was pinched. Tim looked at her in alarm; there were tears streaming down her cheeks. "That woman thinks she saved her child. At least she thinks that. It is all we could have done for her." (240)

Eileen's brief mention of cannibalism seems out of place here, yet Eileen clearly is recognizing this new world of no laws. They have stolen a car, which she is driving heedless of any traffic restrictions. They have warned people, but have not put their own survival in jeopardy by trying to carry others along. Eileen knows that they must leave their "life" on the pavement. They must adjust to a new set of conditions and they cannot negotiate those conditions under the rules of the old world. It is important here that these are not simply the responses to a run of the mill disaster. Because Eileen has known Tim, she understands what the comet's impact means. Eileen is not simply trying to benefit herself in a momentary lapse of police protection. Rather, she knows that police protection is wholly absent and wholly meaningless (that is why the mention of cannibalism may not be so out of place, Eileen is looking forward here). "If . . . When. When we've got to high ground, when we know what's happening, we can start thinking civilization again. . . . Until then, we survive" (240). Eileen here knows the advantages of living in civil society—she does not need to be convinced that life would be better were it rule bound. But she also knows that the social contract, while not a luxury, does require time and energy—two things that are now needed to meet the current crisis in order to survive.

Eileen stands out for recognizing very quickly what the consequences of the comet's impact are ("no one will ever be safe again" (255)). The novel goes back and forth among a variety of survivors of the immediate aftermath and many do not understand how the world has changed. One contrasting response is that of Alim Nassor, the black power broker/criminal introduced above who organized a group to rob houses in Beverly Hills the day of the comet, figuring (and rightly so) that many people will have fled leaving their houses available for robbery. As a burglar Nassor works efficiently ("even *he* followed orders when the need came" (206)) and he is quick to recognize the opportunities that the hysteria around the comet might produce. But he is still thinking about the world as it is now: stealing items that he can most easily "fence" and working on what he might come back to steal later. Only after he sees the dual shadows cast by the sun and the falling comet does he start to think about how the comet's fall will radically change the world that he has known and yet produce a world that he thinks himself particularly well placed in which to survive and even thrive.

Nassor quickly rallies his men to go to a cabin high in the hills. He organizes his men and they survive off of the cattle and other foodstuff (although they lose the car filled with Harvey Randall's carefully created postapocalyptic stash when one of his followers in a drug induced frenzy burns the car). They only leave this safe space when they are forced out: "A lot of honkies with guns came and took it away" (442). Nassor reflects on the world that used to be and the world in which he now finds himself.

> There had been a crazy world, with laws drawn up by gibbering idiots, and unbelievable luxuries: hot coffee, steak dinners, dry towels. Alim wore a coat that fit him perfectly: a woman's mink coat, as wet as any sponge. None of the brothers had anything to say about that. Once again, Alim Nassor had power. (442)

There is a social contract at work here. Nassor's men follow him, perhaps recognizing both the power that he had prior to the comet's fall, but also acknowledging that with Nassor's leadership they are more able to get food and shelter. "They all needed him. None of the rest could have got them this far, and they all knew it" (443). Nassor falsely believes his leadership to be built on natural superiority, but the novel clearly illustrates that his power rests on the fact that others acknowledge and thus authorize that power. They have consented to his leadership and they expect certain things in return. As their lives worsen the pressure on Nassor to produce the security that a Hobbesian sovereign signs up to provide increases.

Nassor is not simply trying to keep his group together; he is also trying to find a place for black people in this new world. This second urge leads him to make the mistake of joining up with the group that becomes the novel's anti-social contract and the enemy that must be defeated for the new and true social contract (on Senator Jellison's ranch) to flourish.

So the novel presents two sets of individuals trying to work out both their survival and their long term flourishing in this new state of nature. How each group comes together and establishes organized rule illustrates the ways in which the novel argues for a Hobbesian social contract.

The Social Contract

Senator Jellison helpfully owns a ranch in a valley adjacent to the foothills of the Sierra Mountains, a ranch to which he has gone prior to the comet's impact, ostensibly to watch more clearly the comet's path past earth. But, as noted earlier, he has also stockpiled resources and has prepared for the possibility that the comet will land. Once the comet crashes down he has the advantage of being out of the path of the tidal wave and the ensuing floods that cut off his part of the valley from most of the California coast. The reader is led toward the ranch because Tim Hamner and Harvey Randall are both heading in that direction.

The immediate aftermath of the comet is less traumatic and so Jellison and the local farmers can discuss the meaning of the comet fall on the day of the impact. The rain, warm and salty from the displaced oceans, will go on for weeks and the farmers all realize that this will kill this year's crop. Dams will overflow and burst, filling the nearby San Joaquin valley. Decisions about moving usable goods from nearby towns in the valley to the foothills are made quickly, although questions initially remain about how such goods will be distributed. These decisions imply a functioning organizational system. But this is not an organization, but rather a loosely convened set of people who are doing what they wish and can to augment their survival and will work together if they share goals. Jellison is not in charge. His authority is not recognized by all, and the entrance into the social contract must be unanimous. If the decision is not unanimous then those who do not agree to the system live in the state of nature with those who have chosen to enter the contract—such a situation challenges the security that the social contract is supposed to produce.

It might seem that these people are not in fact living in the state of nature. Their homes have not been destroyed, their immediate survival is not in question, their local authorities (Mayor, police) are present and one of their national representatives is both present and aware of the dangers facing them. But this is an illusory social contract. At the initial meeting on the day of the comet strike the cohesiveness of the group is already in question. Jellison has knowledge: what does the comet strike mean. But they all must decide what to do about their first impending crisis: refugees. People escaping from Los Angeles and the San Joaquin valley will all come up to the foothills and would expect to be fed and housed. This is a direct threat because there will not be food enough to feed everyone the first year. "We can take care of all those people for a week. Maybe two. Not longer. Longer than that, *somebody's* got to starve. Who'll it be? All of us because we tried to keep a hundred times too many alive for a couple of weeks" (349). George Christopher, Senator Jellison's biggest competitor for leader of this group of individuals, is a local farmer who understands quickly the toll that the refugees will have on their food stores; he also harbors suspicions about "valley people" "hippies" "city people" "tourists."[10] The issue is not simply feeding potentially thousands of refugees; there is also a clear fear that those refugees will be useless. What this discussion reveals, and what Jellison recognizes, is the fear that is awakened by the threats of "locusts," who will come and destroy all they have worked to produce. "George looked around at the sea of faces. They were not hostile. Most were filled with shame—fear and shame. George thought that was the way he looked to them, too" (359). This fear, as evidenced in part by the recognition of shame, is an acknowledgement of what has changed. This is no longer a world with room for charity and brotherhood; rather it is a world of threats and not simply of refugees, but also of the death of the organized system to which they had become accustomed, a system where someone else dealt with the difficult questions.

The farmers of the valley decide to set up a roadblock in order to protect what they have and to give refugees time to move on, further into the mountains, and potentially build something of their own to protect. (And George Christopher decides on his own to blow up one of the bridges leading towards town.)

Jellison has a far reaching goal of going beyond the mere survival that his people desire:

> We can rebuild it, and this time we'll do it right. We'll spread beyond this one damned little ball, get human civilization out all through the solar system, to other stars even, so no one thing can knock us out again (363)

Given that surviving the winter is a pressing concern, the desire to colonize space might seem a bit premature. Jellison is musing as a sovereign would. He is not simply thinking about day to day concerns; rather he has a perspective about the future. He also recognizes that colonizing space must be a back burner concern for a while:

> But how do we live long enough to start rebuilding? First things first, and right now the problem is getting this valley organized. Nobody's going to help. We have to do it ourselves. The only law and order will be what we can make, and

the only safety Maureen and Charlotte and Jennifer will have is what we can put together. (363)

While the paternalism is clear (Maureen and Charlotte, his daughters, Jennifer, his granddaughter), what is also clear is a recognition of moving from a state of nature into civil society. The valley is currently not fully organized, the people must be convinced that there is no help coming from elsewhere (they must be convinced that they do live in a state of nature). Then they must be convinced that they can take matters into their own hands, they can create a new civil society. They can:

> confer all their power and strength upon one man, or upon one assembly of men, that may reduce all their wills, by plurality of voices, unto one will: which is as much as to say, to appoint one man, or assembly of men, to bear their person; and every one to own and acknowledge himself to be author of whatsoever he that so beareth their person shall act, or cause to be acted, in those things which concern the common peace and safety; and therein to submit their wills, every one to his will, and their judgements to his judgement. (Hobbes, Ch. XVII)

Jellison and his council will become the single will, the single judgment, that will work to protect the valley, first from the needless waste of what few resources they have and later from the attack by the New Brotherhood Army.

By the time that Harvey Randall and Tim Hamner, in separate cars, with separate groups of survivors, arrive, the Jellison ranch area is organized and Jellison's authority has been accepted. This is most clearly illustrated by Maureen Jellison's musings on her new job as inventory agent. She goes from house to house making an inventory of everything useful found in the house. These items, what would clearly be understood as private property in the now absent civil society, are now common property, to be redistributed on a new basis. "They were only too glad to offer everything they had, freely, in exchange for protection that did not exist. . . . [T]he Jellisons were 'the government' which would care for them, as it always had" (405). People are giving up their right to what they once had and they are expecting to receive security in return. Maureen is pessimistic about the ability of the Sovereign entity, her father, to provide this security (which at this stage is security from a long, hungry winter); but despite her pessimism the exchange is Hobbesian and complete: people will give up the rights they have to do anything in their power to survive in exchange for security and assistance in that survival from Jellison. Even the local farmers and ranchers, who have "pride and independence," recognize "the need for organization." In other words, they reject the potential chaos of the state of nature in favor of a system, authorized by Jellison.

Lucifer's Hammer embodies this Hobbesian worldview in that the civil society that is created is one where there is a power center (Jellison and his council), there is a hierarchy of command and there are expectations of the people. They have "authorized" Jellison to protect them. Jellison will "cause to be acted" in that he will create a system for the protection of the community. People may not love the rules under which they live, and they may not appreciate the authoritarian style of Jellison, but in their silence they show their agreement to this new system. "All the Senator's rules made sense, but they were rules, laid down without discussion, orders issued from the big house with nobody to say no except the Christophers, and they weren't arguing" (416). This musing, from Harvey, about the rule that no game be shot within 5 miles of the ranch, reflects the shift from the expectations of a democratic system (one that could have been chosen by the people of the valley) and the more oligarchic system they had chosen to install. This system includes swift and public punishment for those who threaten the security of the town. The four young men and women who killed the Roman family are captured and publicly hanged. "The executions had shocked a number of townspeople. . . . But nobody said anything. The Romans had been their friends. Besides, it could be dangerous to argue. . . . There was always the road, for those who wouldn't cooperate, for those who caused too much trouble. The road." (418).[11] This is a classic description of the realist state. People obey rules because they fear punishment. The people also expect to be protected. If that protection includes harsh punishment for those who break the rules (or try and live outside the rules) then the people see that such punishment is the price of their submission to this system.

Challenging the Social Contract

Not all of the groups post comet fall will make the choices that those in the valley have made. When Harvey Randall finally finds his son, who had gone camping the weekend the comet hit and has been living since with his Boy Scout troop, Andy is living in a different kind of organized community. He and the scout leader are in charge, each of the scouts is paired off with a Girl Scout, who have been rescued from "bikers" that the boys have killed. This community of hunter/warriors derides the valley people as creating a mere "survival machine." Whatever their new vision of the world is, it is not a Hobbesian organization and Harvey will leave his son to live his new life, returning to the contract by which he has decided to abide.

But even this band of Boy Scouts grown up represents a form of living together that represents the basic principles of civil society. The New Brotherhood Liberation Army that Alim Nassor encounters, and joins, represents the opposing force—not life continued in the state of nature—but rather adherence to a set of rules that will produce nothing other than destruction. The anti-social contract that this group represents is found both in the cannibalism by which the group both lives and initiates new members and the principle of human sin that embodies their purpose.

Nassor joins up initially because he knows that his own group is too small to survive. He kills one of his followers who refuses the price of admission to the New Brotherhood, the eating of human flesh; and he initially shares in the power of the group, so the exchange is worth the price paid. Reverend Armitage, the leader of the Army, preaches that the comet fell to kill the wicked and now it is up to these people to "complete His work" (462). Armitage wants to destroy any attempts to recreate the lives humans once had. This culminates in an attack on the still functioning nuclear power plant that symbolizes the opportunity the survivors have to jumpstart their lives post comet.

The New Brotherhood Liberation Army exists as the anti-social contract. By requiring the eating of human flesh as the membership price the New Brotherhood Army both acknowledges and then debases the idea of the social contract. On the one hand choice is possible: eat human flesh or die and be eaten. But is this really the kind of choice that Hobbes famously acknowledges as difficult but still a choice? No, it is not. It might be if the choice were eat human flesh or leave us. But the threat is eat or be eaten and this cannot be a legitimate Hobbesian choice. Instead what we have is a mockery of such a choice establishing a mockery of a social contract. For the purpose of the New Brotherhood is to destroy what is left of humanity in order to honor God's purported intent to punish human overreaching.

> It is God's intent that civilization be destroyed, so that man can live again as God intended. In the sweat of his brow he shall eat his bread. No longer shall he pollute the earth and the sea and the air with the garbage of industrial civilization that leads him further and further from God's way. Certain of us were spared to finish the work done by the Hammer of God [the comet]. (518)

The idea of destroying "civilization" is the destruction not simply of power plants and other mechanical human inventions. It is also the destruction of the idea that civil society—that act of human artifice that pools skills and resources in order for humans to improve the conditions under which they live—is a necessary step in human living together. But using threats of being eaten, and by diminishing human life by requiring ritualized eating of human flesh, *Lucifer's Hammer* describes an inversion of the social contract. Rather than the usual exchange: "I give up my right to acquire what I desire in the state of nature by whatever means I can, in exchange for your providing security," this playacted contract says: "I kill and eat others who refuse to kill and eat me in exchange for my threatening to eat and kill those that we capture tomorrow." This is both a contract into a war (precisely the situation one enters into the social contract to escape) and a contract to destroy human initiative. There is little sense that they are out to create anything; they exist merely to destroy those who have survived.

The members of the New Brotherhood Army, environmentalists, fundamentalists, inner city black people, highlight who (and what) must be destroyed. This group seems to follow a traditional survive—regroup—fight again—live again trajectory that postapocalyptic fiction favors. This enemy highlights two key Hobbesian concerns. First, it clarifies that unless specific allies are made (as Senator Jellison's group makes with the Tule Indians and the Boy Scout group) there is no expectation of peace between organized groups. Second, the war between those groups happens in the rule-absent state of nature. So from the novel's perspective the decision by Jellison's people to use mustard gas is legitimate and does not reflect on any lack of "civilization" on their part. The question of whether to enslave those captured in the New Brotherhood Army's retreat does raise important questions about the kind of civil society Jellison's group is advocating. Maureen advocates that they create a POW camp—using those captured for their labor (and consequently feeding them, a real issue given potential food shortages that winter). To enslave them would, for Maureen "make it too easy to think like a slavemaster" (607). Maureen is thinking through the conditions under which the people of this valley wish to live. They have gone beyond their immediate physical needs, now they must decide who and what they want to be.

In another moment of Hobbesian argumentation the question of who they are coincides with the issue of succession. As Hobbes himself notes succession is an obligation of the current sovereign because succession crises will destroy the security that people entered the social contract to receive. Here the succession crisis concerns Maureen Jellison and which man she will ally herself with: George Christopher, long time rancher in the valley; Harvey Randall, former documentary filmmaker who had an affair with Maureen; Johnny Baker, hero astronaut who lands (with three other astronauts—2 Soviet) weeks after the comet's impact. The obvious choice is Johnny, until

he is killed trying to save the power plant (and thus trying to save the opportunity for these people to create something approximating the dream Jellison
had of colonizing other planets).

The novel presents the best case scenario for using weapons that go beyond our usual just war sensibilities. The enemy is out purely for destruction,
the enemy has proven itself to violate all standards of humanity (cannibalism), the enemy has proven itself to fail at the skills needed to survive in
the post comet world. The triumph of the Senator's people is clear from the
start because the novel is out to celebrate the kind of guided can-do spirit
that these people embody. The Senator's authority allows individuals to do
what needs doing to save the community. It gives Dan Forrester the food
and shelter and materials to make mustard gas; it gives Harvey Randall the
opportunity to prove himself in battle (and thus to prove himself as a worthy
successor and suitor to Maureen); it gives the children of the community a
purpose driven life—and candy bars for the ones who catch the most rats; it
alleviates the futility of working for the future that permeates the conditions
of the state of nature.

The climax of the novel plays out its Hobbesian sensibility in a number
of ways: First, Jellison's community must defend itself and so the authoritative structure of that community is tested and proved to uphold its side of
the social contract. Second, Jellison's embodiment as the Sovereign is maintained up until his death when he whispers, "Give my children the lightning
again" (625) and thus turns the tide in the discussion as to whether they
should protect the power plant against the New Brotherhood Army. Third,
this moment of deciding what to do also clarifies Jellison's decision to use
Maureen to provide legitimacy to any successor to his authority. Maureen
takes Harvey's hand and propels him to the front of the room to convince
people to fight to protect the power plant (in Rick Delanty's words they are
deciding whether to live as safe "as ground squirrels," protecting only their
turf, or they can "make all of Outside . . . as safe as we are" (624)). Harvey
Randall "slapped Maureen's butt and bounded ahead of her onto the plat-
form, moving quickly before the moment died away. Decisions were simple,
now that he knew what he'd be shouting" (625). The community will survive
under a new Sovereign. There will be no succession crisis and the community
has chosen to maintain its survival by advocating for the hallmarks of civil
society. Not a mere survival (not the "survival machine"), rather they will
embrace the possibilities that are denied them in the state of nature: "no
culture of the earth; no navigation, nor use of the commodities that may be
imported by sea; no commodious building; no instruments of moving and
removing such things as require much force; no knowledge of the face of the

earth; no account of time; no arts; no letters; no society" (Hobbes, Ch. XIII). By protecting the power plant they will opt for industry, knowledge, electric razors, and the stars.

Gender and Race

Carole Pateman in *The Sexual Contract* (1988) and Charles Mills in *The Racial Contract* (1997) both outline the ways in which traditional social contract thinking, as that found in Hobbes, is explicitly interested to promote hierarchies based on sex and race. Pateman argues that the traditional social contract is a patriarchal contract and Mills argues that it is a contract for white power. *Lucifer's Hammer* provides a unique look into the inherent inequalities lurking beneath Hobbes' claims about natural equality. *Lucifer's Hammer* ends with the victory of the white men, the subordination of the white women and the literal destruction of non-whites.

Harvey's emergence as the next ruler of the valley community is based on his winning Maureen's hand. And Maureen knows the role that she plays in guaranteeing this new authority: "I'm a goddamn prize in a goddamn contest . . . in a goddamn fairy tale. Why doesn't anyone ever speak for the princess?" (536). But she does not question the need for the authority nor does she do anything with her complaint about being the "princess." She acknowledges her role unhappily, but she does not challenge it. Likewise Johnny, the only black man who is not affiliated with the New Brotherhood Army, must die to save the power plant because there is no place for him in this community. The text makes it seem as though Maureen is choosing between Johnny and Harvey—but what better way to remove the option of the black Sovereign than to have him die heroically trying to save the power plant.

It is also important for the novel that the women choose their subordinate role just as the black members of the New Brotherhood Army have chosen (although as I noted earlier this is an invalid choice) their membership. It seems as though Niven and Pournelle want not simply to present a world where equality based on race and/or sex are dismissed as luxuries; it also seems as if they want to acknowledge the readers' potential discomfort and thus explain the subordination (and extinction) as chosen. Given this the essential racial genocide of the novel is passed over as a rational protection of the only legitimate community in the novel. Niven and Pournelle are not asking their readers to acquiesce to direct racism, the reader simply has to acquiesce to the rational decision to eradicate cannibals intent on total destruction.[12]

This difficulty with the issue of women and minorities will continue in the next two chapters. This may well be, as Pateman and Mills would have it, because the models of the social contract used are themselves inherently problematic. I will argue instead, as seen with the analysis of Octavia Butler in the final three chapters, that it is not the idea of the social contract that is problematic. Rather what is problematic is what is designated essential and what is a luxury, and who it is that does the designating. Hobbes, and Niven and Pournelle, understand security as the reason for entering into the social contract and that security is bodily (as Jellison notes—he wants the women in his life, his daughter and granddaughter, to be safe). This bodily security is based on destroying the primary threats to that insecurity: hunger and then the New Brotherhood Army. But of course this means that security requires the eradication of most and the enslavement of the rest of the remaining black men and women. This happens in the novel as a simple matter of course. And the reader is not likely to protest—they are cannibals; and in postapocalyptic fiction cannibalism is the sign of total inhumanity, and thus an inability to enter into a contract. As Maureen notes, "it made so much sense" (536).

Niven and Pournelle fall into the easy sexism and racism of many post-apocalyptic accounts (*World Made by Hand* and *The Rift*, for example). And in many of these texts it is as if the reader is to share Maureen's standpoint that it all "makes so much sense," but only when inherent superiority—of men over women or of whites over non-whites—is the underlying assumption. If this is not your assumption then these texts reflect a deep kind of non-sense. Why is equality somehow only a luxury? As a reader of the genre the egalitarian novels of Octavia Butler are the exception and not the norm. Yet what is worth noting is not simply that the genre appeals to this male fantasy of protecting the women-folk, but that in noting this these novels are advocating that equalities of race and sex are merely legal. It should be that a Hobbesian account could actually explore what it means to be vulnerable to death when all of the advantages of civil society are removed. Octavia Butler[13] explores this natural equality. Niven and Pournelle give no real argument against this natural equality. In fact it seems that in the initial aftermath that the women who survive do so because of the know-how they possess (and not because they are saved by a man).

Hobbesian Postapocalyptic Fiction

Lucifer's Hammer argues for a Hobbesian social contract and it provides a version of the conditions out of which that contract will be chosen in the chaos post-comet. The argument is hypothetical, but it fleshes out the realist worldview under conditions that are plausible. The novel promotes an authoritarian style of government chosen by the people in order to protect their lives and the possibility for those lives flourishing. The novel also promotes a kind of white male fantasy—put women in their place and show who is really boss. The novels of the next two chapters share some of the aspects of the white male fantasy, but they argue differently for what it is supposed to be that just "makes sense."

Notes

The chapter title is from Hobbes, *Leviathan* (Indianapolis, Indiana: Hackett Publishing, 1994 [1668]), XII: 9 (76) (Chapter, paragraph, page number).

1. For example, William Forstchen, *One Second After* (New York: Forge Books, 2009), John Christopher, *Wrinkle in the Skin* (Brooklyn, New York: Brownstone Books, 2000), e-text *Lights Out*, Walter J. Williams, *The Rift* (New York: Eos, 2000). Most apocalyptic films start with a Hobbesian premise of violence after societal breakdown: *Mad Max, 28 Days Later, Escape from New York, The Quiet Earth, Twelve Monkeys, Omega Man, Planet of the Apes, Doomsday, Waterworld, Soylent Green, The Day the World Ended, Panic in Year Zero, Ever Since the World Ended.*

2. He has won both the Hugo and the Nebula awards multiple times and *Lucifer's Hammer* was nominated for a Hugo. Both Pournelle and Niven are members of a group of science fiction authors who have advised the US government on homeland security issues.

3. *Lucifer's Hammer* was reviewed in the *New York Times* briefly as "one of the most ambitious disaster novels to date" (November 13, 1977); Mike Davis, "Why LA is a Synonym for Disaster," *LA Times*, August 16, 1998 cites *Lucifer's Hammer* in his article about the popularity of disaster films and books that destroy Los Angeles as "rooted in racial anxiety;" recently Oliver Morton, "In Retrospect: *Lucifer's Hammer*," *Nature* 453, June 26, 2008, 1184, reviewed the book calling it a "broadly plausible cataclysm."

4. This inability to really think through equality nicely illustrates the criticisms of social contract thinking found in Carole Pateman *The Sexual Contract* and Charles Mills *The Racial Contract*.

5. The potential sexism of seeing Maureen as primarily a beautiful woman can be read as a consequence of the values of civil society, not as a claim challenging the natural equality between the sexes. I discuss *Lucifer's Hammer* and gender equality later in this chapter.

6. This failure includes a decidedly racist and genocidal twist where virtually every African American living in California will die (other than the astronaut—who will only die, heroically, later in the novel).

7. This is a common theme in postapocalyptic (and disaster) fiction. Those who recognize the event for what it is and see what the consequences might be are mentally more prepared. This is fully explored in Butler's *Parable of the Sower* in Chapter 6.

8. This is one reason why I find postapocalyptic films so disappointing. They revel so much in the violence of the event and the spectacular special effects that little time is able to be spent thinking through the aftermath.

9. This is why so many postapocalyptic accounts recreate reactionary political visions. Every postapocalyptic account that involves the creation of a new civil society is working through some kind of utopian impulse. Sometimes the memories of what civil society was hold the characters (and the author) back from really rethinking what civil society could be. That means that the hypothetical inhabitants of social contract thinkers' states of nature have an advantage over the hypothetical inhabitants of these postapocalyptic worlds. Octavia Butler is one of the few authors who recognizes this tension.

10. One of the farmers also says that "niggers" will come. He then starts to and then refuses to retract his claim, acknowledging that the black farmer that lived down the street was fine, but that "city niggers, whining about equality!" would show up.

11. While I have no evidence that Cormac McCarthy has ever read *Lucifer's Hammer*, there is an added chill in this repetition of "the road" when you imagine McCarthy's world. In his world there is no valley stronghold, but there is reason to believe that anyone sent on the road here in *Lucifer's Hammer*, would experience a life not unlike that of the father and son of *The Road*.

12. It is important to note here the difference between the racism of *Lucifer's Hammer* and that of a book like William Pierce's *The Turner Diaries*. *The Turner Diaries* is asking the reader to agree with a white supremacist view of the world; *Lucifer's Hammer* is simply asking the reader to agree that cannibals should be killed. It just happens to be that the majority of the cannibals are black.

13. There are other feminist postapocalyptic accounts, although many make the opposite claim that women, not men, are somehow best suited to life absent civil order. Leigh Richards' *Califea's Daughters* and Marge Piercy's *He, She, It*.

~

CHAPTER THREE

"Industrious and Rational"

John Locke and Alas, Babylon:
The Rational Life Postapocalypse

At first glance it would seem that Hobbes has the corner on the postapocalyptic fiction market. The genre tends toward violent excess and authoritarian response, and postapocalyptic films are particularly enamored of the state of nature as chaos theme. But if postapocalyptic fiction is understood as a particularly American genre, then the appeal of the Lockean account is clear. It would be strange not to see postapocalyptic accounts that seek to affirm the very story that we use to justify the legitimacy of our own state. Oddly, however, the Lockean postapocalyptic account is definitely in the minority. A Lockean world of free and rational individuals out to protect their bodies and their property is not the primary thrust of the postapocalyptic genre, which likes to highlight the chaos that emerges from the end, not its inconveniences. The Lockean postapocalyptic account will be a cleaner and less stressful account. It will highlight humanity's essential ability to see what needs to be done to pursue one's best interest. If enemies must be defeated, they will clearly be designated as less rational and they will be fairly easy to defeat. A Lockean postapocalyptic account will not include cannibalism.

Alas, Babylon,[1] by Pat Frank first published in 1959, describes the experiences of an All-American Florida town that survives the nuclear war that wipes out most of the Southeast and cripples the U.S. Frank states in the preface that he wrote the book after a conversation with someone about the potential aftermath of a nuclear war between the U.S. and the Soviet Union. Frank notes that this man had no way of understanding what this war could possibly mean. "To someone who has never felt a bomb, bomb is only a word." He wrote *Alas, Babylon* to try and explain what this war, this kind of bombing could mean. But he does so from the outskirts. He tells almost nothing about those who die in the blast ("Most of those who died in North America saw nothing at all, since they died in bed, in a millisecond slipping from sleep into a deep darkness" (123)); and there is little information about the refugees that arrive in Fort Repose with radiation sickness. The focus is on the citizens of Fort Repose. These people will experience the aftermath, but none of the immediate chaos of the war. This Lockean account, even more so than the Hobbesian account, celebrates the ability of humans to rise above the conditions of their lives.

Nuclear war is a potentially odd choice for the Lockean account because its aftermath is so extreme. David Brin (author of the postapocalyptic *The Postman*) writes a foreword to the 2005 reprint of *Alas, Babylon* and he notes that Frank underestimates the impact of the radiation. But Brin notes that in Frank's novel "the characters are not only knocked down by cruel fate. They get to stand up. He lets them try and rebuild. It's no fun. But there is perseverance. And there is hope" (xi). Again Brin describes Frank's characters as "basically good, capable of cooperation and deserving—if possible—a second chance" (xi). This basic goodness is what I would describe as its essentially Lockean character. Because it is not so much a moral goodness that the characters have, rather it is a work ethic that reflects a Lockean rationality: the human drive to improve the earth on which we live.

Locke

Where Hobbes describes the state of nature as a state of war, Locke clearly distinguishes the state of nature from a potential state of war. The state of nature can turn into a state of war, but there is nothing inherent to the condition of lawlessness that necessarily produces war. The state of nature is for Locke, primarily inconvenient. People in the state of nature are free and rational and desire to work hard to build and improve on the earth and it would be easier for them to do this work if someone else were in charge of dealing with those who seek to take advantage of the hard work of others.

Locke, like Hobbes, believes that humans are equal. Likewise he believes that humans will come together to choose a Sovereign in order to avoid exigencies of the state of nature. But Locke's description both of human nature and of human motivation illustrates a shift in the realist political outlook that the previous chapter outlines. While Hobbes argues for laws of nature, in the state of nature the only law that truly governs us is the law of self defense. For Locke the laws of nature hold sway in a different way, because we are both commanded by reason and ordered by God to acknowledge such laws:

> The state of nature has a law of nature to govern it, which obliges every one: and reason, which is that law, teaches all mankind, who will but consult it, that being all equal and independent, no one ought to harm another in his life, health, liberty, or possessions: for men being all the workmanship of one omnipotent, and infinitely wise maker . . . and being furnished with like faculties, sharing all in one community of nature, there cannot be supposed any such subordination among us. (*Second Treatise*, Ch. II: 6, 9)

Humans are equal in that they are all made by God and possess the same faculty of reason. Reason then dictates that we "ought not" to harm another—not bodily and not by taking or destroying another's possessions. So, unlike Hobbes, who said we could do what needed doing to survive in the state of nature, and who also denies that there is property (which is a convention that can only be sanctioned with state rules) in the state of nature, Locke answers that we should recognize others' "life, health, liberty [and] possessions."

Locke understands that some might not do as they ought and so by the next paragraph he clarifies what one can do to punish those who transgress the laws of nature. What matters here for thinking through the different descriptions of human motivation is that Locke begins with what we ought not to do while Hobbes begins with what we are able to do. Hobbes describes humans in the state of nature as wholly free. Locke distinguishes between "liberty" and "license." A Lockean postapocalyptic account will follow this distinction: what are we free to do? What would go beyond the laws of nature for a rational person to do? Randy Bragg, the protagonist of *Alas, Babylon* represents the Lockean hero. Rational, self interested but also aware of his responsibilities to those around him in concentric circles: family, friends, neighbors, townspeople.

The rational state of nature where people enjoy their property, that with which they have mixed their labor, turns into a state of war when those too lazy ("noxious creatures") to do their own work invade the fruits of the labor of others. In such a case you have the right not simply to protect yourself and your property, but to punish the transgressor:

> But force, or a declared design of force, upon the person of another, where there is no common superior on earth to appeal to for relief, is the state of war: and it is the want of such an appeal gives a man the right of war even against an aggressor, tho' he be in society and a fellow subject. Thus a thief, whom I

cannot harm, but by appeal to the law, for having stolen all that I am worth, I may kill, when he sets on me to rob me but of my horse or coat. . . . Want of a common judge with authority, puts all men in a state of nature: force without right, upon a man's person, makes a state of war, both where there is, and is not, a common judge. (Ch III: 19, 15)

This "right of war" is like Hobbes' right of nature. But the circumstances in which it arises differ. For Locke there must be an aggressor, and that aggressor—the preemptive striker—acts against the law of nature. Part of why one is legitimately able to punish the transgressor is because they have proven themselves to be unworthy of the mutual respect that usually governs relationships in Locke's state of nature.

Having the right to punish transgressors in the state of nature makes that state ostensibly more peaceful (in that there is a means of trying to deter others from stealing) but it is also both inconvenient and potentially unfair. Part of what the "common judge" can do is deal objectively with a law breaker. If someone steals from you and you are also the punisher you are likely to let your anger overwhelm your capacity to rationally assess the appropriate punishment. This is potentially harmful and always inconvenient for those who must do the punishing. We move from the state of nature into civil society to solve this inconvenience. By choosing a "common judge" we free up time and energy from pursuing and punishing transgressors in order to improve the earth and amass property.

Hobbes thinks that rational people (interested in self protection) will readily agree to give up their right to everything in order to gain security. If they know they are secure such people will go on to do what secure people do: build, trade, grow, discover. For Locke people are already doing this building in the state of nature, but they are distracted by the need to protect what they have built and so they will agree to give up the right to punish transgressors in order to focus their time on property improvement.

God gave the world to men in common; but since he gave it them for their benefit, and the greatest conveniencies of life they were capable to draw from it, it cannot be supposed he meant it should always remain common and uncultivated. He gave it to the use of the industrious and rational, (and labour was to be his title to it;) not to the fancy or covetousness of the quarrelsome and contentious. He that had as good left for his improvement, as was already taken up, needed not complain, ought not to meddle with what was already improved by another's labour: if he did, it is plain he desired the benefit of another's pains, which he had no right to, and not the ground which God had given him in common with others to labour on, and whereof there was as good left, as that already possessed, and more than he knew what to do with, or his industry could reach to. (Ch. V: 34, 21-22)

This classic description of the right to property and the explanation of what we are to do with our bodily labor (improve the earth) and how we are to understand those who fail to do so ("quarrelsome and contentious") clarifies how the rational person is to understand his obligations and the obligations of others. We are to work hard to create an improved world—one that reflects our capacity for industry and inventiveness. We should expect others to do the same and we should leave them alone when they do so. However, if someone tries to impede our ability to be industrious then we must be prepared to show them the error of their ways.

Locke promotes the acquisition and improvement of property. But he also cautions that we can only take what we can use. Not only should we not take something that we cannot use, we also should not complain that someone else might take that property for their own use. To complain is to pretend that you have a right to more than you can use, which is a claim that you have the right to waste. There is no accumulation simply for the sake of being rich. One's accumulation must both work to improve the world and must do its own work. Because the primary focus is on property acquisition and the principle of world improvement, when people do move from the state of nature to civil society they do so in order to receive greater protection of their property than they could receive in the state of nature.

> Where-ever therefore any number of men are so united into one society, as to quit every one his executive power of the law of nature, and to resign it to the public, there and there only is a political, or civil society. And this is done, where-ever any number of men, in the state of nature, enter into society to make one people, one body politic, under one supreme government; or else when any one joins himself to, and incorporates with any government already made: for hereby he authorizes the society, or which is all one, the legislative thereof, to make laws for him, as the public good of the society shall require; to the execution whereof, his own assistance (as to his own decrees) is due. (Ch.VII: 89, 47-48)

The body politic can, as a unit, accomplish what people in the state of nature had to do singly: make laws for the protection of property. They have "set a judge" who will "decide controversies" and thus they no longer have to bother with trying such cases on their own. This latter concern is of particular interest in the postapocalyptic account where it seems someone is always willing to transgress on what little you might have managed to carve out for yourself in the post event world. A Lockean account would stress the people's desire to not simply stop such transgressors, but to provide a community where such transgressors would never attack.

The only way for this civil society to come about is through the consent of those in the state of nature. People in the state of nature share the inclination to come together and create a civil society. We share the desire to protect ourselves and (for Locke) our property. Thus we consent to government, and we live under a legitimate government when we think of the laws it passes as ones to which we have consented.

> The only way whereby any one divests himself of his natural liberty, and puts on the bonds of civil society, is by agreeing with other men to join and unite into a community for their comfortable, safe, and peaceable living one amongst another, in a secure enjoyment of their properties, and a greater security against any, that are not of it. (Ch. VIII: 95, 52)

In *Lucifer's Hammer* we see people mourning the loss of civil society and trying hard to create some semblance of a life recognizable to them as secure. *Alas, Babylon* shares the desire for security, but it focuses far more on the successful re-creation of a meaningful society. One where people are self reliant and creating an improved world. *Alas, Babylon* stresses far more the "enjoyment" of one's property and it ends with the achievement of a "comfortable, safe and peaceable" community.

Alas, Babylon: Randy Bragg, Lockean Hero

Alas, Babylon, unlike *Lucifer's Hammer*'s sprawling cast of characters, has one protagonist, Randy Bragg. All of the action of the novel concerns Bragg's home and the community that he creates out of the small group of houses built along the Timuacan River in this north central Florida town. This focus on Randy shifts the attention from the universal concerns of survival in *Lucifer's Hammer* to a sustained focus on one exemplary, rational man. The state of nature that emerges in *Alas, Babylon* reflects Randy Bragg's essential character. At the beginning of the novel Randy is a somewhat bored and disaffected son of the town who lives in his deceased parents' home (that he co-owns with his more successful brother, Mark, who is in the Air Force). Randy drinks too much and is not quite sure how to fill his days. He is currently dating a young woman, Lib, who wants him to leave Fort Repose and go to a big city; but he has also dated a woman, Rita, who encouraged idleness and drinking. For Randy, as ultimately for many in the town of Fort

Repose, nuclear war brings about conditions that allow him to realize what he is capable of. Fort Repose succeeds in part because it is possessed with a Lockean idea of the American Dream: let me work hard to create what I can and then leave me alone.

We first learn of Randy through the eyes of Florence Wechek, the local telegraph operator, raiser of exotic fish and birds and self-described Clara Bow look-alike who describes Randy as "a hermit, and a snob, and a nigger-lover, and no better than a pervert" (6). The latter charge centers on Randy's habit of viewing Florence's home with binoculars. She thinks he is looking at her, when in fact he is watching birds. We learn from Florence that she had voted for Randy, although we do not know the office. We learn from Florence that Randy's home is the "big house."

Randy, musing about his loss in the primary election for the state legislature, notes that his loss stemmed from his inability to give the proper response to the loaded 1964 election question "where do y' stand on the Supreme Court" (8). Randy's answer was "I believe in the Constitution of the United States—all of it" (9).[2] Randy's failure to assuage the racist concerns of Florida's citizens might seem to be a minor anecdote to characterize Randy Bragg. But this anecdote does more than just assure the reader that Randy is not an opponent of desegregation. Rather we get a picture of the world in which Randy is living, a reason why Randy is failing to thrive in that world and an indication of what Randy stands for—and what he would stand for if given the chance. He allies himself with the Constitution; he eschews telling people what they want to hear just to get elected; his allegiance "as voter and soldier" goes beyond the particular concerns of Timucuan County. Randy is an American hero: moderate, willing to work hard without selling out, intelligent, handsome and aware of complexities. He does not live in a world that can embrace such characteristics. He drinks bourbon with his morning coffee. He looks for exotic birds. He is aimless and has no reason to commit to anything.

Under these conditions a nuclear war will bring out a world in which Randy Bragg can thrive. *Alas, Babylon* is one of the most Swiss Family Robinson-esque of postapocalyptic fictions. There is little death, little mayhem and a lot of rising above difficult circumstances. But the novel still follows a traditional trajectory: survivors who must figure out how to eat, how to protect themselves and how to build something new. The script that they follow here is wholly Lockean. When the bombs fall and cut the town off from their power source, their delivery systems, their connections to the wider world, the people of Fort Repose must decide how to respond. How they respond illustrates a Lockean approach to human motivation both in and out of the state of nature.

As with some of the key characters in *Lucifer's Hammer*, here too Randy Bragg is given some warning of what is to come. His brother sends his wife and children to live with Randy for fear that something might happen and Randy uses the 24 hours prior to their arrival to stock up on food, liquor, gasoline and medical supplies. Again we have the lesson that stocking up can help, but is neither the key to either survival nor flourishing in the postapocalyptic world. Here Randy's preparations illustrate how one cannot prepare for something like a nuclear war. While there are no great moments of packing a jeep with spices, Randy falsely thinks that buying out the meat counter and increasing his dairy delivery will help prepare the house for its three new inhabitants and the coming war. The loss of electricity and the end of the milk delivery system show Randy's all too common inability to really understand the end.

There are conditions that help Randy Bragg and his new family: he lives along a river (water and fish), in an orange grove (food and vitamin C). The Henrys, a black family (descendants of the slaves owned by Randy Bragg's ancestors) that lives adjacent to his land, grow corn and have an extensive vegetable garden. They also have the requisite know-how about living off the land under trying circumstances. The people who live close to the Braggs, including the nosey telegraph operator Florence, all have some postapocalyptic skill to bring to the table. And those who don't (Randy's girlfriend Lib's mother, a diabetic who is deathly afraid of snakes) do not live long. The obstacles that this group faces include the immediate worries about radiation, longer term worries about food and the threat of outsiders hungry to take the products of the hard-earned labor of Bragg and his neighbors.

"Industrious and Rational"

Frank is careful to describe a world of humans primarily motivated by self interest to work hard to preserve their own lives, property and families. From the moment that the first bombs fall we see a number of characters move into action. Those characters that are not able to immediately deal with these new conditions will quickly die out. Randy goes into town right after the first two bombs fall to get a doctor for his niece Peyton, who has been blinded after witnessing one of the explosions, and to pick up extra supplies. On the way to town he passes a wrecked car and an armed former chain gang. These two scenes illustrate the kind of state of nature that *Alas, Babylon* presents.

He first sees the wrecked Sedan: "In this second Randy made an important decision. Yesterday he would have stopped instantly. . . . When there was an accident, and someone was hurt, a man stopped. But yesterday was a past period in history, with laws and rules as archaic as Ancient Rome's. Today the rules had changed. . . . Today a man saved himself and his family and to hell with everyone else" (98). Randy does not simply drive by the wrecked car so worried about his niece that he had to rush into town. Instead we hear his wholly rational analysis of what it means that these bombs fell. Randy assesses that the laws have changed, that whatever social contract of which he was a member on the previous day was no longer binding. He shows that he was clearly obligated by the earlier contract "when there was an accident . . . a man stopped." He understood the obligations of being a man in a civilized world. Such a man would stop to help someone, particularly to help a woman. Randy assesses that the new contract is simply familial: protect your own. It would seem that we see here, almost instantaneous with the bombs falling, a recognition that the state of nature has come into being. However, Randy does stop his car. He does make sure that there is nothing he can do to help.

"[T]hinking himself soft and stupid . . . [he] examined the wreck" (98). There is nothing he can do, the woman is clearly dead. But Randy has proven his resilience. He would abide by the contract, even when the contract seems not to be binding. "Randy knew he would have to play by the old rules. He could not shuck his code, or sneak out of his era" (98). This sentiment (and it could be interpreted as mere sentiment—an emotional attachment to a way of living that is now irrational) reveals Randy's core: a rational understanding of who he is and where his obligations lie. Locke says that

> Every one, as he is bound to preserve himself, and not to quit his station wilfully, so by the like reason, when his own preservation comes not in competition, ought he, as much as he can, to preserve the rest of mankind, and may not, unless it be to do justice on an offender, take away, or impair the life, or what tends to the preservation of the life, the liberty, health, limb, or goods of another. (9, Ch. II, para. 6)

Randy must be able to recognize that when his own preservation is not being threatened he is obligated to the "preservation of mankind." Randy is not motivated by the fear that this car wreck is a decoy for outlaws. Checking on the woman in the wrecked car is Randy's way of accomplishing his obligation to humanity. His reaction in the case of the chain gang reveals his recognition of why the conditions of the situation matter for determining the proper obligatory response.

"On River Road he passed a dozen convicts, white men, clad in their blue denim with the white stripe down the trouser leg" (106). They have clearly escaped, are carrying weapons and could certainly be a threat to someone.

But Frank's analysis here is striking. After noting that the convicts are white (so there is no knee jerk reaction on the part of the reader about non-white convicts) he then goes on to have Randy explain why they must have killed their guards: "The guards, some of them, were dour and sadistic men, skilled in unusual and degrading punishments. It was likely that any breakdown in government and authority would begin with a revolt of prisoners against road gang guards . . . with realization, rebellion . . . had been almost instantaneous" (106). In any other postapocalyptic account the sight of armed convicts who had killed their guards would be the sign of the violence of the state of nature emerging.[3] Instead we get a rational explanation and even justification for the convicts' escape. The language of rebellion in this Lockean context sets out a legitimate form of rejection of the guards' authority. It would be wrong, it seems, for the convicts to escape when the government was in power, because then the degrading treatment by the guards would be sanctioned by the state. But now that the state is gone the authority of the guards is gone and the guards' past mistreatment of the prisoners results in their death/punishment.

The convicts never reappear. They are clearly not a threat to Randy and he is not overly concerned when he sees Florence leaving to go into town. He warns her about them ("don't stop") and leaves it at that. So the convicts do not represent the beginning of mayhem. Their freedom is again a sign that the social contract has been threatened. But their actions are described in rational terms and there is no indication that other rational people should overly fear them. Yes, one should be cautious. But Randy feels no obligation to police the freedom of these convicts or to punish them for the deaths of the prison guards. It is almost as if Randy thinks that doing "justice to the offender" has been done retroactively: the prisoners were treated poorly by the guards, the guards have been killed by the prisoners and now it seems as if Randy must think that the escaped convicts will simply go on their way trying to fend for themselves. These escaped convicts are not the "quarrelsome and contentious" that Locke notes are not the recipients of God's bounty on earth. These expected enemies turn out to be not dangerous and so we see a world where mistrust is not rampant. Later when Randy does confront an enemy that enemy is described as an outlier, not the norm, not fully human.

State of Nature Is Not a State of War

Before we encounter the enemies that shift the state of nature to a state of war, I want to first introduce how this state of nature works. We know it as a state of nature because some, who have become accustomed to the

benefits and care of the state, cannot survive in a world absent such advantages. As we have already seen, Randy notes the absence of governmental
authority on his drive into town after the bombs fall. Fort Repose reflects
a spectrum of realization about the consequences of the bombs falling. On
the one hand many people seem wholly wrapped up in their own personal
needs: "People were tensed over their wheels like racing drivers, even
while moving at normal speeds, mouths set, eyes fixed, each intent on a
personal crisis" (100). There are long lines at the gas station and the stores
are crowded (although people are still using money, a clear sign that they
still recognize governmental authority). Disorder is fully present in the
Inn, a winter time retirement community for retired Northerners. Written
in short elliptical bursts, the residents surround the managers demanding
to know when breakfast will be served, why they cannot get a phone line,
when the televisions will work again. "A retired major general, in full dress
uniform and displaying all his ribbons, burst out of the elevator. 'Attention!' he cried. 'Attention, everybody! Let's have order here. You will all
please be quiet. There is no cause for alarm!' Nobody heeded him" (101).
This remnant of what authority meant prior to the bombs falling now appears as something grotesque. The residents of the Inn are clearly unable
mentally, or physically, to adjust to world where they will not be cared for.
Eventually most of the residents will die and the novel's tone about their
deaths is merely resigned.

The local doctor, Dan Gunn, notes, three days after the bombs, that the
residents are ignoring his warnings about the need to dig latrines; instead
"every morning they wake up saying that things will be back to normal by
nightfall, and every night they fall into bed thinking that normalcy will be
restored by morning" (160). These people will die in the state of nature pretending that perhaps this is nothing more than a few nights without power
after a snowstorm. Their inability to recognize what has happened illustrates
their lack of rational judgment and their inability to be self-sufficient. Others
in town, by day three, have moved beyond running on the bank for funds
to hunkering down and protecting what they have from those who may not
have stocked up. But the mood in town is merely disordered; it is not violent
or chaotic. Again there is a focus on the private: the few people that are out
in town move quickly, "shoulders hunched, eyes directed dead ahead. There
were no women on the streets, and the men did not walk in pairs, but alone
and warily" (154). This description implies some form of mistrust. The lack
of women is clearly an indication that it would not be safe for women to be
out. And the refusal of the men to walk together indicates suspicion over
people's motives. On the other hand there has been little violence to warrant

such a reaction. This is not a "war of all against all," rather this is a rational self interest on display in the public arena.

Two cases of violence, one actual and the other potential, still reflect Locke's contention that violence in the state of nature is the exception, and not the norm. First are the drug addicts who have broken into the medical clinic and killed an officer and the older doctor in town while searching for a fix. Dan Gunn notes, "poor old Jim was something of a puritan. If he'd given them a fix he might have gotten rid of them" (158). This little claim indicates that the addicts could be dealt with and only Jim's puritan anti-drug sensibilities (that have no place in this post nuclear world) killed him. The second are the group of four young men who circle the shattered open window of the drugstore watched by the owner; "they were outwaiting Old Man Hockstatler" (154). These are crimes of opportunity or, in the case of the drug addicts, crimes of a kind of perverse necessity. This is not a description of a town under siege by marauding packs of cannibals.

Adjusting to the abrupt transition from civil society to the state of nature is difficult because the tools we use to negotiate and succeed in civil society have little place in the state of nature, but abandoning them in favor of new more useful tools means "shucking your code" as Randy was not willing to do. And so people wait in long lines to buy food with money carefully taken out of bank accounts, yet within three days the store shelves will be all but empty and the cash will be useless. While this maintenance of the norms of civil society could be used to ridicule these characters or even to highlight how out of touch they are with their new reality, I think instead that these scenes show how the novel describes humans as being essentially grounded. Locke describes humans as being in a "state of perfect freedom" but importantly not a state of license. This perfect freedom extends to their ability to "order their actions, and dispose of their possessions and persons, as they think fit, within the bounds of the law of nature, without asking leave, or depending upon the will of any other man" (Ch. II: 4, 8). The transition to the state of nature requires realizing that one does not have to "ask leave." And yet that does not mean that one should immediately start looting.

We are raised in civil society with an expectation that we will follow a set of rules. Those rules, insofar as we live in a legitimate system that we have chosen, are part of a large governmental framework and hierarchy. When the framework seems to disintegrate there is uncertainty about whether or not the rules still hold sway. On the day the bombs fell the police chief is directing traffic, by day three, after one police officer has been shot by the addicts, police presence is largely non-existent. The rules, and the norms that surround those rules, do not fall away like shackles at the moments the bombs fall. *Lucifer's Hammer* depicts looting and murder within moments of the comet's strike and the earthquake it produces. This fits both with a Hobbesian understanding of rules[4] and it contrasts with the more Lockean fading of rules and shifting of norms in *Alas, Babylon*. Locke clearly states that "he has not liberty to destroy himself, or so much as any creature in his possession, but where some nobler use than its bare preservation calls for it" (Ch. II: 6, 9). The maintenance of the vestiges of rules (except among the elderly, who are shown to be prone to irrationality) illustrates a willingness not to fall into license. Likewise, those who are more likely to license, the "vultures" lurking outside the drug store are in the minority.

Civil Society

The tension between the perfect freedom of the state of nature and the license that can shift us into a state of war reveals a time period when the rational inhabitants of the state of nature are going to be thinking about the advantages of entering into civil society. *Alas, Babylon* walks a fine line on this question, recognizing the importance of the idea of consent to political authority to confer legitimacy, but also using the vestiges or remnants of the federal government to externally authorize the political authority that emerges.[5] In order to read *Alas, Babylon* as a Lockean account I need to show signs of consent to the authority of Randy Bragg. To do this I will discuss first his clear authority in his own household and then extend the argument to his initial forays into acting authoritatively in Fort Repose and finally his performance of authority in his capture and punishment of the highwaymen who assault Dan Gunn. What is clear here is that while the novel does not present a perfect communal moment where the inhabitants are seen to sign a social contract (and that moment was largely absent in *Lucifer's Hammer* as well), it is careful to stress both moments of consent and the parameters of the role of authority.

On the one hand *Alas, Babylon* is out to celebrate the self sufficiency, industry and organization of the community surrounding Randy Bragg's home on the Timuacan River. Their life post war is a state of nature in the absence of external authority. But it also illustrates what work people are capable of doing when they are freed from meaningless rituals, customs and bureaucracy. As in many postapocalyptic accounts, there is a stress here on how much better off some of these characters are since the bombs fell. But they clearly face difficulties. Too much stress on the success of the Bragg community might minimize the work that they put into it. Four months out they face critical shortages (gasoline, matches, needles) and threats to their existence (something is eating chickens and has taken one of their pigs). Randy leads this small community as head of household. He makes decisions, not so much because the people there have chosen him to do so, but because in this small community he possesses the natural superiority of age, sex and race. When threats come to the larger Fort Repose community Randy will have to legitimize his claims to authority as that natural superiority will not extend to the town itself. Randy is the owner of the "big house," the center of the community (and he will not opt for communal ownership as will happen in the next chapter). He has masculine authority over his sister-in-law, Helen, her children, his girlfriend, Lib. He holds masculine and age related authority over Florence and her friend Alice. The other white male characters clearly acknowledge (and thus have acquiesced to) Randy's authority. Dan Gunn, the doctor, is happy to be able to do what he needs to do to care for the larger community by letting Randy make decisions about food and security; this is simply an efficient distribution of labor. The Admiral, who has the only short wave radio, and Randy's girlfriend's father both acquiesce out of their age, but also their recognition that Randy respects what they can give the community. The more difficult case is that of the neighboring black family. Do they acquiesce or is there a claim about natural racial superiority?

The Henrys, the African American extended family that has owned land adjacent to the Bragg's home for generations, has a clear edge on providing benefits for the community. They owned the chickens and pigs; they knew where to find wild sugar cane; they had the extensive vegetable garden. The novel is less clear on their full acquiescence to Randy's authority. Many white characters in the book presume that as a white man Randy Bragg has authority over them. Randy recognizes the unequal arrangement in the food supplies and declares that they must all help the Henrys protect the food supply. They share the eggs from the Henrys' chickens (which are delivered to the Bragg house every day) and they will now share the responsibility for guarding them. This is not a vision of racial equality.[6] But the question is whether it is to be read as a vision challenging Lockean claims of natural equality. I would argue that, as in *Lucifer's Hammer*, we as readers are supposed to see the hierarchies that emerge as simply "making sense." It just happens to be that the novel puts forward the white man, Randy Bragg, as the hero who rules and the black man, Malachai Henry, as the hero who must die.

The novel is struggling with the ideal of equality, both in that it is bogged down by the racial and gender norms of its time (publication in 1959) but also because of a tension seen as well in social contract thinkers when thinking about what natural equality means. Surely some are more talented than others? So does that not deny natural equality? Hobbes solved this by claiming that despite talents each of us is vulnerable to death and could be killed, in one's sleep, by a plot bringing together the talents of many. We can all kill and be killed for Hobbes. Locke understands natural equality somewhat differently, however.

> Though I have said above, (Chap. II). That all men by nature are equal, I cannot be supposed to understand all sorts of equality: age or virtue may give men a just precedency: excellency of parts and merit may place others above the common level: birth may subject some, and alliance or benefits others, to pay an observance to those to whom nature, gratitude, or other respects, may have made it due: and yet all this consists with the equality, which all men are in, in respect of jurisdiction or dominion one over another; which was the equality I there spoke of, as proper to the business in hand, being that equal right, that every man hath, to his natural freedom, without being subjected to the will or authority of any other man. (Ch. VI: 54, 31)

So no one of us can be legitimately ruled by another without the one being ruled giving consent. But talents exist, by birth, by age, and by extension we can say by sex or by race. Randy benefits from being the son of the "big house." He has employed members of the Henrys family; he has run for office (and Florence voted for him). There are reasons why those living near him might "pay observance to those to whom nature, gratitude, or other respects, may have made it due." The children do so through birth (age). Dan Gunn, the Admiral and Lib's father do so through alliance and benefits. The women do so through habit and the Henrys, I would argue, do so through an alliance that the novel does not wish to make too explicit. In other words, as I said earlier, the novel does not want to be an argument for racial equality. And yet buried in its tale of struggling to survive after nuclear war (and in its ending where the school in Fort Repose is desegregated), *Alas, Babylon* uses the state of nature like setting of the post nuclear blast to argue for a Lockean kind of natural equality. Randy is shown to be worthy of respect, because he is able to act in a way that will benefit the community.[7] And the members of the community, in recognizing his "just precedency" will then consent to his ideas.

That the novel argues for Randy's "excellency" is clear when Randy has to go into town to face the first postwar town-wide crisis. Randy wants people to help bury the radioactive body of Porky Logan (who had beaten him in the primary election for State Legislature), and was trading in radioactive jewelry stolen from the contaminated zones of Florida. Randy has to present himself as an authority figure that the townspeople could reject or accept (with consequences). Randy first approaches Bubba, the town undertaker, recognizing the vestige of his office, although it is clear that Randy does not think that Bubba will simply bury Porky for the town. Bubba instead "made a little speech" to those gathered for daily trading, outlining the need for cooperation and what Porky, the former State Legislator, had done for the community. This speech and the command it implied is ignored and even laughed at by the traders (again evidence of the state of nature).

Dan Gunn, the medical expert, sets out in conversation with Bubba and Randy the threat. They must bury dead bodies to avoid disease and they must bury radioactive material to avoid exposure. But Dan Gunn is not going to appeal to the community. He is the expert, but he is not an authority figure who can get the townspeople to act for the common good. Instead it is Randy who speaks up, Randy who sees that "it was necessary that he act" (215). He acts by drawing his gun, "so that it was a menace to no one in particular and yet to each of them separately." He then names five of them and declares "you have just volunteered to be pall bearers."

> For a long time no one had ordered them to do anything. For a long time, there had not even been a boss on a job. Nobody moved. Some of the traders carried handguns in hip pockets or holsters . . . [Randy] was going to shoot the first man who reached for a weapon. This was the decision he had made. Regardless of the consequences he was going to do it. (216)

On first read this might seem to be an illegitimate use of force. Randy could simply be seen to threaten these men. Instead the scene should be read as appealing first to the sense of communal preservation and second to the recognition ("you have just volunteered") that Randy does not have the power (or the authority) to make them do this. He will shoot to protect himself. But he is not saying that he will shoot to force them to bury Porky. Randy must make clear to them that this burial needs to be done. The scene ends simply "the five men followed him and he holstered his pistol" (216).

Two things are going on here. First we see an example of the "covetousness" that Locke discusses as unworthy of the rational person who will improve the earth given to him by God. Why has Porky Logan died of radiation poisoning? Because he looted jewelry stores in places outside of the blast zones to trade for whiskey in Fort Repose. The others who have contracted radiation poisoning were the ones who traded the whiskey. None of these men were involved in the "improvement" of the earth. Rather all were expressing mere self interest and desire. Second we see Randy taking on a job for the good of the community; but he does not do so simply out of some sense of munificence. Instead Randy sees this as an opportunity to clue the townspeople into their interconnected lives. At this point, four months after the bombs have fallen, people are going about their lives in individual family units. They trade for goods and they trade news about the war, but they do not work together to benefit anyone. Some fail to even work hard to survive (the poor whites in Pistolville are eating their dogs) and the novel promotes the Lockean view that those who fail to work hard when conditions are roughly equal disqualify themselves from the status of full, free, rational human beings.

Randy succeeds in getting men to help him bury Porky's radioactive body both because he does so from a potentially threatening position, holding a weapon, but more so because he simply speaks with authority. The other men all had weapons and they could have easily rejected Randy's plan by shooting him. But again, the novel shows here both Randy's ability to get others to do what he wants them to do and that the others will recognize that burying this body is something that needs to be done. This is not simply a moral argument about doing what is right; it is a self interested argument where Randy is in a position to clue them into what is in their self interest. So these men consent to Randy's description of their volunteering for this job.

After this incident Randy goes home and hears on the radio that the acting President is deputizing all members of the National Guard in the contaminated zones. This announcement confers authority on Randy by an external source. But that source has little legitimacy for the town of Fort Repose. Being in a contaminated zone means precisely that no one will come to their aid and that they are on their own. So Randy's ability to get people to follow him without the external justification of his National Guard uniform, attests to the people's acquiescence to his authority. Importantly he demands very little from them, and he faces the next threat to community without "volunteering" anyone. Thus he recognizes what his job is: to preserve the town and punish transgressors to their well being.

By the time Randy has to deal with the deeper threat of "highwaymen" he will fully accept his role as protector and judge. The burial of Porky Logan is Fort Repose's first move towards the creation of civil society: the recognition of a threat to the well being of the community as a whole, and the agreement on a process to redress that threat. Randy's capture and punishment of the highwaymen reflects the community's more rigorous move toward the social contract.

And this is done, where-ever any number of men, in the state of nature, enter into society to make one people, one body politic, under one supreme government; or else when any one joins himself to, and incorporates with any government already made: for hereby he authorizes the society, or which is all one, the legislative thereof, to make laws for him, as the public good of the society shall require; to the execution whereof, his own assistance (as to his own decrees) is due. And this puts men out of a state of nature into that of a common-wealth, by setting up a judge on earth, with authority to determine all the controversies, and redress the injuries that may happen to any member of the commonwealth; which judge is the legislative, or magistrates appointed by it. (Ch. VII: 89, 47-8)

The key here is the setting up of a "judge on earth" in Randy. That must be seen as a legitimate move by the people of Fort Repose and it must be clear that if they were going to reject Randy, they could. The novel must make clear that the people of Fort Repose "authorize" Randy's actions.

"Quarrelsome and Contentious"

It is noteworthy that Randy gains his authority through dealing with the inconveniences of the state of nature: the need to defend and punish trans-gressors of the law of nature. When the vultures stop being in the minority or start infringing more obviously on the freedom of the rational and industrious then Locke is clear that punishment of such breakers of the laws of nature, the dictates of reason, is wholly legitimate and that we are all authorized to protect what we have from those "noxious creatures" (Locke, 11, Ch. II, para.10). *Alas, Babylon* has few examples of the "noxious creatures" as a reas-surance that most people are obeying the laws of nature. The inhabitants of Randy's corner of the Timucuan River are shown four months after the bombs have fallen, to be highly organized and all working hard for their own benefit and that of the community. They are hungry, but not starving; in fact most characters are described as being in excellent shape. They have a good supply of water from their wells yet their showers are cold.[8] Everyone has a job to do and each is encouraged to be innovative in thinking about new food supplies and new conveniences for their postapocalyptic life. Randy muses that he misses music, coffee, cigarettes, but not whiskey. Whiskey could only be used medicinally as an anesthetic. Randy's vice from before the bombs is no longer an issue for him, showing again his ability to face these new circumstances clear eyed and with an eye to the community's well being.

When Dan Gunn is attacked by the highwaymen, "Randy felt nauseated, not at the sight of Dan's injuries—he had seen worse—but in disgust at the beasts who in callous cruelty had dragged down and maimed and destroyed the human dignity of this selfless man. Yet it was nothing new. It had been like this at some point in every civilization and on every continent. There were human jackals for every human disaster" (241). Randy clearly shares with Locke the assessment of these attackers as "noxious." He describes them as sub human: beasts, jackals that have attacked "the human dignity of a selfless man." Dan Gunn, in recounting his story, had noted his liking of a local family because they "were cheerful, industrious, and thoughtful" (247). Thus he clarifies his own Lockean worldview: these are precisely the terms on which someone should be praised. As a doctor (a point that Dan Gunn made clear to his attackers) any rational person would acknowledge that he both had little to steal and that he had skills that any rational person would recognize and want to protect. Thus these attackers attacked for no rational reason. Their own self interest was not even being followed; when Randy and his colleagues catch up with the highwaymen they find that the female of the group has "goofed off with some bastard with a bottle" (277) (probably after drinking the whiskey that Dr. Gunn kept to use as anesthetic). Unlike the single minded escaped convicts, these are people simply leeching off of the work of others to sustain a life of drunken abandon.

Randy approaches the capture and punishment of these highwaymen systematically and in a way that reflects both his acceptance of this as his job, but also his recognition that he needs to signal to the town that he is taking on this job (thereby allowing them to signal their lack of consent). After hearing the president's announcement about being deputized, Randy remarks "I have been legally designated" as being in charge. He describes getting the men of Fort Repose to help him bury Porky: "I had no authority. Now I do have authority, legally" (221). But Randy is putting too much on the words of a president who is hundreds of miles away and is not able to back up his authority at all. He succeeded on the town green not simply because he had a gun and was willing to use it (everyone there had a gun), but because those men chose to be "volunteered." They consented to his request.

After Randy hears of Dr. Gunn's attack, he goes into action as the judge and prosecutor. The novel simplifies the movement into the social contract by utilizing the external source of authority. But Randy both acknowledges that he is in charge and also announces that to the people of Fort Repose, both in the prior case of Porky's body, but also here by posting a series of announcements. Randy's movement into the role of leader is then symbolically cemented by his marriage to Lib. Now he can truly be the head of household of the river community. Randy begins from the claim "I'm going to execute them" (241). This is said "in a monotone." He is not being visibly passionate. This is not a merely emotional decision. Instead Randy is doing the only thing that can be done with the "noxious creatures" who seek to destroy the natural rights of the members of his community.

He sets out in a series of systematic steps, each one of which acknowledges the bounds of his authority, the rights of his community members and his rational preparation to find and punish the aggressors. He meets with the Admiral to devise a war plan; he visits Rita Hernandez in Pistolville to request the use of a truck with gasoline (that can be used to lure the highwaymen into attack, Lib's idea); he goes to town and posts a set of rules on the town green.[9]

Those rules establish for Fort Repose their movement from the state of nature to civil society. And the posting of the rules illustrates that Randy is seeking to authorize his actions not simply through the president's deputization. Prior to his posting of the rules Randy learns that the attackers have also attacked the Hickey's, the beekeeper family that Randy had been admiring for their hard work a few days earlier. The highway men had killed the older Hickeys. Their children had escaped into town. Here Randy responds "raging for immediate retaliation" (266). He moderates that feeling by appealing to the Admiral, who counsels him to stick to his original plan: "These people operate like beasts, Randy. Having gorged themselves in the night they sleep through the mornings, perhaps through the whole day" (266). Again is the presentation of these violators of natural law as sub human. So that the need to move into civil society is not based on the impulses of humans striving to survive in a difficult world, rather civil society is needed to deal with those few who fail to appreciate their own capacity to work hard and improve the earth.

The rules Randy posts cover the basic boundaries that the Fort Repose community will set: the four orders cover Randy's own position of authority and the deputization of other guardsmen, the need to boil water because of a small typhoid outbreak, and the penalties for "robbery or pillage, or for harboring highwaymen, or for failure to make known information concerning their whereabouts or movements, is death by hanging" (256). He later adds an order covering the need to register marriages and births. These orders are posted on the town green. The orders cover the minimal kind of government that is needed for the people to be able to thrive, working on their own. There is the presentation of Randy's position "assuming command of Fort Repose and its environs." Randy then notes that others who have been deputized or (with military experience) who might want to volunteer to form a company to protect the town. There is the warning about typhus and an establishment for the punishment for harming members of the community or their property. The addition of marriage and birth certificates simply closes out this minimal protective government. This government will protect people and property; it will inform people of threats that they will have to face themselves, and it will be a community in that information about household dynamics will be recorded.

Randy acts in accordance with the expectations of a legislative power that rules by the consent of the people. He makes the laws public. He limits those laws to people's primary desires.

> And so whoever has the legislative or supreme power of any common-wealth, is bound to govern by established standing laws, promulgated and known to the people, and not by extemporary decrees; by indifferent and upright judges, who are to decide controversies by those laws; and to employ the force of the community at home, only in the execution of such laws, or abroad to prevent or redress foreign injuries, and secure the community from inroads and invasion. And all this to be directed to no other end, but the peace, safety, and public good of the people. (Ch IX: 131, 68)

These laws will secure Fort Repose from threats external (highwaymen) and internal (typhoid). These laws also make the community one by requiring the registration of marriages and births (a requirement that Randy makes retroactive back to "the Day"). The "peace, safety, and public good" of Fort Repose is Randy's primary concern. He is not setting out laws whereby people are required to pay him, he relies on the workings of his own family and extended household. He is not out to regulate people's behavior except where that impacts their good and the good of the whole.

Only after posting these laws can Randy commence finding the highwaymen. So he does not act as "supreme power" until he has announced his intention to do as such. He is transparent about being the power of the community. He need not be transparent about his plan to capture the highwaymen; once he is in power it is his job to capture and punish them. His plan is to lure the highwaymen to attack a truck, seemingly filled with goods, that is driven by Malachai, one of the Henrys, the black family that are Randy's neighbors. In the truck will be Randy, the Admiral and Lib's father Bill. It is Malachai's idea to drive and Randy is reluctant to relinquish this position of prime mover in the plan. Randy is wearing his uniform, to signal his position of authority, and Malachai notes,

> "Sir, that uniform. It don't go with the truck."
> "They won't see it until they stop us," Randy said. "Then it'll be too late. Anyway, all sorts of people are wearing all sorts of clothes. I'll bet you'd see highwaymen in uniforms if they got their hands on them."
> "That ain't all, sir," Malachai said. "It's your face. It's white. They're more likely to tackle a black face than a white face. They see my face and say, 'Huh,

here's something soft and probably with no gun.' So they relax. Maybe it gives us that extra second, Mister Randy." (270)

This strategy plays up on the racism of the highwaymen (who we know are white from Gunn's description). It also illustrates some weakness in Randy's own reasoning. He thinks his clothing may not matter, and yet he is wearing a uniform for a reason, and a good one at that. If the highwaymen had uniforms they would be worn precisely to fool people into thinking that their actions were sanctioned by some acknowledged authority.[10] Randy also expresses a certain amount of skepticism about Malachai's ability to play this role: "He had confidence in Malachai's driving and in his judgment and courage. But it was the driver who would have to do the talking, if there was any talking, and who would have to keep his hands off the pistol" (270). So Randy does not seem to trust Malachai's ability to play the role successfully: to speak to the highwaymen in a way that will not rouse suspicion and to refrain from shooting first. Malachai convinces Randy with repeated uses of the term "sir" and the honorific "Mister Randy" that clearly infantilizes Malachai and represents his acknowledgement of the authority Randy has over him. Randy acquiesces once the Admiral steps in to back up the strategic advantage that Malachai's driving will play. This small scene offers yet another window into the interesting racial politics of Alas, Babylon.[11]

Once they finally encounter the highwaymen they are "herded" into an ambush (and Randy once again compares them to animals: coral snakes). Malachai's plan proves to be correct; the highwaymen refer to him as "boy" and clearly have no respect for Malachai as a potential threat. (Malachai also clearly knows how to "play" them "acting dumb and talking dumb" (275)). In the ensuing shootout Malachai is shot in the stomach (and subsequently dies, both showing how right it was not to let Randy drive, but also illustrating another example of the 'killing off the black character' in American film and literature).

One of the highwaymen is left alive and he is tied up and taken for his public hanging in the town green. They cannot find Dan Gunn's medical bag, but Randy does have the foresight to take their guns and extra ammunition. "He was thinking ahead. There would be other highwaymen and this was armament for his company" (278). The next day the surviving highwayman was hanged on the town green. "Randy ordered that the corpse not be cut down until sunset. He wanted strangers to be impressed and spread word beyond Fort Repose" (283). On that same day seven men in Fort Repose volunteered (without Randy's 'persuasion') to join the Fort Repose Provisional Company. Randy also made public who had been killed and what they had done. On a separate notice he announced Malachai's death in the service of his community. Thus Randy again performed the job of leader: he protected his community, he announced that protection as a potential deterrent to others and he honored the life of a "rational and industrious" member of the community who had died trying to protect it. The remaining 30 pages of the novel are anticlimactic from the standpoint of protecting Fort Repose. But the ending does illustrate a few more Lockean points concerning the advantages accrued from human effort and the preferred form of government.

Alluded to earlier is the solution to the lack of fish where Peyton and Preacher pool their talents (Peyton's youth and Preacher's lifetime on the river) and catch an excellent string of large fish. The second problem was the lack of salt and this is solved by Helen (Randy's sister in law) remembering that the journal she read to Dan while he was recovering included a discussion of a salt lick 15 miles north on the river. They go to the salt lick in the sailboats, (refitted motorboats invented by the Admiral). The salt, the crabs (that congregate in the part of the river near the lick), the fish and the armadillo steaks that Ben has produced illustrate a bounty of ingenuity and earth's providence. Peyton further proves her own resourcefulness by searching through parts of the attic others had ignored, finding a foot pedal sewing machine, kerosene lamps, a woodstove and other leftovers from the house prior to the age of electricity. It is at this moment of bounty, where the life of the community is clearly thriving, that a helicopter from the US military lands, bringing potential escape from this contaminated zone.

The thriving inhabitants of the Bragg community hear about how the rest of the United States fared during the war (which they learn that the US did win). The population is radically diminished ("I doubt if we have the population of France" (314)). There is no power, little food and epidemics. Life in Fort Repose starts to look quite good in contrast. Other than the lack of power, they have a food supply and an organized community that is not living under martial law. When they ask Randy if he wants to leave he muses:

> This was Randy's town and these were his people and he knew he would not leave them. Yet it was not right that he make this decision alone. He looked at Lib without finding it necessary to speak. She knowing what was in his mind, simply smiled and winked. He said, "I guess I'll stay, Paul." (315)

Others in their riverside community concur, admitting that life is more fulfilling now than it had ever been.

And so *Alas, Babylon* ends on a pioneering note. This small group of survivors will remain in their Florida community, rebuilding it themselves and making it what they wish. The lives they will lead will be difficult, and they are likely not to move beyond the nineteenth century for quite awhile. But everyone will have an essential role to play in the well being of the community. Male or female, black or white, everyone will be needed and everyone's work will be important to the community's flourishing. Towards the end of the novel, after various crises have been solved, the children return to their schooling (now the responsibility of parents) and Caleb, the black son of the Henrys, arrives for classes on the first day. "Randy was a little surprised. He saw that Peyton and Ben expected it, and then he recalled that in Omaha—and indeed in two thirds of American cities—white and Negro children had sat side by side for many years without fuss or trouble" (300). The next generation of post-war inhabitants of Fort Repose might attain racial equality. That equality will be eased by the death of Malachai. The only other age and sex appropriate man to challenge Randy's power is gone. Thus the novel ends on a note that goes beyond the hopeful. Yet, again, the reader is asked to simply go along with the lack of consent offered by the Henrys and the women (absent Randy's shared glance with Lib). As a contract this is one limited to a few select white, male characters, and the novel is presented in such a way that we will not question those limitations.

As a novel out to instruct the reader about the potential horror of nuclear war, *Alas, Babylon* may well fail. But as a description of how a group of rational and sensible people can overcome the destruction of catastrophe and rebuild a community based on the importance of private property, *Alas, Babylon* succeeds. In so doing the novel emphasizes a very familiar American story—a young man can't find his way in the world without a challenge. What better way to show the world what he is made of than to rally his community to self sufficiency after a nuclear war?

Notes

The chapter title is from John Locke, *Second Treatise of Government* (Indianapolis, Indiana: Hackett Publishing Co. 1980 [1690]) V: 34, 21 (Chapter, paragraph, page number).

1. Reviewed in *The New York Times*, Orville Prescott, March 20, 1959; *Alas, Babylon* has experienced a small amount of scholarly interest, usually in contrast to the author's primary interest. Cf. Wagar (1982), Sponsler (1993), Booker (2001), Abbot (2006), Foertsch (2007).

2. "He had not framed the right kind of answer: the moderate Southern quasi-liberal, semi-segregationist double-talk that would have satisfied everybody except the palmetto scrub woolhats, the loud-mouthed Kluxers and courthouse whittlers who would vote for Porky anyway." (8). Randy is unable to explain the intricacies of his views on desegregation (it needs a generation, he says). But in this novel what is interesting is that Frank gets to have it all ways. He gives Randy the line that Randy could not use and thus the readers of *Alas, Babylon*, first published in 1959, do not need to worry that this postapocalyptic account will end up being a justification for racial equality, even though that is one of its conclusions.

3. And the freed convicts are a common ploy in postapocalyptic fiction. *Jericho*, the postapocalyptic television show, used escaped convicts in season one as a way to terrorize the town.

4. For Hobbes rules are like shackles: external constraints that keep us from doing what we might wish to do to better our situation. In this sense any loss of rules results in an increase in freedom. Locke, who sees a difference between freedom and license, does not think either that rules are like shackles or that the absence of rules would produce mayhem.

5. Jeffrey Porter, "Narrating the End: Fables of Survival in the Nuclear Age." *Journal of American Culture* 16 (Winter, 1993): 41-47. Porter argues that *Alas, Babylon* exemplifies a kind of pleasant military dictatorship under Randy Bragg. I counter this claim with the moments of consent that are present in the novel.

6. Cf. Jacqueline Foertsch, "Extraordinarily convenient neighbors": African-American characters in white-authored post-atomic novels. *Journal of Modern Literature* 30, (Summer, 2007): 122-138. Foertsch analyzes both the Henrys and Rita Hernandez, the woman of Pistolville that Randy has rejected in favor of white, educated Lib, as examples of the continued ways in which novels like *Alas, Babylon* simply reinscribe racial hierarchies after the end (135).

7. But many other members of this community are also shown to have natural talents. Preacher knows why the fish do not seem to bite in August and he helps Peyton, Randy's niece who is shown to chafe against the prescribed roles being given to girls, succeed where others have failed. She knows enough to ask for Preacher's help (others ignore him because of his age and race).

8. The enticement of a hot shower is used by Harvey Randall in *Lucifer's Hammer* to try and convince the people of Jellison's valley to save the power plant. The emphasis on cleanliness here in *Alas, Babylon* again illustrates how the novel presents the main characters as admirable and industrious.

9. In the midst of these preparations the community along the river is faced with another threat. Something, human or animal, is attacking the chickens and pigs. This is a natural threat. Randy knows it needs to be solved, but he also knows that he need not solve it. Ben, his nephew, ends up shooting and killing the dog that was attacking the chickens. By doing so we see how the natural and the noxious must be faced in the same way.

10. The postapocalyptic television show *Jericho* uses this scenario when a marine brigade comes to town and "requisitions" supplies. The townspeople discover that these are not marines and that they have killed the marines and stolen the uniforms in order to use their authoritative force to steal from the town.

11. These are of particular interest as the author, Pat Frank, was in the military at the time of desegregation. Randy, the character, notes fighting in Korea with black soldiers, and this experience has changed his racial views. But Randy also falls into his racial superiority easily. The novel seems to gently challenge him (and the reader) on these points.

~

CHAPTER FOUR

"Man is born free; and everywhere is in chains"

Rousseau and Malevil: The Responsibilities of Civil Life

The two previous chapters each concerned novels arguing that the state of nature is a condition from which we desire to escape. For Hobbes (and *Lucifer's Hammer*) it is because the state of nature is violent and scary; for Locke (and *Alas, Babylon*) it is because the state of nature is inefficient and does not have a sure system for dealing with the "quarrelsome and contentious." This chapter takes up the last classical social contract thinker, Jean Jacques Rousseau, whose view of the state of nature is different from either Locke or Hobbes, and whose understanding of the motivations for entering into the social contract is also different. Rousseau emphasizes who we become when we decide to enter into the social contract. We gain "civil" and "moral" liberty through the act of agreeing to laws that we give to ourselves. This chapter analyzes two postapocalyptic accounts, each of which reflects different parts of Rousseau's theory. First Robert Merle's *Malevil* reflects the Rousseauean motivation behind entering into the social contract, not to escape from anything harmful in the state of nature, but rather to achieve a sense of morality; second is *Into the Forest*, by Jean Hegland, representing a return to the state of nature and a rejection of civil society.

Hobbes and Locke use the state of nature in order to explain how we move into a social contract through a mechanism of choosing to give up some natural rights in exchange for security of self and property provided by a legitimate sovereign power. Thus both *Leviathan* and the *Second Treatise* move from descriptions of the state of nature to the social contract to civil society. Rousseau, on the other hand, separates his argument about the state of nature from his argument about civil society. By separating the issues in two different works, the *Discourse on the Origin of Inequality* and *The Social Contract*, Rousseau clarifies that it is not the conditions of the state of nature that motivate our entrance into civil society. Rather it is our self-conscious desire to live under a legitimate authority that provides the necessary motivation. *The Social Contract* focuses on the move to civil society and argues that we can move from the state of nature to an illegitimate civil society and that since living under a legitimate system is our primary motivation the primary focus should be on the social contract itself and not on the state of nature.

This means that Rousseauean postapocalyptic accounts will look different than the Hobbesian and Lockean ones that use the apocalyptic event, state of nature, social contract, civil society trajectory. The two accounts I discuss in this chapter approach Rousseau from different directions. *Malevil* reflects the concerns of *The Social Contract*: how can a group of people legitimately follow orders if no one has any natural authority over another? *Into the Forest*, on the other hand, reflects Rousseau's interest in the state of nature and it ends without any move into civil society, but rather with a retreat into nature. *Malevil*, which seems more similar to *Lucifer's Hammer* and *Alas, Babylon* with a small group of survivors struggling after a nuclear war, maintains an argument about the relations among the survivors stressing how they are to remain fully human under these trying conditions. *Into the Forest*, on the other hand, concerns only two main characters, both teenage girls, who find that survival means rejecting other people and moving back into nature.

Rousseau: Noble Savage vs. the General Will

Rousseau, like Hobbes and Locke, is concerned that natural inequalities (strength, age, experience, intelligence) might be understood to confer political inequalities. Hobbes solves this by declaring natural inequalities meaningless once vulnerability to death is realized. Locke comes closest to rationalizing that inequalities by nature (certainly inequalities in either rationality or effort) should result in some form of political inequality. But Rousseau most forcefully faces up to the question that if people have a variety of talents conferred by nature then do those talents justify the talented having the right to make the less talented do what they would otherwise have not chosen to do? He famously opens *The Social Contract*: "Man is born free; and everywhere he is in chains. One thinks himself master of others, and still remains a greater slave than they. How did this change come about? I do not know. What can make it legitimate? That question I think I can answer" (1, I). Rousseau is not asking how some come to order others to act; rather he is asking whether and why such orders could be legitimate. Hobbes and Locke claim that no one would follow the orders of the illegitimate. We might give up our property to the robber (who is not technically stealing, for Hobbes) but we do not think of this as legitimate and for Locke, at least, we know that we have the right to punish such a transgressor. But Rousseau acknowledges that sometimes we convince ourselves that such orders are legitimate. Again, legitimacy is the key: how should we properly understand what a legitimate civil society would look like? And conversely what does illegitimate force look like?

Postapocalyptic accounts are as relevant for thinking through this focus on legitimacy as they are for thinking through the conditions and/or the mechanism of the state of nature.[1] A focus on the state of nature and a focus on legitimacy are not radically different in their consequences. Hobbes and Locke use the state of nature to explain how a legitimate civil society emerges. But Rousseau is concerned that we may not move so easily from the state of nature to a legitimate state. We may enslave ourselves, to custom or to expectation. More importantly we need a mechanism to understand whether or not our own civil society is legitimate. Hobbes and Locke might be misread to be saying that *any* move from the state of nature to government produces legitimacy. The idea that we move from the state of nature to civil society, through the social contract, in order to accrue benefits to ourselves contributes to this potential misreading, and *Lucifer's Hammer* and *Alas, Babylon* both emphasize the advantages of civil society, not necessarily the legitimacy of civil society. *Malevil*, on the other hand, is clearly interested from the beginning of the book to question legitimacy. *Into the Forest* wrestles with the legitimacy issue from a different perspective: when is it better to turn away from the possibility of illegitimate government? Might not a life in nature without politics sometimes be better than enslavement?

Rousseau uses his description of the state of nature in the *Discourse on the Origin of Inequality* to show how the conditions for illegitimate government emerge. But this description of the state of nature is also famous for its references to nature as a place of authenticity: the noble savage makes of nature what he can and thus while not a full human being, is at least not chained to convention.

If we strip this being [human], thus constituted, of all the supernatural gifts he may have received, and all the artificial faculties he can have acquired only by a long process; if we consider him, in a word, just as he may have come from the hands of nature, we behold in him an animal weaker than some, and less agile than others; but, taking him all round, the most advantageously organized of any. I see him satisfying his hunger at the first oak, and slaking his thirst at the first brook; finding his bed at the foot of the tree which afforded him a repast; and, with that, all of his wants supplied. (*Discourse*, I, 47)

The apocalyptic event performs the "stripping," yet few postapocalyptic accounts describe humans in such gently animalistic terms. Usually the animalistic is synonymous with the violent (as seen in the previous chapter with the repeated use of the term "beast" to describe the highwaymen). For Rousseau human beings in nature have minimal desires and are able to fulfill those desires easily. What is admirable about these humans is that they are not distracted by the "artificial faculties." They may follow the dictates of "mere appetite" but that is sometimes better than following the dictates of fashion.

Humans possess a capacity for betterment—a capacity for "perfectibility" that Rousseau does not think is shared by other non-human animals. We "have a share in [our] own operations, in [our] character as a free agent[s]" (*Discourse*, I, 52). In nature we are faced with a series of choices. We need to guard ourselves from choosing the path that might turn perfectibility into a mere automaton, performing at a high standard in accordance with the wishes of another. If we cannot choose moral liberty then it is better to simply be naturally free. "So long as they undertook only what a single person could accomplish, and confined themselves to such arts as did not require the joint labour of several hands, they lived free, healthy, honest, and happy lives, in so far as their nature allowed" (*Discourse*, II, 83). So nobility in nature goes beyond the following of appetite over custom; it also includes that one is largely alone. Too much interaction with other humans raises the potentially dangerous competition that emerges from our perfectibility. *Into the Forest* reflects this rejection of human society in favor of happiness with "rustic huts" (*Discourse*, II, 83).

Rousseau is not counseling that humans should stay in nature, in part because his target audience is so disconnected from nature that the trip back would be nearly impossible. He does recommend in *Emile* that a child (male) should ideally be educated in nature, so that he can stand up to the artifices of conventional society. Rousseau's readers would be members of illegitimate civil societies and not noble savages. But in the postapocalyptic context only Rousseau has an option that promotes staying in nature. Where Hobbes and Locke, and the postapocalyptic accounts that follow them, promote establishing a set system of laws, Rousseau, and the accounts that follow his lead, do not see law as a sufficient sign of a well working society.

The mere existence of law is not enough for Rousseau to claim that a legitimate civil society exists. Nor does the absence of law represent an automatic reversion to the state of nature.

> The subject of this present discourse, therefore, is more precisely this. To mark, in the progress of things, the moment at which right took the place of violence and nature became subject to law, and to explain by what sequence of miracles the strong came to submit to serve the weak, and the people to purchase imaginary repose at the expense of real felicity. (*Discourse*, I, 44-45)

The state of nature may in fact produce conditions that convince us to enter into illegitimate states (and worse yet to think that those states are legitimate). So what is the "real felicity" that we seem to reject in order to attain "imaginary repose"? In part Rousseau believes that the systems into which we contracted under Hobbes and Locke represent such "imaginary repose." We think that survival, protection of life and property, are the goals of civil society. But for Rousseau the goal of civil society is different.

> We might, over and above all this, add, to what man acquires in the civil state, moral liberty, which alone makes him truly master of himself; for the mere impulse of appetite is slavery, while obedience to a law which we prescribe to ourselves is liberty. (*The Social Contract*, 1, VIII, 178)

We enter into the social contract with the goal of attaining this moral liberty. We enter into the social contract with an eye to becoming a full human being—one who obeys laws given to oneself. The social contract represents an opportunity not simply to attain security or efficiency, rather the social contract is the vehicle through which we mature as rational creatures. It is the means by which we free ourselves from the chains of custom and appetite and link ourselves with other like minded individuals to become something greater in its whole than in its parts.

The "general will" is the sovereign entity of this contracted civil society. For Hobbes the sovereign had to protect and defend life, and for Locke the sovereign had to protect and defend life and property. But for Rousseau **we** are the sovereign. And what we are primarily protecting is the community itself. The general will is the common interest and "the Sovereign, merely by virtue of what it is, is always what it should be" (1, VII, 177).

> What makes the will general is less the number of votes than the common interest uniting them; for, under this system, each necessarily submits to the conditions he imposes on others: and this admirable agreement between interest and

justice gives to the common deliberations an equitable character which at once vanishes when any particular question is discussed, in the absence of a common interest to unite and identify the ruling of the judge with that of the party. (2, IV, 187)

The social contract produces a universal, unanimous decision to act for the good of the whole. The people entering the contract, who have interests (particular wills) of their own, suppress those particular interests in favor of the common interest. If there is no common interest on a particular issue then it is not an issue for which the general will can have a stand. But the social contract is not merely the "sum of all particular wills" rather it is "the sum of the differences" (2, III, 185). In other words you remove from the common interest the "pluses and minuses that cancel one another." What matters here is that the decision to enter the social contract is not thus simply a decision of self interest. You are not simply signing the contract in order to achieve your particular will. Rather you sign the contract because you recognize and desire to bring about the common interest. That interest may well go against your own particular interest. If you choose (after signing the contract) to go against the general will Rousseau's famous response is "that whoever refuses to obey the general will shall be compelled to do so by the whole body. This means nothing less than that he will be forced to be free" (1, VII, 177). This freedom is the previously discussed moral liberty, not the Hobbesian or Lockean freedom of doing what you wish to benefit yourself.

The clues to look for in the Rousseuaean postapocalyptic account include a recognition of the group as a group (as "a people"). The interests of the group as a self sustaining entity should reflect that the individuals can be more than they were without the group. In *Alas, Babylon* we saw characters who became more than they were before the war. But that was not a Rousseauean move to moral liberty. That was a Lockean move to self determination that was able to find an outlet under post-war conditions. The post-war conditions that *Malevil* represents create the need for a community.

Malevil

Written in 1972 by French author Robert Merle,[2] *Malevil* was an international bestseller, and first published in English in 1975.[3] The novel follows a small group of French men, friends since childhood, who survive a nuclear war in the wine cellar of the owner of Malevil, a thirteenth-century castle.

The four friends (Emmanuel, Meysonnier, Colin, Peyssou) are supplemented by Thomas, who has been renting a room in the castle and La Menou, the cook, and her mentally impaired son Momo. They are joined by two more women (one young) and another young man after the father of this group tried to steal one of Malevil's horses. This small group learns of other survivors in a nearby town and there will be the ubiquitous postapocalyptic fight against a group organized in a way contrary to the tenets of modern political thought.

Lucifer's Hammer and *Alas, Babylon* are both present tense narratives, but *Malevil* is written retrospectively, as a journal started months after the initial incident. So that from the very first page we discover not hints of what might happen, but deep contemplation about life "before" and life "after" the bombs. The novel opens with rumination on Proust's memory trigger, the madeleine, and how Colin had lived such a moment through a discovered bag of tobacco. This incident allows the narrator to muse on the very idea of memory and the past: "I envy Proust. At least he had a solid foundation under him while he explored his past: a certain present, an indubitable future. But for us the past is doubly past, our 'time past' is doubly inaccessible, because included in it is the whole universe in which that time flowed. There has been a complete break. The forward march of the ages has been interrupted. We no longer know where or when we are. Or whether there is to be any future at all" (7-8). This analysis of the meaning of the idea of the past in a postapocalyptic world promises that *Malevil* will spend less time on the need to make insulin or find salt, and instead will analyze how we live in a world absent both a past and a future.

Malevil contemplates the existential meaning of such a world ending event and uses the political and social arrangements of the residents of Malevil, in contrast with those survivors in the neighboring town of La Rocque to explore what makes human life worth living. And *Malevil* concludes similarly to *Alas, Babylon*, praising the opportunity that the conditions of post war life have produced. This use of the postapocalyptic landscape to work out utopian visions of what life could be like counters some of the warning that the account is also out to produce. And *Malevil* explores the lost opportunity of realizing in time how life can flourish. Readers of *Malevil* learn (as the reader of Rousseau learns) how to identify the illegitimacy of our current lives. Two particular incidents in *Malevil* bring home this lesson of the harms of illegitimacy. Both incidents illustrate the principles behind the social and political arrangements at Malevil. The first concerns the "women question" and the second the renegades in La Rocque.

The Woman Question

Malevil recognizes that survival and potential flourishing in this world will require thinking carefully about interpersonal relations. While there are plenty of typical postapocalyptic moments in this novel—they struggle for food, they must deal with those more desperate—much of the novel explores the internal reactions to this war and Emmanuel works from the start to ensure that the group at Malevil become a community. This community is essentially one of the men at Malevil. The older women play a wholly secondary role. The younger women, however, prove to be one of the primary issues around which the identity and legitimacy of this community will turn.

Emmanuel, the narrator and ostensible lord of the manor, writes the narrative, although Thomas, the outsider among the group of friends, includes his comments at the end of many chapters. From the outset there is a concern that humanity may simply die out, although the narrative itself raises the possibility of future generations. Thus the organizing of the inhabitants of Malevil matters not simply as a way to ease them into certain death of the species, but rather models an appropriate way to achieve a new political order under these circumstances. On the very first night after the bombs fall, Emmanuel refers to plans for Malevil with the term "we." "'What do you mean?' Peyssou said 'Malevil belongs to you, doesn't it?' 'No, Peyssou, it doesn't,' I said, shaking my head. 'All that is finished, in the past. Suppose I die tomorrow from an illness or accident, what would happen? Where's our lawyer? Or our laws of inheritance? Or even our heir? Malevil belongs to those who work in it, and that is all there is to it'" (134). This is a recognition of the state of nature and simultaneously the moment where the first step towards a Rousseauean social contract is realized. By referencing the absence of lawyers and laws of inheritance Emmanuel is noting that the rules under which they used to live were both absent and irrelevant. The laws have no meaning and there is no mechanism to enforce them.

Beyond this, however, Emmanuel is both helping to establish a community at Malevil and a principle (shared work) for the justification of that shared ownership. He is rejecting the interpretation that only he could make the property communal because of course Emmanuel owns Malevil. But by referencing the principle of shared work producing shared ownership, Emmanuel is indicating that he is not giving Malevil to the community, rather that through labor, Malevil simply belongs to the community.

Rousseau says that before any talk of a social contract can come about there must be "a people" who can enter into such a contract. This is not simply a group of individuals, rather it is a community. "It would be better, before examining the act by which a people chooses a king, to examine that by which it has become a people; for this act, being necessarily prior to the other, is the true foundation of society" (*The Social Contract* 1, V). Emmanuel has given such a foundation for the inhabitants of Malevil. By articulating that Malevil is to be shared by those who work for the community, Emmanuel has moved this disparate group of individuals to a community, a people who now share in Malevil's land, stores and animals. Each of these characters had a role to play in Emmanuel's life as owner of Malevil, either as employee, tenant or friend, but now they will belong to Malevil as equals. Only La Menou seems put out, "by saying that Malevil belonged to everyone I had reduced her to a lowest common denominator and stripped her of the power and glory of her position as sole mistress of our ship after me" (135). Emmanuel then describes La Menou as pretending that he had not declared Malevil common property, thus restoring her own position at least in her own mind. This incident reveals that the sharing is largely among the men of Malevil. La Menou's role as cook and primary caretaker of domestic tasks does not change after the shift in ownership. This raises the issue that drives much of Malevil's plot—the question of women.

Unlike the other accounts discussed here (excepting *The Road*, which is not concerned with the perpetuation of the species) there is a clear sexual imbalance at the outset of Malevil: six men and one woman (who is post menopausal). This is part of why Emmanuel begins his journal by questioning the idea of the future: if there are no children who will grow and have children themselves after your own death then to what extent can we be said to have a future?[4] Emmanuel's interest in the woman question is not simply for procreative purposes. For Emmanuel "woman" represents much of what is good about life. But to be such a "woman" one must be young. His sexual interest reflects his desire to be fully understood as a man. He had no wife and no children before the bombs, but he did have a woman, Birgitta, who came to Malevil every summer. La Menou, because of her age and her status as employee is not really a woman. The first woman that the community encounters, Miette, is accompanied by another post-menopausal non-woman, La Falvine. Miette is young, sturdy, and ironically, mute. Once Miette joins the community, Emmanuel's principle of sharing comes up against the conventional views of his compatriots.

Miette is the step-daughter of the "troglodyte" who lives in a cave near Malevil. She is the victim of sexual abuse by her step father. This family has survived the bombs and try to steal one of Malevil's horses. The family is described as "brutish, dour, immoral, and worse still, poachers" (176). These are Rousseau's savages of nature minus any real noble characteristics. The father (who Emmanuel will kill in the raid that reveals Miette) has kept his family to himself and built a self sufficient farm whose peculiarities are of particular use to the community at Malevil. The father insisted on growing his own wheat and he raised only male animals. This solves Malevil's bread deficit and the absence of male animals that had heralded the end of horses. Upon his death the father is compared to a "Cro-Magnon:" "Underhung jaw, low forehead, jutting eyebrows. But after all, think of him washed, shaved, manicured, hair cut short, his well muscled body tightly belted into a new uniform, and he wouldn't have looked any more primitive than many a good commando officer" (189). His skills in the "Art of War," which included his highly accurate use of a bow and arrow (a silent method of poaching animals from Malevil prior to the war) illustrate both his savagery, and also thus his preparedness for life after the bombs.

But there is no place for such a man in Emmanuel's community at Malevil, which can benefit from his preparations for life after the bombs, without being threatened by his pre-political savageries. And so he is killed by Emmanuel, and his wife, son and step daughter, plus his animals and food stores will all be used to benefit the Malevil community. Because the "troglodytes" attacked Malevil without provocation and have been beaten by Malevil the inhabitants of the cave farm accept with no complaint Emmanuel's power over them. "I had conquered and killed the tyrant. So now I was in the tyrant's place myself, surrounded by an almost religious aura, and everything was my property" (204). The difference between the mature and rational inhabitants of Malevil, capable of politics and living by a principle of mutual dependence is wholly absent among those left after the father's death. The woman, La Falvine, seems to only know how to obey and simultaneously to undermine. The son, Jacquet, now sees Emmanuel as a larger than life hero who has destroyed the monster (his father) in his own life. Only Miette can interact with Emmanuel as an odd kind of equal.

The mere existence of the male animals would have greatly benefitted the Malevil barnyard, but it is Miette who proves to be the greatest asset of the defeated household. She is initially described in glowing terms: "dark eyes and luxuriant hair"; "breasts high and rounded liked bossed shields, high buttocks, well-muscled legs"; "I admired everything about her, totally, even her peasant awkwardness" (205). Miette is beautiful in a fleshy, highly natural way. Her beauty is not found in her clothes or her education; rather she is beautiful because of her youth, her health, her abundance.

She "radiated light and warmth." "She was a magnificent human animal, this future mother of mankind" (206). That she is also mute only proves that she exists for Emmanuel to play out a series of ideas in communal living. He has no interest in forcing Miette, nor does he have much desire to engage her in analysis of what it means for her to be the only fecund woman among six men. As he returns to Malevil that night, with Miette riding behind him on his horse, Emmanuel imagines himself a medieval baron returning to his castle after a hard fought war: "Of course it wasn't quite the same. I hadn't raped Miette, and she wasn't captive. On the contrary, I had freed her from captivity" (212). Miette is a perfect female blank slate. She is not encumbered by the conventions and expectations of a woman of Emmanuel's class and education who might have lived in town. Instead Miette is fully innocent of town conventions and simultaneously fully aware of natural passions. Miette fits Rousseau's description of a woman:

> The first thing that they ought to learn is to love their duties out of regard for their advantages. This is the only way to make their duties easy for them. Each station and each age has its duties. We soon know our own, provided we love them. Honor woman's station, and in whatever rank heaven puts you, you will always be a good woman. The essential thing is to be what nature made us. A woman is always only too much what men want her to be. (*Emile*, 386)

Miette is perfectly of nature. She embraces her duties. Whether those be mere obedience to Emmanuel and the other men, willingness to work in the kitchens and stables with La Menou, or providing a sexual outlet for the men of Malevil, Miette performs her duties good naturedly (and silently).

Emmanuel's plan is that Miette cannot simply "marry" one of the men and so he proposes that she be shared among them, to whatever extent she agrees. Emmanuel presumes that his former role as leader of the small group of friends (and his relationship with Thomas) will compel the men to follow his views. His primary argument in favor of the principle is that he chose not to simply make Miette his own at her cave. "I could perfectly well have had Miette and then come back and said, 'There it is fellows. Miette's mine, my woman, my wife. Hands off everyone'" (228-9). Emmanuel's presumption that such a proclamation would be acknowledged and respected by everyone speaks to the kinds of rule to which he is appealing. He seems to think that such a "first come, first served" or perhaps "finders keepers" mentality still holds sway even after the bombs have destroyed systems of law and so many conventional practices.

Emmanuel also presumes that his fellow men will respect his decision not to declare Miette as "my woman, my wife." He thinks that his logic will move them towards a principle of polyandry.

> "It is my opinion that Miette must not become anyone's exclusive property. In fact Miette isn't property at all, of course. Miette is her own mistress. Miette can have whatever relationship she chooses with whomever she likes, whenever she likes. Do you agree?" (229)

Emmanuel presumes that their initial reticence is due to the ingrained nature of the principle of monogamy. Laws may be destroyed, but systems and institutions in which people were raised would take more than just nuclear bombs to destroy. But in fact the men reject Emmanuel's principle on the basis of their own communal standard. First Emmanuel revises his own principle to say that if Miette wanted to choose one of the men "to the exclusion of all others" then such a choice was not acceptable. And so we immediately see that the idea of Miette being "her own mistress" is not really the case.

Thomas exposes Emmanuel's desired principle, that "Miette sleeps with all of us" and declares it "totally immoral" (229). The men must now work out a moral principle for Miette, a principle that, like sharing Malevil itself, will help shape who they are as a people. Emmanuel's argument is that the conditions of their current lives demand it. "We're being forced into it simply by necessity. Because Miette is the only woman here capable of producing children" (230). While Emmanuel does not go through all of the details here, the presumption (erroneous as it might be) seems to be that if Miette is impregnated by all of the men at Malevil, serially, then her offspring, only being half siblings could legitimately procreate with one another or, failing that, if female, could procreate with any man not her father. If this were Emmanuel's real principle then you would think he would be far more careful about the rotation—it would surely matter that they know the paternity of any child if the world is being repopulated simply by Miette's offspring. Emmanuel's friends reject the principle, arguing simply, that they do not wish to live based on such an appeal to necessity.

"Sharing a woman with a lot of other men, no. I say no," says Peyssou (231) and all the others concur. The primary issue here is the nature of the community at Malevil. On the one hand this could be seen as a rejection of Emmanuel's principle of sharing; but more importantly it is a rejection of Emmanuel as the voice of the general will of Malevil. This was a debate over the common interest that Emmanuel thought he could win with appeals to their childhood rememberances of Adelaide, a shop keeper noted for having "helped [the friends at Malevil] over our adolescence" (230). The friends also reject Emmanuel's retorts to Thomas' claims that such an arrangement would amount to prostitution. (No, says Emmanuel, for a prostitute is paid.)

Emmanuel reels from his failure to win the day: "I had lost a vote! I had been beaten! . . . I was deeply mortified" (231). This mortification can only be healthy for the community at Malevil, for despite Emmanuel's claims that Malevil was to be shared, this incident did reveal his presumption that the others would do as he wished.

The community at Malevil faces this first potential breach in their unanimity over an issue that simultaneously references both the future of humanity and the particular sexual desires of one man. They maintain their community in part because Emmanuel is the only outlier. Emmanuel follows their will (he is "forced to be free") even though he contends that "this respectable social system of theirs was absolutely doomed to break down in a community of six men who had just been issued, as it were, a single woman" (232). The irony of Emmanuel's obsession with Miette is that he acts, in his journal, as if once the issue has been decided that it simply ceases to matter to anyone. He describes the actions of the next day without reference to the decision and ends this entry with the next threat to the community—the visit by the priest Fulbert. But Thomas, editorializing at the end of the journal entry notes that the very next night Miette makes her choice: Peyssou. And the sexual politics of the story will continue as Miette will favor each of the men in turn, as Emmanuel had desired, except that she will avoid Emmanuel himself. Miette believes that Emmanuel's German girlfriend Brigitta is still in residence at Malevil (and clearly she also believes that the girlfriend has been locked up in Emmanuel's room). Once she is disabused of this idea she quickly adds Emmanuel to her rotation. And so Emmanuel wins his argument while simultaneously having lost his hold over the men at Malevil. Miette is hardly playing Sophie to Emmanuel's Emile. But Miette does reflect a kind of female Emile—a woman who is fully comfortable in her own skin and able to make her own decisions without obsessing over conventional mores. That Merle describes her as willing to sexually service all of the men cheerfully may well indicate his own version of the postapocalyptic male fantasy.

The incident reveals a desire for communal agreement on those issues that will help identify who the people at Malevil want to be. The "woman question" becomes the primary focus of their community insofar as Fulbert uses it to excoriate Malevil to the surviving townspeople in La Rocque, the neighboring town. The ubiquitous battle for identity and survival in *Malevil* then reflects both the advantages of Malevil's Rousseauean political arrangements (and thus the disadvantages of Fulbert's tyranny) and the character of Merle's Rousseauean political fantasy.

General Will vs. Tyranny

From Fulbert's initial appearance at Malevil demanding a cow for the infants of La Rocque, his soft-pedaled tyrannical impulses are clear. Posing as a priest he has clearly terrorized the people of La Rocque into cowed religious submission. La Rocque represents illegitimate rule wrapped up in a medieval presumption about divine will—a standard move for the enemy in postapocalyptic fiction which, excepting the *Left Behind* series and its ilk, promotes a modern secular view about human political organization. Emmanuel chides the people of La Rocque for failing to do their political duty and letting Fulbert rule over them illegitimately. Upon his initial arrival in La Rocque Emmanuel brings a side of beef and loaves of bread for exchange. When he hands the food over to the butcher the surrounding townspeople, described as "thin looking and oddly subdued" (316), argue that it should be distributed immediately. But there is clearly a fear that this goes against the practice of Fulbert, who seems to be in charge of food distribution and uses that distribution to reward obedience and punish those who try and go against his authority. Emmanuel tries to get them to vote on whether or not to distribute the food right away and after a moment of "stunned surprise" only two townspeople vote for the proposal and only one against. They all look to Fulbert's spy among the townspeople, and Fabelatre tries to sneak away to inform Fulbert of Emmanuel's arrival. The town is fearful and while everyone clearly wants their share of food, only three are willing to voice their opinion one way or another.

La Rocque must be freed from the tyranny of Fulbert. This tyranny works both because Fulbert claims ecclesiastic authority and because he holds all the food. The cobbler Marcel acknowledges that the people let Fulbert take the power.

> "We must be fair. In the beginning Fulbert did a lot of good. He was the one who made us bury the dead. And in a sense he was the one who gave us back the courage to go one. It was only gradually, with Armand [the muscle] behind him, that he began putting the screws on. . . . The trouble, really, was that we weren't suspicious enough at the start. He has a tongue like honey, that Fulbert. He told us that all the groceries had to be brought up and stored in the chateau, to prevent looting. . . . It seemed rational at the time and we did it." (326-7)

Likewise it seemed rational to put all the weapons, ammunition, livestock and food stored in people's houses in the chateau, and "one fine day it dawned on us that he had everything up there in the chateau" (327). The people of La Rocque thought it would be safer to keep their food in one place. But more so they thought their lives would be better if they just let Fulbert take care of things for them. In this they abdicated their responsibility as citizens and they soon realize that by giving everything up to Fulbert they had un-wittingly given him illegitimate power over them. And yet they are also so fearful that they will not act to overturn that illegitimate power (they are in the process of turning force into right). "There's no community life" (337), Marcel complains. And while he initially seems to mean that there is no work for the community to do together, he also means that there is no sense of community. The people of La Rocque are not in fact "a people."

They are held together by fear and that fear is compounded by Fulbert's claims of being a priest. Emmanuel quickly catches him in a lie that reveals he is not in fact a priest, but the people of La Rocque are convinced of Fulbert's worldly power (backed up by Armand) and by Fulbert's spiritual power. The few people of La Rocque not held in Fulbert's sway, who fully recognize the illegitimacy of his rule, are shunned by the rest of the townspeople: "I noticed that none of them dared so much as go near Judith, Marcel, or Pimont, as though the power of the Church had already laid the trio under its interdict" (356). In a world where you might see people recognizing the limits of political and ecclesiastic power (neither of which could keep the bombs from falling) the people of La Rocque seem to almost desire that power as a child might look to the parent to solve problems. Emmanuel, who gives a brief horse riding exhibition in order to create time for Miette's sister and a young asthmatic or-phan to escape from La Rocque, describes the townspeople awaiting the horse show as transfixed as if watching television. "I was now their TV, and they were already deep in their normal numbed and blissful spectator state" (351). He goes on to describe "their childlike happiness" clarifying that the people of La Rocque have abdicated their capacity to form a general will.

Like people in the state of nature who are seduced by the products of competition to think that natural talent legitimizes force, the people of La Rocque have become Rousseau's people "everywhere in chains." For the reader of *Malevil*, then, the unfreedom of the people of La Rocque is con-trasted with the free, communal life of the people of Malevil. The people of La Rocque are not simply unfree because of Fulbert's tyrannical use of power. For example, Marcel, Judith and Pimont are not unfree, even though they are constrained by Fulbert's rule. Rather the people of La Rocque are largely unfree because they have submitted to an illegitimate power: "The citizens, having fallen into servitude, have lost both liberty and will. Fear and flattery then change votes into acclamation; deliberation ceases, and only worship or malediction is left" (*The Social Contract*, 4, II, 249).

Thus to free themselves they need to do more than just get rid of Fulbert, they need to see that it is in fact their obligation to form a community so that they can live under rules that they have given themselves. The defeat of the enemy force that will inevitably rise up will prove the advantages of Malevil's freedom, while also freeing the people of La Rocque from their self made chains. The idea in *Malevil* is not the Hobbesian use of a threat to cement the community ties. Rather here it is that the strength of the already formed community proves that the threat is able to be rebuffed. The people of Malevil do not come together in order to protect themselves. They came together (particularly the men) in order to form a community that expressed their humanity. Even when the group votes to give Emmanuel executive authority in times of emergency they do so unanimously and as a community.

Emmanuel is fully comparable to Fulbert because he has also been voted as Abbe of Malevil, in part to keep Fulbert from trying to install a priest inside the walls of Malevil, but also to reflect the spiritual concerns of the Malevil community. Emmanuel is chosen as their communal soul. First, he is *chosen* and second, part of what he aims to do is to allow the members of the Malevil community to decide for themselves their religious/spiritual direction. Again we see Emmanuel rejecting the dogmatic and narrowly understood Catholic doctrine that Fulbert is promoting. Emmanuel is promoting a Rousseauean civil religion. He claims "in my opinion any civilization needs a soul" (374). This will be Rousseau's "civil profession of faith" (*The Social Contract* 4, VIII). Emmanuel needs "as social sentiments without which a man cannot be a good citizen or a faithful subject" (4, VIII, 276). It is not that the people of Malevil need all profess the same faith; rather, they must all consent to a set of beliefs about who they are, and those beliefs extend to the spiritual. "After all, it's not necessary to believe in God to have a sense of divinity in the world" (475). And so Emmanuel can marry Thomas and Catie (despite his remark that such a marriage is "folly" given the continuing realities of the disparity between numbers of men and numbers of women). That marriage will be seen as sanctioned by the community and will thus be strengthened and can provide the community with a variety of socially sanctioned sexual outlets.

This communal tie is essential once Vilmain, the "cannibal" of *Malevil*, has overtaken La Rocque and commences his preparations for attack on Malevil. Fulbert is a petty tyrant using religion to control the people of La Rocque to work for him so that he can live out his days without laboring. And he is easily overthrown by Vilmain. Vilmain desires both more and less than Fulbert. He is not thinking about human flourishing; he only desires to win—to kill and rape the people of La Rocque and then the people of Malevil and then anyone else left alive, at the end of which he will presumably just kill the rest of his men. Vilmain is the cannibal of postapocalyptic fiction, although he does not literally eat human flesh. Emmanuel rallies his people, recognizing what Vilmain represents.

> To Vilmain, conquering Malevil means simply acquiring a base for his plundering expeditions. If the human race is to continue, then it will owe its future to little groups of people like ourselves, who are trying to reorganize an embryo of society. People like Vilmain and Bebelle [his henchman] are parasites and beasts of prey. They must be eliminated. However, the fact that our cause is a good one doesn't necessarily mean we're going to win. (474)

The stakes are clear. The cannibals, the "beasts," the non-humans must be destroyed. The people of La Rocque are children—children who can be raised to the maturity of adulthood. But Vilmain and his willing followers have no place in the world. Further Vilmain's villainy reveals Fulbert's willingness to go along with such villainy. Fulbert excuses both the killing of the guard at La Rocque upon Vilmain's arrival and the "excesses" that Vilmain's chosen men inflict upon the women of the town.

Not surprisingly, the people of Malevil defeat Vilmain and his men and they consequently go back to La Rocque and reveal Fulbert's complicity with Vilmain's crimes (they also sit by while the people of La Rocque kill Fulbert with their bare hands). Finally they talk with those members of the town who always understood Fulbert and work to set up an election for town council and mayor that will include these individuals and Malevil's own Meysonnier as mayor. This micromanagement of the affairs of La Rocque might be seen to betray the core of self determination that the men of Malevil keep positing in Rousseauean ways. The micromanagement can be seen in two ways: One, it is a protective gesture. They cannot afford to have La Rocque fall under the influence of another parasitical leader. Two, it is the only way that the men of Malevil can see to allow the people of La Rocque to grow up—to cease being children who expect their leaders to solve their problems. This chosen slate of candidates will not simply do the difficult work of governing in La Rocque, rather they will push the people of La Rocque to learn to govern themselves.[5]

It is precisely this goal of self government, of finding a place and a community where one can live on the basis of laws that one gives oneself, that both rules and is denied by Hegland's *Into the Forest*. Illustrating this otherwise unexplored option: retreat, the force of the usual move into civil society is clear. *Into the Forest* does not move from the state of nature into a civil society (legitimate or illegitimate), but rather moves from the edges of a civil society into a variety of states of nature. The novel is not out to argue the necessity of political life for human flourishing. Rather, *Into the Forest* gives a version of satisfaction with Rousseau's "rustic huts." This rejection of civil society is less than compelling and reveals the ways in which the social contract is still a potentially valuable vehicle for human well-being, despite the unattractive contracts outlined in the previous novels.

Into the State of Nature

Unlike all of the accounts discussed thus far, *Into the Forest* does not have a singular apocalyptic event. Thus the movement into a world without rules is gradual and sneaks up on the characters. There is no nuclear war, no comet, no plague. There are epidemics, there are power outages, there are terrorist attacks. But for these protagonists who live at the end of a dirt road 30 miles from the nearest town in Northern California, the end of the world happens slowly. Beyond the kind of postapocalyptic events that happen on the outskirts of the novel is the "what if" sensibility of its protagonists, teenage sisters Eva and the narrator, Nell.

Into the Forest, by Jean Hegland, was published in 1996 and represents a departure from the texts I have been analyzing and a glimpse into the upcoming chapters. This is not the boilerplate postapocalyptic account. There are no pyrotechnics, no grand moments of survival, no tidal waves to outrun, no bombs to survive and no cannibals to destroy. Instead we have a small family, primarily two teenage daughters, already living through what they thought was the end of their world, the death of their mother by cancer prior to the novel's opening. This is still a postapocalyptic novel, yet its concerns are smaller and less utopian. This novel gestures towards the concerns that I'll discuss through Octavia Butler in the following chapters, but its apolitical conclusion leads me to a Rousseauean reading of its retreat to the natural world. Thus the trajectory of this novel is not to go into town and link up with other like-minded people and return to the safety of the woods and recreate community along some other lines. Rather their trajectory goes from replanting their vegetable garden to discovering the native plants that surround their home and offer as much sustenance as the carrots and tomatoes that they are growing. "[The earth] would present on every side both sustenance and shelter for every species of animal" (*Discourse*, I, 48).

The daughters, Eva and Nell, have always lived in the woods of Northern California and were home schooled. Eva dances and Nell wants to go to Harvard. Their lives may be different from the usual mass of characters that experience the end of the world (for one thing they are, like Lauren Oya Olamina, teenagers) and yet they reflect on the end of the world in ways that most of the characters do who are working out already determined scripts of survival. They experience a similar trajectory of survival, and they have enemies they have to defeat, although here those enemies include not simply other humans, but also loneliness, uncertainty and a constant struggle against what might seem to be the futility of trying to survive in a world that is not likely to simply revert to normalcy any time soon.

Into the Forest opens as *Malevil* does, with a journal entry that explains retrospectively how it is that these characters, the two sisters, come to be alone in a leaky cabin in Northern California without electricity and eating wormy flour and dusty jars of canned fruit. It is Christmas Day and they celebrate by lighting the last of their candles. They also exchange gifts and Eva's gift to Nell is the notebook in which Nell, the narrator, now writes their story. She remembers Christmas one year ago, the first since the death of her mother, when she and her sister tried to bring their father back into the memories of the happy family they once were. But at that Christmas the power outages had already begun.

> Last winter when the electricity first began going off, it was so occasional and brief we didn't pay much attention. . . . Perhaps it took longer than it should have for us to suspect that something different was happening. But even in town, I think the changes began so slowly—or were so much a part of the familiar fabric of trouble and inconvenience—that nobody really recognized them until later that spring. (12)

They may have missed the meaning of the power outages over shock at their mother's death and the normalcy of occasional power outages in their remote home, but it is clear that everyone was failing to see what the reader recognizes as obvious. This "familiar fabric of trouble and inconvenience" offers a common thread connecting *Into the Forest* with Octavia Butler's *Parable* series. Unlike the all abiding can-do spirit that permeates the three earlier postapocalyptic accounts, this novel describes how the end sneaks up on you. Endings, and even the violence that they might bring, are absorbed into our everyday understanding of our lives. We cope, sometimes better and sometimes worse, and heroics don't always involve armed rebellion against the obviously evil.

In literal terms the characters of *Into the Forest* are as heroic as the characters of any of the other accounts (or more so). But in fictional terms there are few outward heroics. There is no great battle in which the survival of the main characters culminates. There is no great invention that will guarantee either the survival or the flourishing of Eva and Nell. Rather what we do see are the quiet everyday heroics of keeping going under circumstances that are clearly extreme, although in contrast to the conditions of living of the other books seem almost advantageous.

Into the Forest also faces up the proto-utopian fantasies of simple living that *Lucifer's Hammer*, *Alas, Babylon* and *Malevil* all promote. Here we see towards the beginning of the novel the mention of how the difficulties, power failures and food shortages, have produced

> along with all the worry and confusion there came a feeling of energy, of liberation. The old rules had been temporarily suspended, and it was exciting to imagine all the changes that would inevitably grow out of all the upheaval. . . . Even as everyone's lives grew more unstable, most people seemed to experience a new optimism, to share the sense that we were weathering the worst of it and that soon . . . America and the future would be in better shape than ever. (17)

This is not the backward looking realization that life has become more meaningful once it became more simple that seems to come at the end of many postapocalyptic accounts. Rather this is the reaction of a 17-year-old to the initial excitement and energy of a change in the status quo. Everyone is gripped with the energy of problem solving, and the newly found communal spirit that accompanies circumstances that are difficult but not dire. There are occasional references to people elsewhere whose experiences of this near end are not quite so accommodating: people walking out of Los Angeles in search of potable water, rioting, new strains of AIDS and the flu. And Nell is able to contextualize the community spirit: "People looked to the past for reassurance and inspiration. At the library, the supermarket, the gas station, and even on the Plaza, we listened to talk about the sacrifices and hardships of the Pilgrims and pioneers" (17). Reference is made to the character building effects of privation. Are these platitudes the result of the slow moving end that people do not recognize? Or is it an attempt instead to really diagnose the end from its initial inconveniences and the snow day excitement of something different to the eventual depressed slog through a virulent flu pandemic and the desperate grasping that life must be better someplace else?

By giving us the end through the eyes of a 17-year-old girl whose experience is singular and not entirely understood, the reader experiences some of the confusion that follows from this portrayal of the gradual disintegration of modern society. While Nell and Eva initially work with their father to put in a more extensive vegetable garden and to prepare the house for a winter without central heating, they really begin their postapocalyptic experiences hanging onto the lives they lived before the end. Eva still dances for hours every day with a metronome, now that there is no electricity for music. Nell still studies obsessively trying to make up for any ground lost before she can apply to Harvard after everything gets better. Each presumes that this is only a temporary glitch and that their lives will return to some sense of normalcy. While such a refusal to see the end for what it is signaled a sure death in the three preceding accounts, here it highlights a reasonable transition from their childhood reality of relying on their parents for everything other than their own future goals to the automatic adulthood of having to feed and house and protect themselves after their father's death.

They begin with the ubiquitous cataloguing of potentially useful items not likely to be manufactured again—the rolls of toilet paper, the plastic containers, the matches, the laundry soap, the needles and aspirin. These foraging projects reveal a life of memory that as children they had both lived within and entirely ignored. "Even something simple as a mixing bowl seemed to fill with a childhood's worth of cake batters when we lifted it off the shelf, examined it, tried to imagine its current and future uses, to assess its value, trying not to dwell on the last sweet lick we had tasted from its depths" (38-9). Nell and Eva are facing state-of-nature-like conditions, but it is as if they must first live through their last vestiges of civilization as they knew it before they can acknowledge that state of nature.

They encounter two men in their postapocalyptic life in the woods. First, Eli, the boy from town that Nell had started dating in the months following her mother's death; second, the nameless man who rapes Eva, impregnating her. Eli hikes out to their house months after Nell and Eva's last trip to town to tell them that he and his brothers are going to walk to Boston where there are rumors of power and jobs. Nell initially says she will go with him (after resuming a sexual relationship). She sets off with him back towards town, leaving Eva behind in the house, only to realize the next morning that she could not leave her sister behind. It is not that Nell realizes that she *should* not leave her sister (this is the reader's response "how can you possibly leave her alone?") and it reflects the real equality that exists between these two siblings. There is no reason why Nell thinks that she should not leave her sister alone, in a falling down house 30 miles from a dying civilization. Rather it is that she cannot leave her sister. Her identity, once wrapped up in matriculation at Harvard, is now wrapped up in a life with the only person who knows her past.

Her only real explanation to Eli that morning is "I can't" until he forces her to admit that "I can't" simply meant "I won't." For better or worse, the sisters will have only themselves, and importantly for the structuring argument of this book, the two of them will make the only community that the novel admits. At the end of the novel, when they decide to abandon their home and live in the tree stump they had used as a childhood playhouse, Eva says to

Nell: "This is a real adventure. His was only an escape" (236). The "his" here is Eli, and Eva is clear that escape is impossible; adventure is the only option available. Escape is problematic not simply because the idea that Boston has power and jobs is a fantasy common to the disaster mentality that "life must be better someplace else."[6] Eva is also making an existential point here: there is no escape. They always are where they will be and so the only option is to make of that reality something worth doing. Perhaps her use of adventure is too flippant, but Eva, having lived through so much, is not simply claiming that it would be fun to live in the woods for awhile. Rather she is declaring what their lives will be: that which will happen, hazards and excitements. They will be living in the future and the past (escape) has little application to their present lives. Nell worries that in the woods they might die of starvation, of illness, and Eva laughs, "We could run out of food or get sick right here. . . . Nell, *people* have been dying for at least 100,000 years. Dying doesn't matter. Of course we'll die" (236). Eva wants a life, a future, a place to raise her son that is not simply made of the remnants and detritus of a civilization now gone. Nell's last act is to reject her desperate piling up of books that she wants to keep for herself and for Burl, her nephew. Instead she keeps only three, the book about the native plants of Northern California, the book of stories about the Pomo Indians of the same region, and the index to the encyclopedia that she has been reading. "Perhaps we could create new stories; perhaps we could discover a new knowledge that would sustain us. In the meantime I would take the Index for memory's sake, so I could remember—and could show Burl—the map of all we'd have to leave behind" (239).

Nell and Eva are embarking on an adventure entirely different from the movement to the social contracts that are the centerpieces of *Lucifer's Hammer*, *Alas, Babylon* and *Malevil*. Here we see a rejection of the social contract and the creation of a small, familial group that will maintain life in the state of nature. The real question is how we view this embracing of the state of nature. On the one hand I have presented it here in contrast to *Malevil* as a Rousseauean choice to stay natural. Importantly this is a choice, and in making it Nell and Eva have moved a few steps away from Rousseau's savage who simply follows his natural passions. The choice is presented as a practical one stemming primarily from a security concern. Eva has found footprints in the road leading to their home. "He's come back," Nell says, referencing the man who raped Eva. "Or someone like him," Eva replies. But security means more than simply escaping from this potential rapist. Security means realizing that "the past is gone. It's dead. And it was wrong, anyway." When Nell wonders why their lives were wrong Eva replies doggedly, "This is our life. . . . Like it or not, our life is here—together. And we've got to fix it so we won't forget it again, so we can't make any more mistakes" (232). Stripping their lives of the vestigial benefits of civilization is the one way to gain this security. It puts them out of the reach of travelers, but more than that it puts them fully into their adventure of living in the forest, off of the land.

This is not a pioneer's dream, they will not build a house and plant crops and put up a fence. Nor is it fully to be understood as a retreat, although there is something about their adventure that seems a little like returning to the womb. We are supposed to see the choice as freeing and Eva's final wild dance "with a body that had sown seeds, gathered acorns, given birth" (240) as more authentic than the classical ballet for which she was training. As with Rousseau's counseling of Emile, Nell and Eva will learn to live without the artifice of civilization. This matters more here because such artifice is clearly only going to ever be the decayed accoutrements of a life long gone.

And Burl will become the savage child Rousseau praises: "The children, bringing with them into the world the excellent constitution of their parents, and fortifying it by the very exercises which first produced it, would thus acquire all the vigour of which the human frame is capable" (*Discourse*, 48). And yet there is something disappointing in this ending; and it is disappointing for Rousseauean reasons. I see little cause for celebration when Nell and Eva and Burl move into the stump that Nell and Eva had once used as a childhood playhouse. Maybe we do not become more full human beings by entering into the social contract. Maybe we do not gain moral liberty by learning to live under laws that we give to ourselves. But we do gain something. To live as hermits, hidden away in the forest, eating acorns and berries is as potentially humanity ending as having everyone simply take their suicide pills as in *On the Beach*.

Notes

The chapter title is from Jean Jacques Rousseau, *The Social Contract* (London and Melbourne: Dent, 1983 [1762]) I;1, 65 (Book, Chapter, page).

1. *Lucifer's Hammer* could be read through a Rousseauean lens of how we should understand legitimacy, where the New Brotherhood Army would reflect the illegitimacy of mere force and Jellison would represent the rightful authority of the general will. But *Lucifer's Hammer* is not sufficiently Rousseauean for that second move, about the general will, to make sense.

2. Merle is best known for his 1969 novel (made famous by the movie) *Day of the Dolphin*; *Malevil* was made into a movie, released in France and West Germany in 1981.

3. Interestingly it has never been rereleased, despite the recent spate of postapoca-lyptic fiction and the new edition of *Alas, Babylon.*

4. This is the primary issue in PD James' *The Children of Men,* which opens at the death of the youngest person left on the planet, 18 years after the last child was born.

5. *Malevil* ends on a less than hopeful note. Emmanuel dies of appendicitis and the community struggles again to find the right kind of leader. But elections are maintained and even the more dictatorial style of Colin is solved through his death thwarting a raiding party.

6. This raises an issue crucial to understanding the mindset of rebuilding in post-apocalyptic fiction—the central characters are never looking to escape elsewhere. Instead they commit to staying put, to building a society on the ground where they stand.

~

CHAPTER FIVE

"Maybe Effort Counted"

John Rawls and Thought Experiments

The previous three chapters each outlined how postapocalyptic fiction can mirror the thinking of the traditional social contract thinkers, Hobbes, Locke and Rousseau. These thinkers use the state of nature—a space without the controlling power of government and rules—to reveal human beings as they really are. With humans thus revealed each then outlines how and why humans such as these would come together: by choosing a formal political structure that will satisfy their needs and create a community, an artificial body within which all who choose to do so shall live. In creating this community the parties to the social contract have established the principles of justice for their community. The literal states of nature described by Hobbes, Locke and Rousseau and fleshed out by *Lucifer's Hammer*, *Alas, Babylon* and *Malevil* provide evidence justifying the kind of political community each creates. The appeal of the novels is that each uses an apocalyptic scenario to throw its characters into a realizable state of nature. The reader is to see herself in this world and to imagine acting and reacting in the ways the characters in these novels do. Thus readers would seem to categorize themselves as "malevilians" or "alas Babylonians" in that these novels would seem to capture what the reader would imagine as her reaction to nuclear war (for example). These novels emphasize the link between the conditions of the state of nature, the characters who survive that state and the nature of the political community created.

Three particular limitations to the theorists and novels discussed in previous chapters have emerged. The novels do give shape and heft to the states of nature described by Hobbes, Locke and Rousseau, but their detailed presentations also open up gaps. First, in the drama of the state of nature the limitations of the choices available to the characters become clear. In making these states of nature real, the novels simultaneously make them less believable, less hypothetical. Second, the characters who are making these choices are often as limited as Hobbes, Locke and Rousseau imagined hundreds of years ago: the main characters are virtually all male and white. (*Into the Forest*, which gives the only extended analysis of female characters, has those characters retreat further into nature.) In giving voice to the choosers these novelists are limiting their appeal. Finally, the authors' goals for the communities in question, while in line with those of their theoretical counterparts (security, property and civil liberty), reveal an inability to grasp the nature of human vulnerability and the conditions needed to confront that vulnerability.

So perhaps when exploring the reasons why we come together and the shape of the political community that we form we should utilize a more abstract, more strictly hypothetical, but not speculative, space. This is John Rawls' move from the state of nature to the original position. Rawls is firmly within the social contract tradition, but instead of describing a time or space where humans as we know them are without the structure of agreed upon rules, Rawls chooses a thought experiment: imagine yourself not knowing anything particular about yourself, your attributes, your talents, your position in society, and then imagine that self choosing principles of justice. In Rawls the reader does not think about how humans might act if they were not bound by the rules of society; instead the reader thinks how she might think about justice if she did not know who she was. How would she distribute what Rawls calls the primary social goods?[1]

This chapter explores Rawls' shift to the abstract, using a short story by Octavia Butler (1947-2006), "The Book of Martha," to illustrate Rawls' hypothetical reasoning. Butler's work is steeped in the genre of postapocalyptic fiction. She won Hugo awards for the short story "Speech Sounds" (1984) and the novelette *Bloodchild* (1985), and Nebula awards for both *Bloodchild* and *Parable of the Talents* (1999). In 1995, she was awarded a MacArthur "genius" grant. The *Xenogenesis* series (1987-1989) and the *Mind of My Mind* series (1976-77) both consider postapocalyptic themes and even *Fledgling*, her last novel, was a kind of postapocalyptic vampire story. Butler often explores life after some sort of cataclysmic event: a plague, war or alien invasion. She is less interested in glorifying the violence of such events than in exploring how people learn to live together under such conditions.

The two succeeding chapters will focus on the *Parable* series, the longest and most human of her postapocalyptic works. In this chapter I look only at the short story "The Book of Martha," which reflects a less developed but strikingly Rawlsian perspective. The story, which is not so much post-apocalyptic as it is an attempt to avert an impending cataclysm, provides an introduction to the concerns that Butler brings to the idea of humans living together. Rawls' rewriting of the social contract means removing the state of nature as an imaginative space of living without government in favor of a thought experiment, the original position. Butler follows through with this thought experiment, but under different conditions, and in a different kind of fictional space and voice. The space is imaginary: both dreamed and about dreaming. What significance do these differences have, for our understanding of Rawls and of the entire social contract tradition?

Rawls

Published in 1971, *A Theory of Justice* revived the social contract as a mechanism for understanding the nature of justice and the nature of political community. *A Theory of Justice* offers an argument for the principles of justice that humans would (ideally) choose to live under and a method for humans to understand how (and why) they would choose those principles. The initial motivation for the argument is to show why a rational person would not choose to live under utilitarian principles of justice. A utilitarian principle of justice would seek to define justice in terms of the good, in terms of what would produce the "greatest good for the greatest number." In arguing against utilitarianism, Rawls returns to the idea of the social contract and the question of how we are to understand justice for a group of people with disparate aims and interests. If we have no shared understanding of "the good," then how can we hope to live together peacefully? Rawls moves the conversation away from the good and back to "the right." This firmly grounds Rawls' theory in the social contract tradition. As should be clear from our discussion of the earlier social contract thinkers, what we agree upon are rules under which we can live, not a goal to live towards. In returning to the idea of the social contract, Rawls returns us to the very process by which we choose principles of justice, a process that reveals our lack of a shared understanding of the good.

Previous chapters have illustrated the ways in which outsider groups focused on shared ideas of the good (e.g. Fulbert from *Malevil* and the New Brotherhood Army from *Lucifer's Hammer*) will inevitably crush dissenting voices. The very description of such groups as proto-totalitarian reveals the way in which we *do* inhabit a Rawlsian world where we understand the primacy of process over any shared goal.[2] The reader of postapocalyptic fiction is familiar with the idea that groups seeking to rule on the basis of a single understanding of the good will crush characters seeking to live freely.[3]

Rawls describes himself as a social contract thinker, and he sees the original position as analogous to the state of nature. He rewrites the idea of the state of nature moving it from a potentially historical or civilization-stage argument to a simply hypothetical thought experiment. This allows him to assert human equality in a more straightforward, although (oddly) less convincing way. The original position creates a hypothetical set of mental constraints that allows humans to deliberate over principles of justice without the potential inequalities of self-interest intruding. "In justice as fairness the original position of equality corresponds to the state of nature in the traditional theory of the social contract. This original position is not, of course, thought of as an actual historical state of affairs, much less as a primitive condition of culture. It is understood as a purely hypothetical situation characterized so as to lead to a certain conception of justice" (Rawls, 11). Just as traditional social contract writers used the state of nature to motivate humans to realizing certain basic facts about themselves (vulnerability to death, desire for security, desire for property protection), so will the original position and the veil of ignorance reveal to us the ways in which we are likely to think about principles of justice absent any particular knowledge about our position, advantageous or disadvantageous, in society.

What we gain from Rawls' shift from a potentially "actual" state of nature to this clearly hypothetical thought experiment is that the parameters of the experiment can be used to more directly argue for what we "would do." Rawls repeatedly claims that the parameters of the original position describe restraints "that we do in fact accept." This is the force of justice *as fairness*. The parameters of the original position can be defended in ways in which the parameters of the state of nature cannot be defended (resting as they are on an imagination of actual lives being lived without government). So as a form of argument the original position is open to philosophical justification in a way that the state of nature seems not to be.

Whether or not full philosophical justification is available for the descriptions of state of nature given by Hobbes, Locke and Rousseau, the previous chapters do provide a kind of hypothetical fleshing out of their presumptions about what the state of nature would look like and what humans, described as reacting to such conditions, would choose. Any reader can argue for or against these with the "what would I do" thought. The strength of Rawls' argument is that one is able to simply go about the thought experiment without worrying about whether to pack spices or move to central Florida or live in a thirteenth-century French castle.

The limitation of Rawls' thought experiment is that absent any particular knowledge about who I am, both my self-understanding (and what I have to say about justice as it pertains to me) and my understanding of equality are made abstract. So that perhaps "I" would accept these principles of justice and "I" would see humans as equal in the original position, but that "I" have to use that abstract reasoning to convince my fully embodied self that I "do in fact" accept such principles and "do in fact" accept such claims of equality. The advantage of the state of nature, particularly the state of nature settings presented in the novels I have discussed previously, is that the reader gains a visceral understanding of why the characters do what they do. This visceral understanding is of particular importance when thinking about human equality, which should be understood at the bodily level, rather than simply at a hypothetical rational level. Rawls is seeking not a visceral reaction, but a rational analysis.

Rawls presumes that free, equal and rational persons in the original position would choose two principles of justice. The first principle, the liberty principle, provides equal distribution of basic rights and liberties. The second principle, the difference principle, holds that an unequal distribution of wealth and social goods is only allowable when positions are open to all and where such an unequal distribution is to the advantage of the least advantaged members of society. Such principles are seen as attractive to any chooser who does not know her own position in society: "[N]o one knows his place in society, his class position or social status, nor does anyone know his fortune in the distribution of natural assets and abilities, his intelligence, strength, and the like. I shall even assume the parties do not know their conceptions of the good or their special psychological propensities" (11). Under such conditions each chooser (rationally self-interested) would want to make certain that principles of justice would work for her advantage. Thus Rawls was initially motivated to explain why someone would not choose utilitarianism as the guiding principle of justice for society. Behind the veil of ignorance choosing utilitarianism is seen as too risky. There is too much chance of ending up in the minority, and if that happened the net amount of happiness in the society would not ameliorate your own individual unhappiness. So instead of utilitarianism Rawls believes a rational person would choose the two principles of justice.

Choosing these principles of justice from the original position then mirrors the movement from the state of nature to civil society. In Hobbes, this movement follows a sequence of rational calculations: the recognition that life in the state of nature is undesirable, the proposed giving up of one's rights to everything (built on others' agreement to do the same), the choice of a sovereign entity and then the authorization of that sovereign authority who in turn agrees to protect us. This is the movement seen in *Lucifer's Hammer*: the characters realize that life is increasingly dangerous, not simply because of the potential lack of food, but because of the existence of the New Brotherhood Army. They recognize that as individuals they have little chance to defeat the Army, or even to hide away and protect themselves. And so a deal is made with Senator Jellison: you protect us and we give up our right to do whatever we can or need to do to survive. We will abide by your rules and you will find some way to defeat this threat. In Rawls' system, the movement from the original position to civil society is more abstract. Choosers agree to principles of justice that reflect their desire for more, rather than less, of the primary social goods. Choosers are not establishing a body politic in the traditional sense. But choosers are setting up the foundational principles that will guide the development and creation of that political community.

For Rawls the key to thinking about principles of justice concerns the *way* in which we think about those principles. In order to capture the necessity for fairness we have to think about justice from a perspective of relative ignorance about our own personal situation. Instead of thinking abstractly about some nebulous whole, we must imagine ourselves as inhabiting any variety of possible positions.

Thinking about a fictional Rawlsian account means thinking through the two parts of his theory: the decision procedure and what it is that is decided. A fictional account might simply focus on the two principles of justice in some way, or such an account might find a way to work through the original position.[4] Octavia Butler's short story "The Book of Martha" reflects a kind of fictional Rawlsian worldview. Highlighting these Rawlsian moments helps to set up the ways in which Butler fully works through the idea of the social contract and the idea of justice in the *Parable* series. Butler likes starting over scenarios,[5] and even though "The Book of Martha" is not itself a postapocalyptic scenario (although it does involve trying to prevent such a scenario) it still requires the main character to think through what it would mean to start over.

"The Book of Martha" as Rawlsian Text

"The Book of Martha" is one of the last short stories Octavia Butler published before her untimely death in 2005. The story centers on Martha, who is visited by God while working on her latest novel. The reader knows from the first line that this figure is, or is narrated to us, as God. "God" tells her that she must make one change to all of humanity in order for humans to be able to survive their "adolescence." Whatever change Martha makes, she will be required to go and live among the changed humans "as one of the lowliest." Thus Martha is asked to change humanity in such a way as to prevent a human-made apocalyptic event. The story focuses on Martha's move from resistance to this request to reluctant acceptance; it tracks her reaction to this God, who is first seen as a "Michelangelo"-like enormous, bearded white man, and finally as a black woman "who could be my sister." The story thus uses Martha's own changing image of God to illustrate her struggles with identity. Those struggles with identity help her to both diagnose and propose a "cure" for humanity.

Martha resists both this request and this God. She does not wish to have the responsibility of changing humans. This reluctance is part of why God has chosen her: that she does not wish for power is one of the best reasons to grant that power to her. "Why should it be my work? Why don't you do it? You know how. You could do it without making mistakes. Why make me do it? I don't know anything" (196). Even here we see the beginnings of the Rawlsian conditions in which Martha is placed. She does not know anything (although her lack of knowledge is obviously not the kind of lack we see behind the veil of ignorance). She understands her ignorance as a fatal weakness. The story does not entirely ameliorate that concern, but it does reveal some potential advantages to her ignorance.

The request that Martha change humanity to prevent an apocalyptic event is contrasted with the conditions under which she currently lives. Her actual life as a novelist is comfortable, filled with work she loves in a home she has chosen. The power she is being given might seem enviable. Martha can literally change humanity, not simply write a novel imagining how humanity might be changed. "You will help humankind to survive its greedy, murderous, wasteful adolescence. Help it to find less destructive, more peaceful, sustainable ways to live" (192). Martha is given not just power, but the power to do good. She can help humans achieve full security. Yet Martha does not want this power, and she does not want God intruding in the pocket of peace that she has worked hard to make for herself. Martha begins from a position similar to that of the survivor of a postapocalyptic event, who cannot get her head around what has happened.

Finally, in the most overtly Rawlsian move, she will have to live through whatever change she chooses from the perspective of the "least advantaged" member of that society. God says: "When you've finished your work, you'll go back and live among them again as one of their lowliest. You're the one who will decide what that will mean, but whatever you decide is to be the bottom level of society, the lowest class or caste or race, that's what you'll be" (193). Clearly this condition is an attempt by God to make sure that Martha is, like Rawls, mirroring concerns of fairness when she makes her decision. Butler wants the reader to think through what it would mean to evaluate the conditions of the world from the perspective of those at the bottom. And Martha herself must decide what the bottom will ultimately be. But it is important to note here that God is requiring an actual sacrifice from Martha. Her choice is Rawlsian, but this is no hypothetical thought experiment. Her real social position will necessarily worsen, and she knows this from the outset.

Martha is not to be seen as the "impartial spectator" decider that Rawls claims classical utilitarianism represents. Martha will "choose" for all of humanity. But she does so not as someone who comprehends the desires of all of humanity. She is better understood as a Rawlsian "representative person." There is no assertion that Martha is somehow a stand-in for all of humanity; her experience is not universal, although her experience may well be particularly useful. Rawls' criticism that utilitarianism "does not take seriously the distinctions between persons" (24), does not hold for Martha as chooser. Utilitarianism, Rawls states "adopt[s] for society as a whole the principle of rational choice for one man" (24). According to this logic, God could choose any fully "rational" person to choose for everyone. But the logic of Butler's story is that God has chosen Martha not because she is an exemplar of rationality. It is the experience that she has had and her profession as a novelist—an imaginer of human lives—that will make her a good representative for thinking through what humanity could be. God does muse regretfully that "it would have been better for you if you had raised a child or two"—a regret, Martha retorts silently, that could have been avoided simply by God's choosing someone else. "I chose you for all that you are and all that you are not," God somewhat enigmatically tells Martha. "I chose you because you are the one I wanted for this" (194). Martha was chosen because her life experiences will impact how she will think about changing humanity, and the eagerness (or lack of eagerness) with which she will approach this task.

This initial scenario, in which Martha is taken out of her time and place, reflects a potential state of nature: she is taken out of the world in which she lives and given the opportunity to change that world (or at least the people within it) any way that she wants. The change that she chooses would be to make humans "a little less aggressive . . . less covetous" (205). But Martha makes her choice abstractly; it is not grounded in an experience of living in an actual state of nature. Martha is not living fully under the conditions God has set for her working out of the problem. Even though she and God will sit and eat tuna fish salad sandwiches by the end of their conversation, they are neither in a place nor in a time. The condition of her choice is like the state of nature in that it is absent any rules or political structure, but it is more like the original position in that it is presented entirely abstractly. The making and the consequences of her choice might be experienced as real for Martha, but the choice itself takes place in a hypothetical "space" created by God to allow Martha the opportunity to think through her task. No one else will happen to wander into this space and everything within the space, which begins as an empty grayness, shifting to a green field with a tree and a bench to her own living room and kitchen, is there because Martha has decided (knowingly or not) to give this space content.[6]

The original position is supposed to produce "a fair procedure so that any principles agreed to will be just" (Rawls, 118). Obviously the situation in which Martha finds herself is neither fair nor likely to produce an outcome with which everyone would agree. Martha seems to fully know who she is, something that would seem to challenge the very premise of the veil of ignorance. She is a novelist working on her fifth novel who lives in Seattle. She has a small house that has a view of Lake Washington. She clearly has a space for herself that she has created and where she can create. We learn little of her life outside of this home and those novels, but we do learn that she was not raised in such conditions. "I was born poor, black, female to a fourteen-year-old mother who could barely read. We were homeless half the time I was growing up. Is that bottom level enough for you? I was born on the bottom, but I didn't stay there. I didn't leave my mother there, either. And I'm not going back there!" (194). Martha knows all of the features of her life that Rawls wants to remove with the veil of ignorance.

However, Butler complicates this self-knowledge by showing Martha's wrestling with the image of God, a wrestling that clearly reflects uncertainty about what it means for Martha to be who she is. God first appears to Martha looking like, as she asks with surprise, "a twice-live-sized, bearded white man?" (190). God replies, "You see what your life has prepared you to see." Martha thinks that she has gotten past or outgrown the racist and sexist structures, not of her world, but at least of her thinking. As the story progresses God changes (without actually changing) from this oversized white man, to a normally sized white man, to a black man, to a black woman ("we look like sisters" (209), Martha remarks). The story thus reveals Martha's changing attitudes toward her own identity and the charge that God has set for her. If Martha is to "borrow" some of God's power, then it is important how Martha understands God. When Martha initially sees God as a "twice-live-sized bearded white man," her perspective on her choice is the typical

God's-eye view invoked throughout the Judeo-Christian West. If Martha acts as this God, she will simply be redoing what has been done in the past. It is only as her perception of God changes that her perception of what she could do to change humanity changes. By rejecting the trappings of authority—God understood as "Michelangelo's Moses"—and ultimately seeing God as like herself, Martha takes on the command God has given. By the end of the story, her only fear is that she might become too accustomed to the power God has bestowed upon her.

This change reflects an important set of criticisms of the Rawlsian method. The veil of ignorance is supposed to provide a procedure that mandates fairness. The veil is understood to be needed because we might be tempted to benefit ourselves and our kind. But such a benefitting implies a fixed understanding of what one's identity really is. Rawls also holds that while the usual societal hierarchies are some of the "general facts" about society we will know in the original position, we should not consider anything about who and where we are in those hierarchies. But Martha learns important lessons from the facts of her specific identity. She learns that *how* she sees the world impacts what she *sees* in the world. This is an essential lesson that feminism, for example, has brought to the conversation about justice. The rational choice of abstract principles has a value, but it ignores the day-to-day lessons about the structures of inequality. Even the list of what one does not know behind the veil of ignorance has had to change to reflect developing views about the kinds of identities that can determine unfair advantage or disadvantage. When *Theory of Justice* was originally published in 1971, the list included class, social status, natural assets, "intelligence, strength and the like" (11, 118). By the time of the publication of *Political Liberalism* in 1993, the list was expanded to include "people's race and ethnic group, sex and gender, and their various native endowments" (25). In *Justice as Fairness: A Restatement*, published in 2001, the list mirrored that of *Political Liberalism* (although oddly it only includes sex and not gender). Traditionally theorists now understand the Rawlsian system of the veil of ignorance to include any attribute that can be used to prejudice people against others on the basis of something "arbitrary from a moral point of view" (thus including sexual orientation, for example). But this very trajectory illustrates why the embodied knowledge of prejudice may be a better standpoint from which to develop principles of justice.

When God finally appears to Martha as a black woman, Martha asks, "If I'm doing it, why did it take so long for me to see you as a black woman—since that's no more true than seeing you as a white or a black man?" (209). God replies, "You see what your life has prepared you to see." Even though

Martha thought of herself as someone who knew about and thus had success-fully resisted the racism and sexism in which she lived—"I just thought I had already broken out of the mental cage I was born and raised in" (209)—she learns that she is still wrapped up in those structures. God replies, "If it were truly a cage . . . you would still be in it, and I would still look the way I did when you first saw me." Seeing God lets Martha see herself, and by seeing herself Martha understands better how to change the rest of humanity.

Martha works through a variety of suggestions about how to redirect hu-man energy; she is in a kind of "reflective equilibrium"[7] with both God and the reader, so that the reader has in essence vetted the various proposals that Martha considers. Her change for humanity is not presented as a done deal: rather she and God discuss the pros and cons of a variety of suggestions Martha makes. God plays the role of helpful advisor, pointing out some of the unintended consequences of some of her ideas. For example, Martha's first suggestion that all "people" be limited to two births would lead to the eventual killing off of the human race. Importantly God neither wields veto power nor exhibits the omniscience that would be beyond the comprehen-sion of ordinary human beings. What the reader gets is a variety of proposals, and the pros and cons of those proposals. This kind of back and forth, while quite artificial in this context, is seen in many of Butler's accounts and re-flects her desire for a more deliberative model of governance. (Chapter 7 will explore this more directly in the model of Acorn, the postapocalyptic society of the *Parable* series.)

The change that Martha finally chooses to make in human beings reflects a kind of Rawlsian understanding; it is procedural and not final. Unlike her initial suggestion of limiting humans to two offspring, her final decision—for "vivid, wish-fulfilling dreams,"—establishes a constantly changing method for moving humanity out of their current fixations. The dreams she envi-sions suggest a kind of embodied version of the original position, of the very choice that Martha herself had to make. "Each person will have a private, perfect utopia every night—or an imperfect one. If they crave conflict and struggle, they get that. If they want peace and love, they get that. Whatever they want or need comes to them" (204). Martha chooses something that will impact everyone and that will be tailored to individuals' own desires. In knowing that one is dreaming one's deepest desires then one has those deepest desires revealed. Thus individuals could conceivably gain the kind of self-knowledge that Martha gains in her interactions with God. Dream-ing the way Martha imagines denies us the kind of lies that we live under, pretending to be something we are not. There is of course no guarantee that we would then use that self-knowledge positively (and God notes that some people might just become addicted to dreaming). But perhaps our self-deceptions will be lessened when we not only know what we want, but also get what we want, if only in a dream. Whatever change in the waking world that comes to humans because of these dreams will be a change focusing on the way that humans see the world (it is focused on the right) and not on what humans are or do in the world (it is not focused on the good). The dream change cannot fully embody the good because it only happens in a dream. Martha recognizes the need for the good to be tailored to individuals. And in dreams one's desire to universalize one's understanding of the good does not have the totalitarian consequences that universalizing the good in the world will have.

The change that Martha makes is interior. "The dreams should satisfy much more deeply, more thoroughly, than reality can. I mean, the satisfaction should be in the dreaming, not in trying to make the dreams real" (204). She does not change human motivation. But she does change the way in which we think about acting on that motivation. By having our dream life satisfy our competitiveness, by having our dream life meliorate our fear, by having our dream life provide the desired glory, we will, when awake, be less likely to act on these motivations in ways that cause violence. In part we are given free rein to do what we wish when we are by ourselves and in our heads, and we will be satisfied (partially) by that. We will literally become the novelists of our own lives writing, in our dreams, all of our deepest desires. By changing the way that humans think about their desires she is shifting human energies, taking the edge off of being human by providing satisfaction in a dream life.

"The Book of Martha" explains the advantages of the satisfying dream world primarily through the softening of the aggressiveness of those who desire to master or destroy others. God indicates that these dreams may give humanity "time" to grow up out of a particularly dysfunctional and destructive adolescence. But there are other unexplored advantages to this dream life. If ending oppression is hampered by the degree to which we are all accustomed to the structures of oppression, then providing a world of dreams that reflect all that one would want to see would allow anyone interested in a world without oppression to actually know what that world would look like. Just as Martha, who thought that she had escaped the mental cage of societal oppression, realizes the extent to which she was still in that cage, so too could someone gain a clearer view of what is missing in this world by dreaming of a world without oppression. It is not only that the power-hungry might find that "the vast, absolute power they can possess in their dreams" could overwhelm the satisfactions of seeking real power over people in their waking lives. But those who are not power hungry, those who have visions for a better world, can also see that vision better realized in a dream world.

This could weaken the pull of the dream world, but it could also show where we are close and where we are far from that dream world. Dreaming of a world absent sexism, racism and other oppressions would make the gap between the dream and the waking life all the more jarring. But the lesson to be learned is not that the waking life would radically change if everyone who experienced oppression realized the gap between freedom and oppression. Instead, this change could bring about what many of Butler's protagonists have to recognize: there is no escape. If there is a gulf between the dream world and the waking world then the only way to begin to make that change is to see the waking world as it is. I use the term "realist utopia" to designate works such as this that demand that we recognize the gap between the world as it is and world as it could be, and place ourselves in the world where we live.[8] "Maybe effort counted" ("Martha" 209). The only way for Martha's change to positively impact human living together is for people to recognize the gap between the dream and the waking life and to act. Effort does matter; it may be one of the only things that universally matters, although effort is no guarantee.

Of course "The Book of Martha" could be read as an after-the-fact example of the kind of change that Martha wanted to bring about. Martha herself is dreaming her utopian dream. She may not identify it as such in her dreaming self, but her dream speaks to her innermost desire to be given power over the whole world—power not just over the world but power to improve the world—to make it a place where humans could potentially flourish, or at least grow up enough to be able to flourish in the future. On that reading Martha is revealed to be someone slightly other than she appears: she is having the dream most satisfying to her, but part of the satisfaction is acting through a refusal of the dream's offer. Martha could, in part, be dreaming that she was a successful novelist and the kind of person that God would come to in order to brainstorm ways of improving humanity. Martha's satisfaction then comes in being chosen by God, in learning about herself through that choice, and in changing humanity. Martha's attitude at the end of the story—looking out of her picture window over Lake Washington—is the attitude not of regret, but perhaps the disappointment that comes from realizing that one's life is not as one has dreamed it. Perhaps Martha dreams this dream every night as a way to make sense of her life.

If this is the story—that Martha is living the dream world that has been created and she is only dreaming that she is the one who created it—then does this reading tell us anything further about the potential connections between Butler's story and Rawls' understanding of the social contract? Perhaps. If we read the story as a description of Martha's utopian dream, then we see the ways in which thought experiments turn in on themselves, creating what their conditions have set up for them to create. Martha lives in a world of utopian dreams, and Martha confronts the reality of that world by dreaming that she is the one who has brought about the world of utopian dreaming: a world where her own talents as a novelist have no place, and so a dream where she could both have her talents and willingly sacrifice them for a larger cause, for the future of humanity. So too might the veil of ignorance simply bring about what its own conditions establish. This can happen in two ways. First, as we have already noted, the nature of the ignorance is ever-changing: as we learn about ourselves as individuals and as communities, so too do we learn what we need to discount to bring about a fair society. Second, the goods that we desire, those things that are to be distributed by the principles of justice, may prove to be less appealing, depending on the kinds of beings we end up being when we think of ourselves in certain ways. All of which is to say that the contracts that we make with one another, either tacit or explicit, depend on the conditions under which we make those contracts.

Civil society, understood in the traditional sense, implies that someone has been chosen to deal with the problems of society. Each of the three previous chapters outlines how part of the acquisition of security includes having someone take on the burden of *providing* security. Senator Jellison, Randy Bragg and Emmanuel Comte are each chosen by their communities to provide what the community felt it could not provide without their authoritative leadership. Butler's work demands, instead, that everyone understand that combined individual effort is the only way to improve the world. Insecurity exists in both the state of nature and in civil society. "Martha" illustrates the threat posed by the sovereign as someone other than oneself through the powerful figure of God. God notes the potential threat of command by indicating at the outset, "If you don't help them, they will be destroyed" (192). There is nothing reassuring about this God: Martha's seeing God as a black woman does not make God any less flippant about what it means to have complete power and knowledge. Martha is still "nauseous with fear" (200) about what she must do. Martha is classically the right person to make this choice because she does not want this power. And she is compelled to follow God's command because she recognizes that it is better to be "ruled" by those reluctant to do so. Martha mistrusts God and she fears both the power that the God figure is demanding from her and the consequences that her decision might have for the rest of humanity. But her fear and mistrust allow her to move cautiously toward a potential change that redirects human energies, rather than reshaping human nature. "The Book of Martha" explores the mindset of one constructing civil society, asking what it means to try and change the world for the better. But it responds from a realist perspective: be cautious.

When in civil society we live lives at the whims of others. This is also true in the state of nature, but there the whims have more to do with accident and circumstance, whereas in civil society one has technically signed up for living under the control of someone else. We think of ourselves as gaining control over the uncertainties of life by entering into a social contract. We seek security, but what we most seek is control. The argument that government is only legitimate when backed by the consent of the people is essentially an argument that people want to think of themselves as in control over who makes decisions for them. Whether it be in the moral language of Rousseau, who claims that any adult would (should) choose to live under laws one gives to oneself, or the quid-pro-quo, mechanistic system of Hobbes, in which we gain control over the chaos of the state of nature by ceding control over our right to everything, social contract thinkers have stressed that the social contract, as a contract, grants us control over our lives. Even when Rawls makes this control abstract, even when he stresses the extent to which this control may well be an illusion, he too recognizes that going through the thought experiment compels us to choose principles that "we do in fact accept."[9]

"The Book of Martha" is criticizing the idea that civil society is the guarantor of peace. In fact, argues Butler, we live in the state of nature, in the world as it is. We live in a world that is radically insecure, where security means first recognizing just where we are. To push Martha toward this kind of recognition, Butler radically unsettles the conditions of Martha's life. But she does this in a surprisingly subtle way, not by destroying the community that Martha has created for herself through some sort of external threat. Instead, Butler simply removes Martha from the conditions of her own life and makes Martha responsible for her new conditions. From her own version of the original position, Butler demands that Martha choose the conditions of humanity, and thereby forces her to clarify the meaning of all that she has created in Seattle. She was not expected to be successful as a novelist when growing up as the daughter of a sometimes homeless woman who could barely read. But she has now made a space for herself and a space for her mother, and she just wants to live and work. Thus when God informs her that whatever change she makes she must go and live "as one of their lowliest" it is easy to appreciate her anger and the irony with which she makes the statement about her origins. Martha has known life as "one of the lowliest," and she has worked hard to get herself and her mother out of that life. Martha is willing, perhaps too sacrificially, not only to return to such a life but also to potentially destroy the desire people have for the products of her profession: novels. "What would happen to her if the only work she had ever cared for was lost?" (205). Can she dream a life of herself as a creator of imagined worlds that others find deeply satisfying? Butler's own questioning of the genre of utopian fiction emerges here, as the reader realizes that Martha will not have a better life after the change she decides upon is implemented. Butler claims, "I don't like most utopia stories because I don't believe them for a moment. It seems inevitable that my utopia would be someone else's hell" (214, afterword). This dislike of utopia is reflected both in Martha's choice of a private utopia for each person, and also in the potential personal hellishness to which Martha is resigning herself.

Octavia Butler's work challenges the very idea of control that undergirds the social contract. "The Book of Martha" begins this work of challenging and yet rethinking the idea of the social contract by presenting a thought experiment that reflects but also goes beyond Rawls' original position. In this short story, this rethinking takes place in the thinking of a single individual. I turn next to the *Parable* series, which presents the United States in the 2020s and beyond as a postapocalyptic society. This series, I will argue, reflects a much broader and more thoughtful approach to the postapocalyptic novel as utopia. Martha wants to change people's dreams, and the following two chapters will explore how other Butler protagonists seek to wake all humans out of their apathy and complacency.

Notes

The chapter title is from "The Book of Martha," 209.

1. The primary social goods are: rights and liberties, income and wealth, powers and opportunities and the social bases of self respect (Rawls, 90-95, 1971).
2. This is also why the *Left Behind* series is not analyzed in this book. The *Left Behind* series, as argued in the Introduction, sets out a medieval understanding of human relations and the overarching role that the Divine plays in mandating a good for human living.
3. In fact this move is so familiar to us that *Alas, Babylon*, the novel most imbued with a Lockean and thus liberal spirit does not even countenance the existence of a force that might seek to maximize the good over the right.
4. Michal Keren, "The Original Position in Jose Saramago's *Blindness*," *Review of Politics* 69 (Summer, 2007): 447-464.

5. Other than the *Parable* series, *Xenogenesis* and *Mind of My Mind* all involve starting over after some sort of event that has radically changed how humans can live their lives. Likewise her short stories often put humans in conditions of living that cause a radical rethinking of how we should live ("Speech Sounds," "Amnesty," "Bloodchild").

6. This space for choosing is mirrored in Butler's work in *Dawn*, the first book of the *Xenogenesis* trilogy and in the short story "Amnesty." Both of these accounts involve women who are being held by aliens and their "space" is itself wholly unknown and for a long time unknowable.

7. John Rawls, *Theory of Justice* (Cambridge: Harvard University Press,1971): 20. Reflective equilibrium is a process of bringing our principles into a public and agreed upon coherence collectively.

8. Claire Curtis, "Theorizing Fear: Octavia Butler and the Realist Utopia." *Utopian Studies* 19, no. 3 (Winter, 2008): 411-431.

9. There is an open question here as to whether Rawls expects us to see our society (U.S.) as thus legitimized; or if we are to see the gap between the two principles of justice and the society under which we do live and thus we are given a mental push toward that which we "would" in fact accept, perhaps compelling us to work towards those principles.

~

CHAPTER SIX

"To take root among the stars"

Octavia Butler's Parable of the Sower and Rethinking the Social Contract

The idea of the social contract is that human beings choose the political authority under which they live. Through the fiction of the state of nature and the description of human nature stripped bare humans come together, recognize their current prospects and decide collectively to form a community guided by agreed upon rules.

> Ideas matter. The idea that the world is a dangerous place is the seed of many militarizing processes. Alternative ideas portray the world as full of human creativity, of the potential for human cooperation, or of opportunities for empathy and mutual respect.[1]

The novels of the previous three chapters respond traditionally and faithfully to both the scripts of the social contract theorists and to the idea of the social contract itself. Octavia Butler,[2] on the other hand, manipulates both the script and the idea of the social contract. She offers an "alternative idea." The essential components are present: a state of nature like setting, a focus on human motivation, the importance of consent and agreed upon rules. Yet Octavia Butler's *Parable* series cannot be understood either as expressing one social contract approach or as simply picking and choosing from a variety of social contract thinkers. Butler is taking the social contract in a new direction. This chapter uses each of the theorists that have framed the earlier chapters to analyze *Parable of the Sower* and to highlight Butler's familiarity with the postapocalyptic genre. First, she shifts the debate away from the Hobbesian, realist framework of fear to the idea of vulnerability;

second, she moves from the individually oriented property seeker of Locke to a position where many (not all) individuals are connected through chosen and sometimes compelled linkages; third, she recognizes the essential nature of the community as in Rousseau but she simultaneously shows the fractures and fissures on which any community is built and may fall apart. Finally, Butler recognizes the attraction of a principle based social contract—where the subject of justice itself is the central concern for any contract—but in doing so she understands the substance of justice as essentially contested and ultimately outside the purview of any social contract.

I argue that *Parable of the Sower* engages Hobbes, Locke *and* Rousseau and I read Butler's novel as setting up a critique of the traditional understanding of the state of nature and the social contract that emerges from it. Is the state of nature predominantly violent as Hobbes would have it and as *Lucifer's Hammer* illustrates? Are people in the state of nature constantly fearful of the actions of others or do people largely do their own things, only paying attention to others when their interests overlap? Is the state of nature a place where the inevitable cannibals seem to always rise up or will it be more like *Alas, Babylon*, a largely peaceful place where most people work cooperatively and the irrational few are easily defeated? Or is the state of nature the place where we can finally sit back and regroup, realizing what really matters to us and making that transition to authenticity that has so eluded us? Are people primarily concerned with who it is that they become in community as in *Malevil*? Or would they prefer to reject the trappings of community altogether, as in *Into the Forest*?

Butler begins with these basic questions. Unlike the earlier novels, the *Parable* series works from a far more complex set of assumptions both about the state of nature and about human motivations. These complexities reflect the questions she has about the traditional social contract theorist's transition from the state of nature to civil society in search of some form of security. Butler questions the significance of fear, the idea of the subject and the ways in which the desires of a set of characters produce their community. By exploring the meaning of vulnerability, she shifts the perspective from which we see the postapocalypse and the interdependence essential for communal survival.

Parable Series

Lauren opens *Parable of the Sower* recalling an incident from the past about which she has just dreamed.

Stars.

Stars casting their cool, pale, glinting light.

"We couldn't see so many stars when I was little," my stepmother says to me. She speaks in Spanish, her own first language. She stands still and small, looking up at the broad sweep of the Milky Way. She and I have gone out after dark to take the washing down from the clothesline. The day has been hot, as usual, and we both like the cool darkness of early night. There's no moon, but we can see very well. The sky is full of stars.

The neighborhood wall is a massive, looming presence nearby. I see it as a crouching animal, perhaps about to spring, more threatening than protective. But my stepmother is there, and she isn't afraid. I stay close to her. I'm seven years old. (5)

On the one hand this passage is ordinary, calm in its description of something largely peaceful. But there are hints that this world is not quite the world we expect. Yes, they are taking in clothes from a clothesline, but this could simply be a sign of their environmental awareness or their lack of money for a dryer. It is hot "as usual" but many places are hot. The stars can be seen more than when the stepmother was a girl. Why is that? Simply because the stepmother lived in a city and Lauren and she may now live in the country? But then there is the wall. "Massive" and "looming" this does not seem to be the mere gates of a gated community. The reader does not know what this wall keeps out and what it keeps in, but it is the sign that all of the other potential clues add up to a world unlike ours in ways as of yet unknown to us. And yet there are also the stars, always setting out a possibility for Lauren of new life elsewhere.

Parable of the Sower is set in Robledo, a small suburb of Los Angeles, in 2024. The book, in diary form, opens on the protagonist's fifteenth birthday, which she shares with her father, the leader of their small walled community. She lives with her father, stepmother Cory and four half brothers. Lauren's diary opens describing the world in which she lives through a birthday baptism trip to a local church.

We learn that her mother died at her birth and that Lauren is a "sharer," she was born with "hyper-empathy syndrome," the result of drugs her mother took while pregnant. This drug, Paracetco, originally produced to combat Alzheimer's disease, was also used by others for the feelings of invincibility and sharpened intellect it produced. Paracetco was the "in" drug for educated men and women. The consequences of Lauren's being a "sharer" are not fully clear until the reader sees her writhing in pain at the sight of other people lying on the side of the road after a night of drinking or after being assaulted. Lauren feels their pain in her own body.

In interviews[3] Butler claimed that she wanted to see what it would be like if people could literally feel the pain of others. Would that make them less willing to cause pain? Would it produce people who were ultimately more caring, and a world that was a better place to live? Butler thinks through this hypothesis in the *Parable* series, where we encounter a number of other sharers. We learn that sharing does not produce the kind of enlightened empathy that causes people to stop and think before acting upon another. Instead literal empathy produces a thorough aversion to pain and either a road to an early death or a handle by which others can gain total control over you. Lauren notes at one point her brother's belief that sharers would make good slaves (269).

She was initially debilitated as a child with the effects of this syndrome. She would bleed when she saw blood and was able to be made wholly miserable by her brothers who would make sure that she saw every pain they experienced. The syndrome is real, but works on the imagination, so that the idea that someone is in pain is enough to trigger that very pain that you imagine. Lauren learns, through the disciplinary demands of her father, to mentally reject the pain, but this is not a perfect system. "To my father, the whole business is shameful. He's a preacher and a professor and a dean. A first wife who was a drug addict and a daughter who is drug damaged is not something he wants to boast about. Lucky for me. Being the most vulnerable person I know is damned sure not something I want to boast about" (10). Lauren's position of vulnerability shapes her understanding of the events of the novel and her motivations to enter into a different kind of community.

On the bike ride to the church in the opening journal entry we see both the impact that her hyper-empathy syndrome has on Lauren and the unsettled world in which she lives. What began as simply a description of a cautious community, one that did not often venture outside its gates for church, becomes a nightmarish ride through empty streets where the riders are flanked and protected by adult males with guns. The people in the streets see Lauren and her family as the privileged, those who live behind walls, no matter how makeshift. Lauren and her fellow riders see people lying dazed, bleeding or dead on street corners where no one pays attention to such things. They see a world decaying from the inside out. "We rode past people stretched out, sleeping on the sidewalks, and a few just waking up, but they paid no attention to us. I saw at least three people who weren't going to wake up again, ever. One of them was headless. I caught myself looking around for the head. After that, I tried not to look around at all" (8). We get little explanation for what happened to produce this. If this is postapocalyptic

Los Angeles, then what and when was the apocalypse? When was the war? Where did the meteor strike? What was the plague?

These questions are not answered fully until the second book, *Parable of the Talents*, when we read the journals of Lauren's future husband who thinks back on this time, the mid 2020s and "the Pox" that the United States has experienced. "I have read that the Pox was caused by accidentally coinciding climatic, economic, and sociological crises. It would be more honest to say that the Pox was caused by our own refusal to deal with obvious problems in those areas. We caused the problems: then we sat and watched as they grew into crises" (*Talents*, 8). Hearing this analysis of the events of the twenty-first century does not put everything into place for us. It is not clear who or what is to blame, although the ease with which humans adjusted themselves to new and increasingly worse conditions surely helped precipitate this culmination of events.

What we most learn from the opening journal entries of the book is that Lauren has an outlook on the world that challenges both her father's strict and traditional religious views. Lauren has developed this worldview through her adolescence and her journal entries begin with passages from Earthseed, her aphoristic musings on the way in which the world works. Earthseed is premised on the central principle of change: "God is change" is its mantra, if it has one. Impermanence and the need to recognize the reality of flux are the starting point for Lauren's philosophy. This is a somewhat surprising philosophy given that Lauren is young and sheltered from the outside world. She attends school within the walls of her community and recently a neighbor who had access to television lost her signal. Now news comes only through sporadic radio broadcasts and information brought home from her father who ventures outside the walls for his job at a nearby college.

But Earthseed makes sense as the novel progresses. Security, whether that be in the form of a patriarchal God (or father) who is going to take care of you, or walls that cannot be breached, or a family that stands together, or a friend who can listen to your concerns without telling on you, is absent in Lauren's life. And yet, her expectations for these potential modes of security are equally low and so when her community is burned down she escapes through a combination of luck and forethought. She has packed a survival pack, she takes time to put on shoes and clothes, she manages to grab a gun from a dead neighbor and thus thwart an attack against herself. And, most importantly, she knows that she wants to leave. The attack on her community is wholly bad, her stepmother and brothers are dead (or seem to be; her father has already disappeared and is presumed dead prior to the attack). The people that she loves are mostly dead, but Earthseed is part of the reason that she will not let herself fall into despair.

Earthseed both describes the human condition and prescribes an attitude towards the world that might help alleviate the feelings of helplessness endemic to postapocalyptic accounts. Outlined in aphorisms that begin each journal entry and occasionally are expanded upon within journal entries, Earthseed is a worldview that is less spiritual than practical in content. Many of the aphorisms describe how humans can be manipulated and the ways in which mob mentalities are developed. Earthseed is focused on action, on shaping circumstance to one's advantage as best as one can. It is not a wholly instrumentalist theory, but it does think about the consequences of any action—short and long term. Earthseed is a belief system based on observation, and yet also anchored by a faith that people should be ruled by "the Destiny." "The Destiny of Earthseed is to take root among the stars." At the opening of this first novel, in the mouth of a poor, teenaged protagonist in a world where potable water and police protection are unreliable such a destiny must be based on faith as it is unreasonable at best and ludicrous at worst.

Part two of the novel follows Lauren, Harry and Zahra (two other survivors of the Robledo attacks) as they travel up the California coast. They attract other travelers, usually those as vulnerable as they are, and Earthseed is part of what informs both the way that they attract others and the tie that ultimately binds them. The *Parable* series models an egalitarian model of unification that recognizes human vulnerability (paying particular attention to the vulnerability of children) without somehow claiming that there is one group that must naturally rule over others in order to save everyone. Butler admits that we come together seeking mutual advantage, but she also recognizes that mutual advantage does not mean seeing everyone as equally able to do or be everything at once. Vulnerability reflects a willingness to change, to join together to improve the situation. So when Lauren, Harry and Zahra initially link up with Travis and Natividad they do so in part because of their vulnerability ("they need us more than we need them"), likewise when they link up with other sharers and other adult child pairs. Even Bankole, the older, solitary male traveler who becomes Lauren's husband is vulnerable and has more to gain from joining the group than the group has from welcoming him (other than the land in Northern California about which they do not yet know). For Butler vulnerability provides a common ground from which the travelers up I-5 will come together and will be open to Earthseed's principles. Their shared understanding of vulnerability allows them to be interdependent and to understand their contractual obligations as multidirectional.

When the travelers arrive, at the end of the novel, at Bankole's sister's farm they again find destruction and again must persevere and start over anew. Bankole's family has been killed, their farm burned to the ground. But the land is good for planting; there are fruit trees and oak trees and space that seem secure from outsiders (despite the farm's having been attacked once). Acorn is founded. The novel seems to end on a happier note. Security, it seems has been been achieved and Earthseed's principles of perseverance, openness to change, hard work and awareness can come to fruition.

From Hobbesian Fear to Vulnerability

An initial read of any Octavia Butler text can seem like a Hobbesian world in action.[4] Earthseed itself notes that "disintegration" is inevitable and that "need and greed" (91) will likely follow. *Parable of the Sower* seems to be the perfect illustration of Hobbes' state of nature. As seen above Lauren worries about the negative consequences of pride, concerned that an overweening pride uses an individual's motivation at the expense of the group in which that individual is embedded. Likewise Lauren is fully aware of the motivation of fear and in fact reminds her fellow travelers more than once that to let down their fear on the road will lead to trouble.

Hobbes is the influence behind many postapocalyptic novels because of the force of his contention that life in the state of nature would be "nasty, poor, brutish and short" and a "war of all against all." These features of Hobbes' argument are useful for an analysis of Butler. More so than any of the other social contract thinkers, Hobbes gives a kind of blueprint for a one dimensional reading of Butler's work.[5] Butler surely captures what "nasty, brutish and short" might look like. Yet she also understands both the motivation for and the way out of that nastiness in a way different from Hobbes, or from Hobbesian influenced postapocalyptic accounts.

Butler challenges Hobbes' claims of human universality in motivation. She too understands fear and the desire for security to be the driving forces of her characters. But she recognizes that fear can take different forms and that security can have different meanings. *Lucifer's Hammer*, in a more typical Hobbesian move, contends that fear and the desire for security undergird all of the rational. Thus the New Brotherhood army is simply irrational, even inhuman, in their persistence in fighting when there is no chance of success.[6] But in *Parable* fear reveals vulnerability to more than just violent death. Further, Butler sees that while the vulnerability that feeds fear is universal, the response to vulnerability can differ radically. To successfully bring people together is to seek out those who neither ignore nor feel shamed by their vulnerability.

Lauren's father initially models for Lauren a traditional, Hobbesian relationship between fear and authority: "It's better to teach people than to scare them, Lauren. If you scare them and nothing happens, they lose their fear, and you lose some of your authority with them. It's harder to scare them a second time, harder to teach them, harder to win back their trust. Best to begin by teaching" (58). Lauren's father teaches everyone over 15 how to use a gun and everyone over 18 helps to patrol the neighborhood. Fear provides the universal starting point underlying the community's cohesion. Lauren's father presents himself and his plan as able to provide security for the neighborhood. But he has no succession plan, he is unwilling to alert his community members to the full extent of their vulnerability and when he disappears on his way home from work one morning his community is left reeling. By teaching his people to fear, but not teaching them of their own vulnerability, his teaching ultimately fails.

Lauren adopts her father's advice to teach people. Earthseed is a teaching tool for Lauren on the road. She uses it both to teach her fellow travelers how to read and write and she expects these Earthseed verses to spur discussion and open the minds of her traveling companions. Earthseed reinforces vulnerability and never reassures that someone else will care for you. Lauren's terror at her father's disappearance is bred of her father's position as sole authority. After he disappears and is assumed dead, Lauren worries, "I don't know what that means. I don't know what to think. I'm scared to death" (115). In the world of Robledo, Lauren's father should have prepared his community for his potential disappearance. Instead he has left a vacuum in which the community's differing responses to fear will leave them wholly unprepared for the eventual attack by the "paints" (drug induced pyromaniacs who paint their bodies) who destroy the neighborhood.

Lauren has seen the increasing dangers of the surrounding world—the increase in burglaries and shootings, the torture and death of her brother Keith who ran away from his father's authoritarian rule. She has broken with her friend Joanne over discussions of the impending dangers and Joanne's refusal to believe that things are as bad as Lauren describes. Lauren learns through her home experience that the world can be a dangerous place and that people should be motivated by fear. Earthseed reflects that learning. But what Lauren learns beyond this is that fear is not a reliable motivator. The human capacity for denying, suppressing or evading fear only increases personal danger. Fear requires recognizing vulnerability. Fear fails when we deny vulnerability.

One example illustrating the failure of fear to spur action is that illusion of escape, whether it be in the form of drugs or virtual reality or savagery, is common in the *Parable* series. Part of the pull of Hobbes' claims about human fear is that the only escape from the state of nature is the social contract (or death). Butler creates a world filled with potential and deeply irrational imagined escapes that are still chosen by people. Keith chooses escape, literally in running away from the neighborhood, and symbolically as he rejects his father's moral code and kills and steals to survive. Keith's torture and death teaches the Hobbesian lesson about escape. But the community in Robledo does not seem to learn that lesson.

Others seek escape in less flashy but equally delusional means. The Garfield family moves to Olivar, a town on the coast that has sold itself to a company who will use and expand its desalination plant to sell water. Lauren understands this as one kind of delusional escape. "Something new is beginning—or perhaps something old and nasty is reviving. A company called Kagimoto, Stamm, Frampton, and Company—KSF—has taken over the running of a small coastal city called Olivar" (105). Lauren's reading has prepared her well for understanding the consequences of the company town. The Garfields will be moving from a house with a garden where they could grow the bulk of their own food to an apartment with no access to a garden. They will be "paid" room and board but no cash outside of that and the stores in the town will all be run through credit given by the company. Debt slavery seems inevitable and Lauren is frustrated by Joanne's inability to see this.

One of the last arguments Lauren's father has with her stepmother is over why he will not apply for membership in Olivar. Cory favors the stronger walls and armed guards paid to protect the people of Olivar. "We could be safe," she insists. But Lauren's father and Lauren herself insist that Olivar is nothing other than voluntary slavery. "I wonder how many of the people of Olivar have any idea what they're doing?" Lauren's father muses. Lauren replies "I don't think many do . . . I don't think they'd dare let themselves know" (108). This is the delusional escape of those who think that vulnerability is not shared. People like the Garfields and Cory imagine that life would be better with higher walls and bigger guns, not thinking about which ways those guns are pointed and whether the walls keep people in or out. Lauren's father reminds Cory as well that this delusional escape is likely not available to their family, given their race. "I doubt that Olivar is looking for families of blacks or Hispanics, anyway. . . . Even if I were trusting enough to put my family into KSF's hands, they wouldn't have us" (108). Even here Butler has Lauren's father use a word like trust, implying that it is somehow his problem with trust that makes Olivar unattractive to him. Lauren turns this around and gives a positive argument for suspicion: "When it comes to strangers with guns . . . I think suspicion is more likely to keep you alive than trust" (108). Suspicion denies the possibility of escape and blocks the potential for delusion. Suspicion heightens her awareness of her surroundings and gives her a foundation from which she accepts members into the group that travels up the California coast. This suspicion is based on the recognition of the danger from those who see themselves as invulnerable.

Lauren is aware of this motivation for escape. Escape is not security, although it is related to the desire for security. Escape will not make you less vulnerable, although escape is based on a belief that you can become invulnerable. But escape uses the fact of desire and the delusional imagining that drugs, voluntary servitude in Olivar, or virtual reality will somehow bring security. While Lauren clearly rejects that option she does not wholly demonize those who have opted for it. Thus Butler rewrites the good/bad, "carry the fire"/cannibals distinction. There are cannibals and they will not be eradicated. Lauren acknowledges the fact of some responding to their vulnerability in this way. She rejects such a response as unreasonable, but she is not out to either demonize or destroy those who make such unreasonable choices.

When Lauren, Harry and Zahra first start out on the road Lauren realizes that she must work against the principles with which she has been raised and the presumptions she has about the world stemming from that upbringing. She knows that she is at a disadvantage on the road having always been surrounded and secured by walls. Part of the advantage of having Zahra along is that Zahra up to age fifteen lived on the streets. Zahra has skills that Lauren and Harry do not have—and one of those skills is a deep mistrust of almost everyone. "Harry and I have been well-fed and protected all our lives. We're strong and healthy and better educated than most people our age. But we're stupid out here. We want to trust people. I fight against the impulse. Harry hasn't learned to do that yet" (161). Harry is motivated to help people, both out of a sense of altruism, but also because he is young and self confident. He presumes that he can outwit or strong arm anyone that they encounter. He has not yet learned that he is vulnerable. Zahra has to teach him that no one can be trusted. And yet it is out of this spirit of mistrust that Lauren also begins to help other people and to attract her small group of followers.

Harry describes Lauren's assertions about how they will have to live on the road as savage: "We don't have to turn into animals" (163). Lauren responds that in fact they are like animals: "We're a pack the three of us . . . if we're a good pack, and we work together, we have a chance" (163). Harry stays in part because of his attraction to Zahra. That attraction is both sexual, but also Harry's desire to protect Zahra gives him a goal and a reason to follow Lauren's lead on mistrust. He will not turn into an animal, but he will adapt certain tactics in order to protect Zahra from harm. If he can describe himself as saving Zahra, rather than protecting himself, then he can justify the behavior he needs to have to survive on the road.

While all of the characters in postapocalyptic fiction are motivated to survive (or at least all who become the main characters; in each work there are a few who simply give up, like the retirees in *Alas, Babylon* who die waiting for normalcy to be restored) each group of characters must work out their own set of principles for survival. One familiar route to survival is the demonization of some identified enemy. Once the enemy is dehumanized then there is no question that one can and should kill him. Lauren largely refuses this move of dehumanization. She does still use her father's language of "coyotes" to describe the fast moving "opportunists" who will take advantage of perceived weakness on the road in order to make a quick burglary. But because of the focus on their opportunism the coyotes are not unrecognizable beasts, "Skinny, scared little bastards out to do their daily stealing" (181). This animalistic description is more descriptive than scapegoating. Lauren is clearly rejecting the coyote lifestyle. But she does not use Earthseed to promote enmity with the coyotes or even destruction of them.

Vulnerability will motivate Lauren to find a place to live far from the coyotes' grasp. And in her Earthseed teaching she will be sure that people are made aware of the coyotes' tactics and people will be prepared to defend against them.

Lauren recognizes that part of what people fear is the impotence of not being able to do anything to protect oneself and protect those one loves. Earthseed sets out practical principles for protection while simultaneously offering no guarantee. Earthseed is a particularly appropriate mindset for a postapocalyptic world. Lauren knows that many people are willing to accept Earthseed in order to promote the hard work of building a secure and self sufficient community on the Northern California coast. Lauren also knows that many of those people do not think of themselves as working toward the Earthseed destiny. Lauren wants the purposeful future driven mentality necessary to produce the Destiny to drive people beyond their immediate day to day needs. She knows that there are times when the Destiny will not be furthered—as they travel up the California coast or after Acorn itself is taken over by followers of President Jarrett. In those times day to day survival is paramount. But for Earthseed such day to day survival also requires learning the techniques needed to do the impossible—people the stars.

And so Butler recognizes the Hobbesian motivation of fear, but in *Parable of the Sower* she examines the content of that fear, vulnerability, and explains how some people seek to solve fear by denying vulnerability whereas others seek to solve fear by abdicating responsibility for their own vulnerability. Butler describes Lauren as rejecting both of these responses to the fact of fear.

From Lockean to Feminist Subjects

Locke, who saw himself as rejecting Hobbes' insistence on fear and the prevalence of violence, shifted human motivation from mere survival to the idea of human flourishing. Locke understands the acquisition and protection of property to be the key motivating factor for humans. This is clear in *Alas, Babylon*, where Pat Frank followed Locke in dividing the characters in Fort Repose into two groups, the "rational and industrious" and the "quarrelsome and contentious." While the motivation for property acquisition is universal, the willingness to work for that property, Locke argues, may not be fully present. Those who refuse to work for their own betterment write themselves out of any contract (like the residents of Pistolville). We are motivated by a desire to protect our property. Security is protection of the body and the property it has produced. But we do not automatically fear that others will attack us and steal from us. Recourse to violence is necessary as a last resort against those who have already failed the Lockean contract.

Butler acknowledges our deep desire for a place to make one's own. The small community that Lauren founds, Acorn, is in many respects a different kind of Lockean model of industry and improvement of the earth. The inhabitants of Acorn, like those of Fort Repose, understand the kind of work necessary to make Acorn a self sufficient community. The inhabitants of Acorn are motivated by an "improve the earth" mentality, but it is one that will produce health and flourishing for the whole community. Butler's ambivalence to the Lockean mindset is shown in *Parable of the Talents*, where Acorn's self sufficiency is destroyed and the members of Earthseed must find a new way to connect to the world. The failure of Acorn is not the failure of its industry. Instead Butler uses Acorn's destruction to challenge the seeming ease of the Lockean contract. Butler also challenges the seeming simplicity of Locke's contract by focusing on a protagonist who is "rational and industrious" and yet she succeeds not simply through her own talents, but through her purposeful decision to connect with others.

The first key difference between the *Parable* series and the other novels examined in the previous chapter (excepting *Into the Forest*) is that the *Par-*

able series protagonist is not a white man in a position of power who learns to live a more meaningful life after the end. Lauren Oya Olamina is young (15 at the opening), black, raised by a Latina stepmother who married her father after her mother's death. She is poor, although not as poor as many. She is the only daughter among four half brothers, two of whom will cause her family (first her natal family and second her chosen family) enormous pain. She is a sharer, a literal empath who feels, and is often debilitated by, the pain of others.

Lauren's race provides a crucial first step towards exploring her subjectivity. She is a young black woman, raised by a strong, patriarchal, Baptist minister black father. But she also has a Latina stepmother, a Spanish speaking home life and she resides in a mixed race community. Her father is the ostensible head of the community in which she lives. She is seen by others in the community as in a privileged position. She is the "preacher's daughter." She is the oldest child to whom much responsibility is given. She is as educated as one can expect a young person in a disintegrating world to be. At 15 she is doing college work with her father and stepmother and she reads voraciously. But she also understands the limitations of her own fractured education.

Who is Lauren as a black feminist subject? She is aware of racism and she references a community incident where a white family and a black family come to blows over the sexual relationship between their children: "The Garfields and the Balters are white, and the rest of us are black. That can be dangerous these days. On the street, people are expected to fear and hate everyone but their own kind, but with all of us armed and watchful, people stared, but they let us alone. Our neighborhood is too small for us to play those kinds of games" (31). But she is not shaped simply by racism as we understand it. When she takes to the road after Robledo burns she recognizes what it will mean to be black on the highway, but that recognition is largely intellectual, not experienced. Even when she settles in Northern California surrounded by mostly white farmers she again recognizes what it might mean to those families that her community is mixed race.

Patricia Hill Collins explains that the self definition of Black women is "distinctive." "Self is not defined as the increased autonomy gained by separating oneself from others. Instead, self is found in the context of family and community—as Paule Marshall describes it 'the ability to recognize one's continuity with the larger community.'"[7] This describes Lauren; and yet too much focus on her context blinds us to Lauren's particular resistance to her "family and community," a resistance born from her own recognition that survival means rejecting one worldview in favor of another.

At the opening of *Parable of the Sower*, Lauren is embedded in a family and community context that has been largely absent in the other postapocalyptic accounts presented here.

Lauren is fully in a family, whereas the usual postapocalyptic survivor survives precisely because he (and it usually is a he) is alone. This survival can be literal—they may not be burdened with a child to hamper their escape, as in *Lucifer's Hammer*, where the children who survive either lived outside the crash zone or were already camping out in the hills. Or it can be that absent a family one is more able to do what needs doing after such an event. Both Randy Bragg and Emmanuel Comte have no familial ties. Randy is responsible for his sister-in-law and his niece and nephew, but those are predominantly ties of responsibility, not ties of love. Lauren's birth family does die, thus potentially freeing her to travel north on her own. Yet she immediately recreates a type of family bond to increase the security of the small group. While she and Harry and Zahra start out as a threesome of healthy young adults (the ideal survivor type), Lauren's invitation to Travis, Natividad and the baby Dominic both expands the group and potentially endangers it. Lauren sees that family ties can help produce security. Lauren recognizes the value of the vulnerability of children. Lauren is seeking to create a "context of family and community" into which these children can be raised.

Children are not an afterthought to this account. Lauren recognizes the importance of children and family type units but not because she herself is a mother. She is not making an essentialist claim that has emerged from a birth experience. In part Lauren is arguing as someone who recently was a child; on the other hand Lauren recognizes that children can soften the edges of others' hostility and provide a reason to look to the future. This focus on children emerges in Lauren's understanding of Earthseed as a set of principles that directs us towards the future: "The Destiny of Earthseed is to take root among the stars." Earthseed will not provide salvation. Rather, hard work will lead members of Earthseed communities to flourish elsewhere beyond earth. This destiny encourages members of Earthseed communities to focus their work on future generations. But this focus is literal and practical and not simply abstract.

Lauren's group grows through the repeated addition of adults and children. Some of these additions are through small family units: Travis, Natividad and Dominic, or the two other sharers, mother and daughter Emory and Tori, and father and daughter Mora and Doe. The group also takes up an orphaned child, Justin, they encounter one night after they are caught between a gun fight that kills the mother of a young child camping nearby. Bringing

Justin along with them is, in many ways, foolhardy. He is young, three, but not as young as Dominic who can simply be strapped to a back. Nor is he as prepared for life on the road as Doe and Tori are from their experiences as escaped slaves. The group discusses the acceptance of the two sharer groups, but they bring in Justin without discussion. It is simply a given that a three year old whose mother has been killed on the road will be adopted by them. This lack of discussion is important as it reflects a shared set of values. They do not adopt Justin because Lauren demands it. They simply take him along, after checking the mother's body and things for evidence of who Justin is and where she might have been taking him.

The Earthseed group values children without glossing over either the responsibility involved in caring for them or the potential many children have for violence. Lauren has seen both the violence that is done to children and the violence children can do. She has seen children who have been both the victims of cannibalism (in the small partially eaten remains seen at abandoned campsites) and the cannibals themselves.

> That night, looking for a place to camp , we stumbled across four ragged, filthy kids huddled around a campfire. The picture of them is still clear in my mind. Kids the age of my brothers—twelve, thirteen, maybe fourteen years old, three
> · boys and a girl. The girl was pregnant, and so huge it was obvious she would be giving birth any day. We rounded a bend in a dry stream bed, and there the kids were, roasting a severed human leg, maneuver it where it lay in the middle of their fire atop the burning wood by twisting its foot. As we watched, the girl pulled a sliver of charred flesh from the thigh and stuffed it into her mouth. (243)

This account illustrates Lauren's way of seeing the world and the eye that she brings to life amidst or after the end. First she clearly identifies them as children, kids. Second there is no horror in her tone. She does not forgive them their behavior, they back away and leave and clearly reject the practice. But she does not fulminate about the presence of cannibals. Finally, the existence of these cannibals is not the sign of impending doom in their world. The Earthseed community does not need to rally together to defeat cannibals. It is as if Lauren is simply recognizing that these near feral children are a part of the landscape. They should be avoided, but they can neither be saved nor need to be destroyed. Lauren has turned away from the clearest instance of the Other in postapocalyptic fiction and walked on. "Fixing the world is not what Earthseed is about" (Lauren to Bankole, 247). Butler does not have Lauren use this incident to prove her ability to destroy the Other. Lauren is a different kind of postapocalyptic protagonist.

Lauren connects herself to these cannibal children by noting their close-ness in age to her brothers. But what she wonders as they leave these children behind is not how this happened to these particular children, but rather how it was that this area, with small farms that seemed to have more food and better water supplies, was succumbing to this practice. "So why were these people eating one another?" (244) This is an open question: why did these conditions, which seem better than some of the conditions they have passed through, produce this practice? But her question is both clinical and based in a need to understand what drives people to act in certain ways. She has no immediate answer. And Butler has created a protagonist who does not need to have such answers.

Lauren is a self conscious chooser who seeks to create a forward looking community. Part of what she had to reject about her own upbringing was that the Robledo community held onto a way of life that was dead. The adults of Robledo thought that the good times would come again. They were waiting for better times to appear. Lauren had no such illusion that waiting would do anything other than put them in the path of their eventual destruction. Lauren is proactive and she is motivated by a desire to begin again under Earthseed principles. She does not possess any particularly mystical qualities, although she is, as Bankole notes, "a very unusual young woman" (235).

She possesses clear qualities of leadership, although those leadership quali-ties are different from what we have seen in the earlier accounts. For example the leaders of the earlier accounts all led in part because of the vestiges or memories that survivors had of them before the event. Senator Jellison is obviously trading on his past office holding to organize the valley people in *Lucifer's Hammer*. The most authoritative of those who help support his power are also all people who commanded respect prior to the Hammer fall. Randy Bragg, although he had lost the race for state senate, was the son of a community leader, the inhabitant of the "big house." He was a military vet and clearly commanded the respect of many (if not all). Emmanuel Comte is the owner of Malevil and the leader of the group of boyhood friends. He sur-renders both his ownership of Malevil and his leadership, but he surrenders it with the knowledge that he once had it and he convinces the inhabitants of Malevil of this in part because of his past authority.

Lauren possessed little power prior to Robledo being destroyed. She is respected as the daughter of her father, valued for the help she provides her stepmother in the community school, but she is young and female and not a leader of Robledo. Furthermore once the community is destroyed only Zahra Moss and Harry Balter even know of Lauren's prior life. The new members simply know Lauren for what she provides on the road. Thus her authority (which she clearly has) comes from her actions among people who do not know her. Tellingly, Lauren is traveling as a man. She and Harry and Zahra thought that their threesome would be less open to attack with two men and one woman. In this sense Lauren is trading on the habitual respect for authority given to men. But Lauren's actions belie her use of her height and bodily strength to demand wariness from potential attackers. Repeatedly Lauren chooses new members through their vulnerability and self consciously references that vulnerability. The community as it grows signs off on new members, although there is no account where Lauren's wishes are outvoted.

Lauren continues this search for new members through their vulnerability. This use of vulnerability does not mean that Lauren is somehow seeking the most abject on the road, although the new members might be seen as becoming more vulnerable once she accepts the two groups of sharers. Each incident includes Lauren going out on a limb to help the person or persons, asking nothing in return. She first helps Travis and Natividad defeat two robbers at the water station and she then shoots the dog who tries to take away baby Dominic on the beach at night. After the first incident, while they were camping adjacent to one another on the beach, Lauren approaches them and asks if they would like to join up.

> "If you two would like to take turns bathing, you can come over and join us. That might be safer for the baby."
>
> "Join you?" The man said. "You're asking us to join you?"
>
> "Inviting you."
>
> "Why?"
>
> "Why not. We're natural allies—the mixed couple and the mixed group."
>
> "Allies?" the man said, and he laughed.
>
> I looked at him, wondering why he laughed.
>
> "What the hell do you really want?" he demanded. (186)

At this point Travis is clearly suspicious of Lauren's overture. They do not join up until the next night, after Lauren has shot the dog attacking the baby, and after another day of following Lauren and Harry and Zahra. "They gave in and joined us tonight after we made camp. . . . Once we were settled, they came over to us, uncertain and suspicious, offering us a small piece of their treasure: milk chocolate full of almonds" (PS, 189). Why does Travis change his mind? The chocolate is a gesture of thanks, but simply saving Dominic is not sufficient reason to join up with Lauren, Harry and Zahra.

They are, as Lauren repeats, "natural allies," and while Travis is "bitter" when Lauren says that Dominic will benefit from the protection of four adults ("I can take care of my wife and my son") he also knows that Lauren is right. Travis possesses a male pride that Lauren knows will not benefit him on the road. She understands that the pride/shame feedback loop tends to overwhelm the needed mutual focus on the goal of group survival. Allie and Jill, the next two who are rescued by Lauren's group and then reluctantly join up also possess a pride/shame focus on their ability to care for themselves. Part of what makes Bankole such an appropriate partner for Lauren is that he possesses little need for displays of pride in his manhood.

Jill and Allie, like Travis and Natividad, are suspicious and not particularly grateful (Jill is, Allie is not) when Lauren's group rescues them from the abandoned building that fell on them during an earthquake. When the group has to fight against attackers who use their rescue to take advantage of the group, Allie still insists, "If you hadn't been the ones to dig us out . . . we wouldn't bother with you at all. . . . We know how to pull our own weight. We can help our friends and fight our enemies. We've been doing that since we were kids" (214). Lauren has to respond to Allie's attitude: "I needed to know what her pride and anger might drive her to" (214). Would she attack Lauren in order to prove that she could take care of herself and her sister? Or would she acknowledge the help that Lauren provided and agree to help this group that helped her (or walk away)? Allie and Jill join the group, again after going through stages of fear, suspicion and reluctant acceptance. After the child Justin is adopted by the group and attaches himself to Allie, and after Jill dies in a later attack, then Allie acknowledges her membership in the group. Lauren does not accept them readily, she notes their own story, prostituted by their own father, thinking, "They would bear watching, but they might turn out to be worth something" (214). This is a potentially cold assessment, but it reflects well Lauren's mode of travel. She is not out to save people, rather she is out to gather potential Earthseed recruits. In doing so she will help who she can when she can, not out of a selfless altruism or rational self interest, but simply out of a recognition of human interdependence.

Community Based Interdependence

Earthseed is a principle used to create "a people." Like Rousseau, Butler recognizes that the social contract cannot simply be understood as the mutual decision of a collection of individuals to join together and form a civil society. Rather this collection of individuals must first see themselves as something beyond the sum of their individual parts. The *Parable* series uses the principles of Earthseed to both tie people together and to feel out their willingness to become members. The characters here are linked to a shared set of guiding principles and not simply to a shared understanding of themselves as moral persons who have chosen to live under rules given to themselves. Earthseed is not simply an ideology tying the characters together. Rather, Earthseed sketches out the conditions under which Lauren believes we already do live. Earthseed guides by setting out claims about human motivation. If you accept its description of the ways of human beings and the world that we inhabit then you are likely to ally yourself with its adherents. But it is the adherents together who must prescribe behavior for flourishing in a world governed by Earthseed.

The conditions for an interdependent community are revealed in the idea of the end. *Malevil* used the fact of nuclear war to awaken a Rousseauean reminder about community and civil liberty. Nuclear war illustrates the fact of our chains and life after the war allows the inhabitants of the castle to come together under the direction of the general will. *Parable of the Sower*, like *Into the Forest*, does not involve one clear cut world-ending event that signals such chains. In *Parable of the Sower* both the need for community and the interdependent nature of community come out of the context of an always already end. *Parable of the Sower* complicates the idea of the end and promotes community as interdependence not simply as authenticity.

As in *Into the Forest*, the *Parable* series is a postapocalyptic account with no specific ending event. The series begins in 2024 and it is clear that whatever series of events has caused this environmental, political and economic upheaval has already occurred. We only see the impact of this series of events in California, first in the southern California town of Robledo and then up the coast to northern California, where Acorn is founded. But Lauren references conditions around the world and elsewhere in the United States. We know that there is drought in the Midwest, cholera in the Southeast and rising waters along the Eastern seaboard. Hurricanes are killing people along the Gulf coast and epidemics of measles are sweeping through the cities of the Northeast. These are all catalogued by Lauren with little surprise; such events are clearly part of her norm. And yet such events spur questions for Lauren:

One hurricane. And how many people has it hurt? How many are going to starve later because of destroyed crops? That's nature. Is it God? Most of the dead are street poor who have nowhere to go and who don't hear the warnings until it's too late for their feet to take them to safety. Where's safety to them, anyway? Is it a sin against God to be poor? We're almost poor ourselves. . . . How will God—my father's God—behave toward us when we're poor? (13)

Lauren seems to be contemplating the disintegration of the east coast from a perspective of relative security. She understands that her community is "not yet" poor, although there are no prospects of paying jobs for any of the young people who are reaching maturity. "The adults say things will get better, but they never have" (13). Is this simply the resignation of a hyper-observant fifteen year old? When Lauren says "but they never have" does she mean that things have never gotten better in her own lifetime or is she indicting all parents, throughout the generations, for making promises that can never be fulfilled to their children? Lauren is not being raised on the usual American dream diet of pulling oneself up by her bootstraps. But she does find the promise of a better world to be empty. She sees no action from her parents or the other adults in her community that could be an indication that things will get better.

Lauren's desire to be prepared for whatever might come is similar to the survivalist preparations of the protagonists of the previous novels, but Lauren is one of the few protagonists whose thoughts about survival go beyond making it out alive. This is what Butler's extended and recurrent "endings" bring to these two novels. There is no moment when the reader can think that everything will be all right. "Things will get better." This is expressed by the adults of Lauren's original home in a passive, detached way. That claim is an external hope—"things" there refers to the outside world. It is as if they are saying that if "we" can simply hunker down then at some point, and by some unseen force, the outside world will change so that one day the gates can be opened and "we" can all emerge, eyes blinking, from some sort of nightmare. Only Lauren recognizes that the only way "things will get better" is if things are *made* better by us.

Unlike a meteor strike or a nuclear war, many of the end of the world events of the *Parable* series are potentially solvable. Many of these events are caused by human action and all are made worse through human indifference and opportunism. Further these events, as seen through Lauren's own experience, reveal a spectrum of class divides. In *Lucifer's Hammer*, *Alas, Babylon* and *Malevil* there is the fiction that the event has destroyed class divides—everyone is in the same position after the event and all must work together ignoring previous divisions between them. This is clearly a lie in those books—it matters that the survivors and protagonists are all property owning white men with power gained prior to the event that is used to their advantage after the event. But still it is a comforting fiction in most post-apocalyptic accounts: if nothing else the end of the world will cause us to ignore class, racial and gender divides. The *Parable* series puts this lie to rest by illustrating the numerous ways that such divides are deeply exacerbated by the apocalyptic events of the series.

The first and most important of these divides is to see the ways in which the apocalyptic events of this series illustrates that the wealthy can "survive" the impact of such events with their class status intact. While the meteor strike of *Lucifer's Hammer* leaves Senator Jellison's ranch intact it has destroyed all of the Los Angeles basin—rich and poor—while simultaneously leaving relatively unscathed all of the valley in which Jellison's ranch is found. Part of the clarity after the meteor strike is that there is, as there will be in the nuclear war accounts, a "ground zero" reality. There is a place where everything is destroyed and then concentric circles where that destruction fades and eventually gives way to communities that need to survive the aftermath, but are relatively uninfluenced by the direct destructive impact of the event itself. But there is no such ground zero in the *Parable* series. Instead we have a wide range of survivors and a wide range of destructive impacts within Robledo itself.

Lauren's walled off neighborhood is getting by, if not thriving. They are increasingly subject to attack from outsiders, but they grow their own food and experience a relative amount of security behind their walls. Zahra notes on the road after the neighborhood's destruction: "Those big walls. And everybody had a gun. There were guards every night. I thought . . . I thought we were so strong" (166). Zahra is speaking from her experience on the streets as a child. Compared to that life Lauren's neighborhood seemed so strong. Lauren saw the weaknesses of her own neighborhood, but she also shows the reader the spectrum of lives lived within the city of Robledo. When she goes out of her neighborhood for shooting practice in the nearby hills she notes first "we rode our bikes to the top of River Street past the last neighborhood walls, past the last ragged, unwalled houses, past the last stretch of broken asphalt and rag and stick shacks of squatters and street poor who stare at us in that horrible, empty way, and then higher in the hills along a dirt road" (32), and earlier on her way to church she recounted that "up toward the hills there were walled estates—one big house and a lot of shacky little dependencies where the servants lived" (8). The postapocalypse is already here for Lauren and she sees how it has left people in different places largely based on where they were before the "event."

The reader could read the destruction of Lauren's own neighborhood as the real apocalyptic event. For Lauren it certainly has a much more world ending impact than the destruction that she knows exists outside of her walls. Lauren has known that this destruction was coming in a way not so different from the knowledge that some people had about the meteor strike in *Lucifer's Hammer*. And Lauren does pack for her future, being sure to have not just water and a gun, but also seeds and books about edible plants packed away in her survival pack. But the *Parable of the Sower* is not presenting the destruction of her home neighborhood as the apocalyptic event; just as *Parable of the Talents* does not have the destruction of Acorn as the apocalyptic event. In both novels these events are world changing for the characters involved. But the books also make clear that world ending events are the norm. Each of the characters in both novels has survived multiple, personal "apocalypses:" slavery, prostitution, rape, beatings. Each has seen whatever he or she has called home destroyed and each has seen members of his or her family killed or kidnapped. Compare this to the relative peace and security of the lives of the protagonists of the other novels. The protagonists of Butler's *Parable* series live in a postapocalyptic world and it is only the reader who is lulled into thinking that walled neighborhoods or isolated communities can somehow keep the conditions of postapocalyptic life from violently intruding.

The postapocalypse is not a singular event whose effects can simply be solved by establishing a new system of rules under which the survivors can defeat the enemy and learn to flourish again. Butler understands the readers' expectations from the genre; and she understands the characters' desire to find a safe place. She challenges these expectations by lulling everyone into a sense of false security that will only be shattered. The kind of ending that the *Parable* series presents, the nature of the postapocalypse it reveals, is deeply connected to the very ideas of security and control that the characters in the novels are hoping to achieve. The dual nature of the lulling and shattering, the lulling of the reader and the lulling of the characters happens simultaneously. Part of what lulls the reader, however, is her own condition of relative security (reading a novel) and desire for both resolution and potential peace through the authority of Butler herself.

What is it that comes to an end when the Pox is ongoing? And what does it mean for the Pox to have ended? As in "The Book of Martha" we are seeing here a group of characters trying to deal with what seems to be the most violent outbursts of humanity's adolescence. Earthseed seems hardly sufficient a worldview to convince people that the killing, the torture, the destruction should end. One of the often cited passages of Earthseed speaks to the way in which civilization acts for the group as intelligence does for the individual. But civilization is no guarantee for group harmony or for collective flourishing (89). As with intelligence, civilization can fail. Earthseed provides once again both the analysis and the iatrogenic balm of our desire for peace.

The Pox has produced an example of the failure of the "adaptive function" (89) of civilization, a failure to serve. But it also explains a failure of understanding. Civilization is to be contrasted with its failure, with the classical state of nature that is illustrated in all postapocalyptic novels. Likewise intelligence is seemingly to be contrasted with its opposite, the failure to adapt to the conditions under which one lives. The failure to adapt is the failure to recognize that change will happen and cannot be stopped. Change, in the spirit of Earthseed can only be prepared for or, in the best case scenario, shaped to one's advantage. This failure to adapt is the failure of Lauren's home neighborhood and the failure of Acorn. The ending is thus not wholly external—these novels are not simply describing how people react to climate change, economic downturn and political upheaval or pandemic disease.

The very idea of the end is so clearly the issue of the novels, particularly the *Parable of the Sower*. Many of the earlier novels focused on either the idea of starting over, such that an ending was necessary to get the plot rolling (*Malevil* and *Alas, Babylon*), or on the possibilities that the end might provide in terms of exciting plot twists and pyrotechnics (*Lucifer's Hammer*). Further while war is avoidable the nuclear wars presented in all of the post-nuclear texts considered (including *The Road* and *On the Beach*) are not presented as avoidable. The reasons why a nuclear confrontation both happened and then rapidly escalated to near total destruction are rarely fully explained. Finally no characters in these earlier novels are in a position to do anything about these wars. This is both a part of the often apolitical nature of the characters' pre-war lives and the ideological spin that ordinary people do not stop (or start) war. The *Parable* series, which also focuses on ordinary people (meaning people not directly in political power), have nonetheless both a better sense about the role that human action plays in these ending events and a sense of culpability for such events.

Lauren mentions a brief nuclear war between Iran and Iraq that "scared the hell out of everyone." "After it happened, there must have been peace all over the world for maybe three months. People who hated one another for generations found ways to talk peace" (PT, 90). The consequences of this nuclear exchange, while briefly mentioned and not deeply analyzed, reveal a more realistic response to nuclear war than the usual Cold War madness of mutually assured destruction illustrated in the descriptive move from one nuclear exchange to total destruction within a matter of hours. More than this, however is that this exchange and the other political, environmental and economic disasters that have also occurred are events with causes and effects. They are not simply external chess moves that get the plot of the novel going. Thus for Butler the conditions of life postapocalypse are fully the subject of the novel. And the only thriving community that can emerge from such conditions is one that first recognizes the conditions under which they all live.

Butler and the Postapocalyptic Genre

Social contract thinkers set out a trajectory: state of nature, coming together, social contract, civil society. Postapocalyptic novels use the world ending event to jump start this trajectory. Octavia Butler is using the idea of world ending events for a slightly different purpose than we have seen previously. On the one hand she is engaged in the idea of starting over and the concept of the social contract. On the other hand she is exploring what it means to end and what it means to begin again. The kinds of postapocalyptic events portrayed in earlier novels and the ways in which those characters negotiated for security differ from Butler's use of a series of world ending events in the *Parable* series to also examine security.

Butler's use of these state of nature-like settings mirrors their use by traditional social contract thinkers, although Butler's work reveals these settings as more likely to be stand ins for the conditions under which many already live. The state of nature, for Octavia Butler's novels and short stories, is not simply a hypothetical construct from which we can argue for the legitimacy for a government chosen by the people. In the traditions of the postapocalyptic genre, Butler's novels are both warnings and prescient descriptions of what happens when a combination of events produces disorder.

Finally, Butler does not use the state of nature to celebrate the violence of either an apocalyptic event or the violence of the aftermath of such an event. Butler's novels have their fill of violence. But the reader is never expected to see that violence as mere spectacle. There is little entertaining in it and while that violence is often presented as a fact of life which the characters must simply recognize when the protagonists react violently to violence it is a cause for relief and yet not pleasure. Butler comes close to solving one of the perennial problems of postapocalyptic fiction as utopian possibility. Such novels[8] seem to argue that the utopian present is the result of the apocalyptic violent past—as if the only way to improve the world is through the destruction of some large percentage of humanity. The novels analyzed in the previous chapters follow on this troubling logic when the characters analyze their present situations as revealing a deeper or more real connection to what is important in the world, as if it takes a nuclear war for someone to think about what might make a meaningful life.

Parable of the Talents clarifies this critique of traditional social contract theorizing. The next chapter illustrates the move from a space where vulnerable people come to create community to a set of principles that provide something better than security: a future.

Notes

The chapter title is from Octavia Butler, *Parable of the Sower* (New York: Warner Books, 1993): 74. All passages are from *Parable of the Sower*, unless otherwise noted.

1. Cynthia Enloe, *Globalization and Militarism* (Lanham, Maryland: Rowman and Littlefield, 2007):161

2. There is far more scholarly interest in Butler than the other novelists (other than Cormac McCarthy). Butler was the focus of special editions of *Obsidian III Studies in the African Diaspora* (2005/2006, volume 6/7), *Utopian Studies* in 2008 (volume 19). A full bibliography of scholarly work on Butler can be found in Ritch Calvin, "Octavia E. Butler Bibliography (1976-2008)," *Utopian Studies* 19, no. 3 (Winter, 2008): 485-516.

3. "Essay on Racism," Scott Simon's interview with Octavia Butler (189-192), reproduced in *Conversations with Octavia Butler*, edited by Conseula Francis (Jackson: University of Mississippi Press, 2010).

4. Peter Stillman notes the Hobbesian character of the world in the *Parable* series (Peter Stillman, "Dystopian Critiques, Utopian Possibilities and Human Purposes in Octavia Butler's *Parables*" *Utopian Studies* 14, 2003: 15-37).

5. I often use her short story "Speech Sounds" when teaching Hobbes because its vision of life a few years after a plague that has robbed people of language so well illustrates what a war of all against all might look like.

6. Such persistence in fighting is not just irrational but also immoral. Part of the force of the "chance of success" criterion in just war thinking (a tradition also informative to and informed by Hobbes) is not simply that we do all seek to survive, but that we *should* all seek to survive.

7. Patricia Hill Collins, *Black Feminist Thought* (New York: Routledge, 1990): 105.

8. e.g. Marge Piercy, *Woman on the Edge of Time*, many novels by Sheri Tepper and Leigh Richards, *Califia's Daughters*.

~

CHAPTER SEVEN

"We can choose"

Octavia Butler's Parable of the
Talents *and the Meaning of Security*

Most postapocalyptic fiction, following the framework of social contract theorists, is interested to explore the movement from insecurity to security. Butler's *Parable* series complicates both what produces insecurity and how confident we should be about achieving security. Insecurity is found typically in bodily harm, including the harm of slavery and sexual assault. But insecurity is also found in the purposeful destruction of one's family, in the uncertainty that one's children are safe, in the loss of loved ones. And security, which can mitigate bodily harm and hopefully forestall familial destruction, can do little for loss.

Political psychologists have shown how reminders of our own mortality ("mortality salience") can awaken the desire to protect oneself—to maintain "worldview defense." With the potential for manipulating human behavior based on reminders of death—what might be simply called the politics of fear—what we need and Butler provides, is an ability to see and use fear in other ways. Postapocalyptic fiction is purposefully fear inducing. But the fear produced by postapocalyptic fiction can be used for different purposes and to serve different ends. In some accounts the fear is used to simply reproduce the status quo in a simpler guise (as in *Lucifer's Hammer*); but in other postapocalyptic accounts, like the *Parable* series, fear is a necessary step towards what philosopher Jonathan Lear[1] calls "radical hope": "What makes this hope radical is that it is directed toward a future goodness that transcends the current ability to understand what it is. Radical hope anticipates a good for which those who have hope as yet lack the appropriate concepts with which to understand it."[2] Under situations of fear, radical hope is one possible (and difficult) response. Radical hope allows fear to be the catalyst for working towards a new future. While *Parable of the Sower* showed that fear stems from the multiple ways in which we are vulnerable, *Parable of the Talents* shows how Lauren, from fear, chooses radical hope. In so doing she is entering into a social contract, although one whose guarantees are far less certain than the ones we have seen earlier.

Parable of the Talents disrupts readers' expectations. Neither our expectations for Acorn, the community founded at the end of *Sower*, nor our expectations for *Parable of the Talents* as a sequel are met. Acorn will be destroyed. Larkin, Lauren and Bankole's daughter, and the other children of Acorn will be stolen away from them and placed into adoptive families. Lauren's own journal only comes to the reader through the editing of her unhappy daughter, Larkin. *Parable of the Talents* is a combination of journal entries from Larkin, Lauren, Bankole (Lauren's husband) and Marcus. So the text is complicated by its very presentation.[3] Having read *Sower*, the reader is inclined to read Lauren's journal entries as they were read there, a simple accounting of her life on these dates. But here the reader must remember that Larkin has put together the journal entries. Larkin does not tell us what she is omitting, nor does she explain why she interjects when she does. Larkin's experience of Acorn and Earthseed, her very understanding of who her mother is and what she has accomplished, complicates the reader's desire to see Lauren as the savior of humanity—as the bringer of security.

Security depends on your viewpoint. Lauren and Larkin have different worldviews, each had desires for the other that can never be realized. And so Lauren learns, more painfully than most parents must, that "her" child is simply a person in the world who happens to share a genetic link. More importantly, the reader encounters insecurity not only as a concept but as an experiential component of reading *Parable of the Talents*, and this experience makes the book's rethinking of security more visible.

Parable of the Talents opens five years after *Sower* ended. Acorn is growing and flourishing, taking part in various business ventures, including growing food, repairing tools, making furniture. We quickly learn, however, that this period of relative peace for the inhabitants of Acorn is simply an interlude, and that they will be attacked again, bringing down yet another catastrophe, once Andrew Jarrett, the "Christian American" presidential candidate, wins the election on a campaign promise to "clean up" the country. Acorn is destroyed, its inhabitants enslaved, its children stolen away and "adopted" into Christian American families. The last third of the novel follows Lauren after she and the survivors of Acorn escape their re-education camp three years after they are first attacked.

Parable of the Talents is neither what the reader expects nor what the reader desires. But it is precisely in unsettling our expectations, both for the genre of postapocalyptic fiction and for *Parable of the Talents* as a sequel, that the reader learns that "leaving the nest" means not going home. And leaving the nest means acknowledging the insoluble fear of loss.

Lauren claims, "we can choose."

> We can choose: We can go on building and destroying until we either destroy ourselves or destroy the ability of our world to sustain us. Or we can make something more of ourselves. We can grow up. We can leave the nest.[4]

Choice is an elusive issue in postapocalyptic fiction, particularly in the novels I have discussed here. On the one hand the protagonists are presented with an event about which they had no choice—no opportunity to do anything that might keep that event from happening. Thus the conditions the event creates are simply a given for these characters. On the other hand each account (mirroring social contract thinkers) involves the necessity of the protagonists' choosing to create something new out of the ruins of the destroyed world. Further, the options presented in the novels of many of the earlier chapters are minimal: either they put in with the cannibals, resign themselves to their eventual death, or they organize and fight back.

These minimal choices might be seen as problematic for the very idea of the social contract, although under the conditions of postapocalyptic fiction such choices are rarely going to be made under ideal conditions. Unless the choice procedure is to be seen as wholly abstract, as in Rawls, any actual choice is going to be mediated by the conditions under which the choice is made. Feminist theorists recognize that choice or consent can still be legitimate under constrained circumstances, as long as the integrity and agency of the chooser is acknowledged. But these novels rarely present the choice as constrained, rather they are presented as obvious. It is not a limitation that the farmers in Senator Jellison's valley must choose to either stand with him or face the forced cannibalism of the New Brotherhood Army (or the possibility of starving that winter). The reader understands that choice is clear and the conditions are simply unfortunate. In contrast, Butler explores the constrained choice[5] and the need for Lauren to recognize how the conditions of choice impact what is chosen.

In the passage above, Lauren is posing a choice between the end of the world as we know it or a new beginning. That new beginning is not to be found here on earth, although the consequences of sending some group of humanity to the stars might bode well for those that remain. Lauren wants Len, her new travelling companion, to understand first that each of us must make such a choice and second that simply doing what we have always done and calling it "natural" or the way things were "meant" to be is in fact a choice to destroy us all. Butler seems to be siding here with the *Canticle for Leibowitz* version of the postapocalyptic account where life after the event will simply move back into the track of producing yet another world ending event. Achieving security means avoiding this eternal recurrence of destruction and emergence out of the ashes only to be destroyed again. To explain this choice of a new security that expresses radical hope, I explain how Butler complicates our desire for a happy ending, what rethinking security entails, and how Earthseed as a framework for radical hope grounds a new social contract.

Happy Endings? Achieving Civil Society

Readers of postapocalyptic fiction might ask why survivors come together in the ways that they do. What are the characters hoping to achieve? What does a happy ending look like in postapocalyptic fiction? The general answer to most of these questions is security—people come together to gain security, they hope to live more secure lives after the chaos of the event and its aftermath, and a happy ending is one where such security has been achieved. This happy ending is seen in *Lucifer's Hammer* and *Alas, Babylon*. Both end with the characters having defeated the event's consequences and the enemies that emerged from that chaos. *Malevil* and *Into the Woods* are more ambiguous. But their ambiguity reflects how those novels understand security. Neither saw security as the well being of the community, rather each was looking for security in a transformative experience that would allow the characters to emerge as full human beings, able to obey the laws they gave to themselves. All of these novels have happy endings: we are confident that the characters have what is needed to achieve success.

Parable of the Sower seems to end on this kind of note as well. The characters seem to have found both bodily security and authenticity. The travelers have reached Bankole's land in Northern California. While the house has been burned and Bankole's sister and family are dead the land is fruitful and the area isolated. The group is gaining in cohesion. Perhaps now they can build a community with the walls of isolation. The novel ends with a funeral for all of their dead and a charge: "Let's go back . . . We've got work to do."[6]

We buried our dead and we planted oak trees.

Afterward, we sat together and talked and ate a meal and decided to call this place Acorn. (*Sower*, 295)

A new beginning has clearly begun and given the violence of the road the reader might think that all will now be well. But as the previous chapter argued, even if this was the only book of the series, our expectations for postapocalyptic fiction would have been unsettled. This disruption of our expectations continues in *Parable of the Talents* and the understanding of security that we ultimately gain is far more nuanced than what we have seen in earlier chapters.

The kind of postapocalyptic event matters for the kind of social contract that the characters are able to achieve. Because the characters of the previous novels see the event as wholly external to them, they can react to that event without having to wrestle with that event. All the event does for those characters is produce a string of effects. Those novels approach the apocalyptic event as a kind of survivalist training that sets up the conditions for the survival game. The *Parable* series complicates this survivalism (even while giving better advice than packing spices) by presenting a series of interlocking events that produce more than just a series of effects. Butler explores the idea of cause, without taking the reader into the minds of world leaders or even municipal authorities. By exploring the causes of insecurity we can expand the opportunities for achieving security and further our understanding what security actually looks like.

The *Parable* series is not postapocalyptic because both novels are set after some singular world ending event from which the characters must emerge and survive. Rather there are multiple events, political, economic and environmental. Lauren experiences the destruction of her home community twice. Both the destruction of her Robledo neighborhood and the destruction of Acorn are embedded in a larger context that helps explain the linear move from existence to destruction. But neither of these destructions is enough to describe the novels as postapocalyptic. As I noted in the Introduction, mere catastrophic events do not produce postapocalyptic fictions. Rather there needs to be a clear sense of world ending—both in the sense that humanity has to consider its potential demise and rethink the possibilities of what it means to be human. The *Parable* series presents a postapocalyptic text where Lauren and her followers see "the Pox" even though others may not recognize the conditions under which they live as postapocalyptic.

Earlier novels explain how recognizing the world ending event as world ending facilitates one's ultimate survival. Death comes to those who want to sit and wait for Federal authorities. No one in the *Parable* series really expects the government to do anything to improve their lives, although many wish that it would. The novels do not open into a "normal" world that is destroyed from the outside. Rather the novels open in a world that is recognizable and yet somehow off. This technique is often used in other kinds of postapocalyptic texts[7] that begin years after an event and only slowly does the reader start to understand that the world was once ours and that these characters are humans as we expect humans to be. Instead with Butler we have a world only slightly off—why the homemade neighborhood walls? Why the failures of the municipal authorities? Why lack of electricity and a reliable water source? In the *Parable* series we understand from the start the motivations of Lauren Oya Olamina; what we do not understand are the conditions under which she lives. As those conditions emerge we see that she understands her terrain as postapocalyptic even though she has no pre-apocalyptic life against which to compare her existence.

What Lauren does have is a clear sense of how things could be. She dreams of a better world while still being firmly rooted in the world where she is. She is not pining for a time long gone when the water ran clear and the police came when called. Rather she is able to see that her world is shifting away from what it had been and that while this is happening to her it is not something that anyone else is going to keep from her. The characters of the novels examined in the previous chapters all used the pre-apocalyptic world to organize their postapocalyptic lives. Lauren has a worldview that demands personal responsibility in shaping the understanding of one's existence. "Shape God" means to shape not the conditions of one's life, which may well be out of one's control, but to shape the explanatory power of one's life.

> Black feminist thought . . . views the world as a dynamic place where the goal is not merely to survive or to fit in or to cope; rather it becomes a place where we feel ownership and accountability. The existence of Afrocentric feminist thought suggests that there is always choice, and power to act, no matter how bleak the situation may appear to be. (Collins, 237)

Lauren is expressing this ownership and accountability. She lives in a world where many have given up, and where giving up might seem sensible. One could give up by simply giving in—by merely trying to "survive, fit in or cope." Butler creates Lauren, a character who refuses to simply get by. And she creates for Lauren a worldview, Earthseed, which will give her a grounding from which she can choose and act. This ground is then the framework for the security that Lauren has.

Earthseed, emerging and developing as it is from the mind of a young woman experiencing multiple oppressions, is a potentially utopian outlook that will spur people to rethink the conditions of their lives and their ability, limited as it may be, to change them. Thus Lauren Oya Olamina displays a mindset from which a new social contract emerges.

Rethinking Security

As I noted earlier, the beginning of *Parable of the Talents* might seem to be the happy ending the reader of *Parable of the Sower* desired. Acorn continues to gain new members although those members still tend to be those vulnerable people rescued from the road or the remaining inhabitants of local farms that have been attacked. Acorn has emerged from the ashes of Bankole's sister's house and there is pleasure in seeing a physical space of safety for the characters we saw so threatened in *Sower*. But this safe space will not be as safe as we desire it to be.

A new threat or a "something old" (19) has destroyed a neighboring farm that grew marijuana. The attackers all wear crusader style tunics with white crosses sewn on them. Lauren links these attackers to the victory of a new president, Andrew Jarrett, a leader of the burgeoning "Christian America" movement that seeks to clean up the post-"Pox" landscape. The positive reactions of some Acorn members to Jarrett's election, reflect the realization that Acorn is not a finished product. It is not finished for Lauren because her goal, the Destiny, goes beyond one flourishing community. But more important for others in Acorn is the realization that they have not yet achieved security. Lauren notes that those who approve of Jarrett and his strong arm tactics are "afraid and ashamed of their fear, ashamed of their powerlessness. And they're tired. There are millions of people like them—people who are frightened and just plain tired of all the chaos. They want to do something. Fix things. Now!" (28). This is the same shame that Harry and Travis had to overcome in *Parable of the Sower*—the shame that fear is somehow inappropriate for a man who is caring for a family.

Once Acorn is destroyed, Earthseed must follow a different trajectory. But the principles on which Acorn is founded will be retained. The bounded space in which Acorn was set only seemed to provide security. That space was not secure; however, the principles will be retained in future Earthseed communities. Lauren explains to Dan Noyer exactly what Acorn expects of him and his two younger sisters; in doing so she outlines Acorn's understanding of the principles for security:

"You don't have to join Earthseed," I said. "You and your sisters are welcome to stay. If you decide to join, we'll be glad to welcome you."

"What do we have to do—just to stay, I mean?"

I smiled. "Finish healing first. When you're well enough, work with us. Everyone works here, kids and adults. You'll help in the fields, help with the animals, help maintain the school and its grounds, help do some building. Building homes is a communal effort here. There are other jobs—building furniture, making tools, trading at street markets, scavenging. You'll be free to choose something you like. And you'll go to school. Have you gone to school before?"

"My folks taught us." . . .

"You might find," I said, "that you know some things well enough to teach them to younger kids. One of the first duties of Earthseed is to learn and then to teach." (81)

Initially set out here are the terms or conditions of staying at Acorn. Dan and his two sisters (aged 8 and 7) are asked to heal, to work and to learn. Acorn will provide medical treatment, housing, food, jobs to do and the training to do them well, and schooling. The girls have already moved into a house with another adult member of Acorn while Dan recovers from multiple gunshot wounds. The community understands that healing does not mean simply physically recovering. Rather these children, like most of the inhabitants of Acorn, must learn to live with the loss of their family members and the memories of their rape, capture and death. In time these children will be adopted into the expanded familial structure that Earthseed promotes. Every child and every parent is linked to another set of adults who will commit to the ongoing obligation of familial care. "No one has to take the responsibility of joining in this way to another family, but anyone who does take that responsibility has made a real commitment" (72). Acorn clearly provides the principles necessary for the security of these children. It will protect them, it will nurture them and it will help heal them and focus their energies on the community itself. However those principles will not magically produce impermeable walls.

Dan asks about Earthseed, about whether they will be required to commit to principles beyond the give and take of community building.

"And this? This Gathering?"

"Yes, you'll come to Gathering every week."

"Will I get a vote?"

"No vote, but you'll get a share of the profits from the sale of the crop, and from the other businesses if things work out. That's after you've been here for a year. You won't have a decision-making role unless you decide to join. If you do join, you'll get a larger share of the profits and a vote." (81)

Staying at Acorn requires their presence at the weekly Gathering: a mixture of Earthseed verses, discussion about community needs and aims, welcomings and funerals. Everyone is encouraged to speak at Gatherings and the community does not see these as negatively proselytizing. "You learn, you think, you question. You question us and you question yourself. Then, if you find Earthseed to be true, you join us. You help us teach others. You help others the way we've helped you and your sisters" (84). Lauren fully understands the advantage to involving children from the start in Earthseed Gatherings, but she also acknowledges that the community will not be limited only to fully committed Earthseed adherents.

So Lauren is presenting to Dan a multi-tiered community whose members must all work and learn and protect the community together. But decisions will be made by those willing to commit to the principles of Earthseed and a greater proportion of the community's profit will be distributed to those who have fully committed. Dan and his sisters are welcome to stay as long as they wish and they will earn the profits of their partial membership.

Importantly Dan and his sisters are recognized as full human beings. There is no claim that because they are children they have no say. In this it is clear that for Butler there is no concrete distinction between public and private for Acorn and for Earthseed (this does not mean that there is no privacy). Dan is told of what Acorn can do for him and what the expectations are that Acorn has of him and of his sisters ("finish healing first"). Dan is not passed over as a hindrance simply because he comes into Acorn without his parents. There is little difference between the way that Acorn reacts to Dan and the way that Acorn reacts to potential adult converts. Dan and his sisters are expected to do the work of Acorn and will reap the rewards of that work (to differing degrees depending on how they decide to interact with Acorn).

Acorn is not promoting a guest worker system. Dan is free to join fully at any time (although all members must work for a year to gain profits). He is free to leave at any time, although because of his age Lauren urges him not to go and try and find his teenaged sisters who were abducted when his family was attacked and his parents killed. In fact he ends up sneaking out one night, fearful of being stopped, and he sneaks back into Acorn a few weeks later having found and saved one of his sisters from her captors. That Dan both escapes and returns illustrates that he does not find the requirements of life at Acorn oppressive. Obviously exit usually implies the freedom to walk out the front door, not to sneak out back at night. But Dan seems here to be running to save his sisters—away from restrictions meant to provide him safety. Dan's escape is not a sign that Acorn is oppressive and Lauren admires his desire to help his sisters.

Dan's family was driving north to emigrate to Alaska (which has seceded) in a "housetruck" a kind of armed and armored RV. They were relatively wealthy compared to most of the people living in Acorn (who arrived there on foot). Dan has the innocence of a boy brought up in relative security (as Harry was represented in *Parable of the Sower*). And he is still reliving the visceral horror of seeing his parents shot, his sisters raped and stolen away. Dan understands security as rescuing his sisters—he is not secure until he knows that they are as well. "I shouldn't be here, living soft, eating good food, and reading books. I've been thinking that I ought to be out, looking for my sisters Nina and Paula. I'm the oldest, and they're lost. I'm the man of the family now. I should be looking for them" (85). Lauren replies that the community has already alerted friends in neighboring towns to be on the lookout for Nina and Paula and she tells Dan that she will need his help going to street markets to look for them. But she worries that his sense of old-est child responsibility will push him to do something that she does not see him as responsible for doing. The contract into the Acorn community that Lauren is extending to Dan shares a focus on what Martha Nussbaum calls "capabilities," "what people are actually able to do and to be."[8] By providing Dan and his sisters with a place to live, an opportunity to heal, an education in which they can participate as learners and teachers, a family structure, a voice at the table, Lauren is indicating what people need initially in order to decide their own futures.

When Nina Noyer, who is found by Dan, refuses to go and help her own kidnapped sisters, three years after Dan has died, Lauren notes regretfully that Nina is not Dan. "And Nina Noyer just wanted to get married and settle down with people who could take care of her and protect her. I don't blame her, but I find I don't like her much" (321). Nina wants to re-inscribe a private life wherein she can be protected by males. Lauren did not think Dan was responsible for going out and singlehandedly finding his teenage sister. But she does respect his attempt to find them. Dan was trying to gain control over a bad situation and he was trying to find for himself security in the knowledge that he had done what he could to save his sisters. This is a kind of security, one that links back to vulnerability and to fear, that is largely unaddressed in the other accounts. Dan recognizes that his own security is linked to the fate of his sisters; he cannot live with the knowledge that they might be alive and enslaved. Nina, his found sister, can live with that knowledge. Lauren notes that she "does not like Nina very much" but she also acknowledges that Nina is a person in the world. This is not a relativist rationalization that there is no moral standard by which Nina could be judged and found wanting. Lauren does judge her, she does find her wanting, but she also accepts that this is Nina's choice to make. So again the reader is left with the uncomfortable world where stolen children will not find their parents; where parents will not find their missing children and instead will have to find some reason other than finding their children to continue living. Nina Noyer understands security in the traditional way—she wants someone to take charge of keeping her secure. But most of the *Parable* characters see security as something more robust than this transfer of responsibility.

I argue that security goes far beyond the protection of body or property as seen in chapters 2 and 3 with the Hobbesian and Lockean accounts. Attaining security is elusive and dependent in part on giving up the illusion of control. Security and control go together because control is often the counterpart to security: we feel secure when we are in control or when we have put someone we trust in control. The *Parable* series plays with this desire for control and illuminates the costs that control demands.

Security is the usual answer to the question of why inhabitants of these state of nature like postapocalyptic settings come together. Characters are motivated through fear to desire security; but the conditions under which they live make attaining that security difficult. The characters must struggle with a world turned upside down—food, shelter, injury and sickness immediately come back to the forefront of the characters' minds. Each novel also presents other characters who must be confronted. These "cannibals" are presented in *Lucifer's Hammer*, *Alas*, *Babylon* and *Malevil* as bands of not quite humans who must be defeated in a classic good vs. evil battle. Butler includes cannibals, but their sub-human status is not fully embraced and she understands that there is no grand good vs. evil battle that will result in a happy ending.[9]

Those ashamed of their fear are the usual state of nature inhabitants who desire security and understand that security as secure borders within which one can act as the community dictates. But these characters are the minority in *Parable of the Talents*. For Lauren and most of her Earthseed adherents, security means both more and less than secure borders of one's civil society. This is in part because the limits of one's civil society cannot be secured in the same way that we think of political entities being secured. Further security extends deeply into the interpersonal. The kind of security that this social contract embraces is one that denies a distinction between public and private. Butler shatters our naive dreams of what security looks like while simultaneously outlining the ways in which recognizing interdependence, which is itself based on recognizing vulnerability, can facilitate (if not produce) security.

The desire for security and the drive to join the social contract is itself motivated by control. We feel more secure when we are in control and we choose the social contract—a system where the legitimacy of the government is based on the consent of the people—as an enactment of that control. Butler's *Parable* series offers a chance to work through the idea of control. This focus on legitimacy signals the modern political philosopher. The contention that the political entity must be validated by the people (not by God and not by blood) in order for a state to exist as a legitimate power wielding entity, is the key characteristic that ties modern political philosophers together. This focus on legitimacy is a way that humans seek control. We may see ourselves as largely powerless within our own systems, but we justify those systems because we see ourselves as controlling their existence. I consented to the state and thus I have control over its existence. Butler challenges not simply this illusion of control, but also our very desire for such control. The transition from *Parable of the Sower* to *Parable of the Talents* is a transition from being in control to recognizing that control is elusive and demanding. This is not a message of surrender. Rather this is a message of a clear eyed analysis of what it is that we can and what it is that we cannot control.

Control

I wanted us to understand what we could be, what we could do. I wanted to give us a focus, a goal, something big enough, complex enough, difficult enough, and in the end, radical enough to make us become more than we ever have been. (392)

Lauren uses Earthseed to give humans a task—a meaningful, big, complicated and messy task. The task—preparing humanity to travel and to live on another planet—will give humans a degree of control over their collective future. Thus Earthseed responds to our desire for control, but not in the same way that we retrospectively think that Manifest Destiny provided the illusion of control to individual families moving west. It is important to understand that the Destiny is not only a collective enterprise (as were those moves west) but it is self consciously acknowledged to be a collective enterprise. Individual control is still going to be difficult to find—but a semblance of species control and perhaps security is available.[10]

Butler's work has always revolved around the theme of control. Her characters are often seeking both internal self control and external control of the others who wish to control us.[11] Further her characters desire control over the conditions under which they live, a control that is often elusive and may well be thought of by Butler as illusory. The *Parable* series can be read as a trajectory of attaining and then losing control over one's life and one might conclude that Butler is a kind of theorist of submission. I would not argue that, although I think there are stories where submission plays a larger role than the Parable series,[12] but I do think that Butler has a kind of stoic sensibility when it comes to issues of control. Epictetus famously claimed: "Some things are in our control and others not. Things in our control are opinion, pursuit, desire, aversion, and, in a word, whatever are our own actions. Things not in our control are body, property, reputation, command, and, in one word, whatever are not our own actions" (Epictetus, *Enchiridon*).[13] Epictetus reflects some of Earthseed's ideas about control and nicely illustrates others through contrast. Earthseed recognizes a clear division between what is and what is not in your own control. The very idea that "God is change" reflects the fact of our inability to keep everything the same. The response "shape God" reflects what it is that we can do in the face of a constantly changing world. The idea that "God is infinitely malleable" illustrates that there is so much that people could do; but being able to "shape God" is not quite the same thing as being in control, particularly if your desired control includes a desire to control a believed to be static world.

The list of what is in our control: "opinion, pursuit, desire, aversion, and, in a word, whatever are our own actions" outlines that we control our interior worlds. The list of what is not in our control: "body, property, reputation, command, and, in one word, whatever are not our own actions" reflects our inability to control the interior worlds of others and the decisions others make. The inclusion of both body and property on the list of what is not in our control would seem to shift entirely away from the traditional social contract thinkers' insistence on a natural right to one's own body and its property. Epictetus is not necessarily saying we have no right to our bodies and our property (he has little to say about the idea of rights); rather what he would be saying is that if we do have such a right, such a right exists alongside our having no control over our bodies and our property. This nicely reflects a feminist concern with the idea (and ideal) of autonomy. Further it is illustrated by Butler with the interactions between Lauren and her daughter, Larkin and her brother, Marcus.

Lauren's hyper-empathy syndrome is the best example of what is and is not in her own control. She cannot wholly keep herself from feeling the pain of others. She can limit the impact of that pain, but she will feel it. "I can take a lot of pain without falling apart. I've had to learn to do that" (*Sower*,

9). The pain is still felt, but Lauren learned how to control her response to that pain. Further there is nothing Lauren can do about Marcus' betrayal of her and Larkin; and after the fact there is little she can do to make Larkin understand how much Lauren loved her.

Parable of the Talents is compiled by Larkin, who is renamed Ashe Vere by her adopted parents. Marcus finds Larkin when she is three; he leaves her in her abusive adopted family and tells Lauren nothing. Further when he meets Larkin as a young adult he tells her that her mother is dead. The trio of Lauren/Marcus/Larkin nicely captures the shifting arguments about control and Butler's use of multiple narrative voices itself reflects the elusive idea of control over the story itself. Seeing Larkin/Ashe Vere's response to Lauren and to Earthseed as compared to the reader's immersion into Earthseed from *Parable of the Sower* illustrates quite neatly the ways in which we do not have control over others' reactions to us.

Marcus Olamina is Lauren's favorite brother that she thought was dead after the destruction of her Robledo neighborhood. Zahra had seen Marcus being thrown onto the burning remains of a house and Lauren mourned him as dead. After Acorn had rescued Dan Noyer and his two younger sisters they commit to trying to find Dan's kidnapped teenage sisters and follow a lead into a nearby squatter settlement where a slave holding pimp has a number of young slave prostitutes, one of whom is said to look like Dan's sister. The girl was not Dan's sister, but Lauren is shocked to see that her brother Marcus is one of the slaves. Lauren buys Marcus from his owner and takes him back to Acorn. Marcus has burn scars from the night their home neighborhood was destroyed and numerous STDs from his time as a slave.

He was "collared" as a slave—controlled through the use of a pain and pleasure delivery collar that was controlled by his owner. "These are the rules: Once you've got a collar on, you can't run. Get a certain distance from the control unit and the collar chokes you. I mean it gives you so much pain that you can't keep going. You pass out if you try. We called that getting choked. Touch the collar unit and the collar chokes you . . . and, of course, if you try to cut, burn, or otherwise damage a collar it chokes you" (142). The collar units make wholly real the notion that we are not in control over our bodies. The collar gives the slave owner immediate access to the slave, who is never free from the possibility that the collar around his or her neck will produce pain. Marcus makes clear that he thought the lucky people were those who died from the pain and that he envied corpses that he walked past.

Marcus' arrival at Acorn is bittersweet for Lauren. On the one hand her brother has returned from the grave. On the other hand he clearly dismisses the work she has done to create Acorn and he disapproves of Earthseed, which he had heard of during his time on the road as a "devil worshipping cult." Marcus had preached to groups of squatters before he was beaten into slavery and he wants to resume that preaching in Acorn. He contrasts his own Christian belief with Earthseed claiming it is simply something that Lauren made up. While Lauren is accustomed to this criticism she is also not planning on cutting Marcus any slack for his misunderstandings of their belief system. Further in the days and weeks following Marcus' arrival at Acorn, Lauren is dealing with Dan Noyer's running away to rescue his sisters, her own much desired pregnancy and Bankole's insistence that he and she move to Halstead, a neighboring coastal town that needs a doctor. In the journal entries from December 19 to February 6 Marcus only comes up as a presence in their house who also thinks that Lauren should move to Halstead: "Why do you want to have a baby in this dump? Just think you could live in a real house in a real town" (155). Marcus clearly does not see this as the insult that Lauren takes it to be. She has rescued him and taken him into a community that she and others have created from nothing. But he sees that community as a dump, a rag tag group of cabins built by hand and a multitude of back breaking work, planting, salvaging, fixing tools. Marcus has not found meaningful work at Acorn, work that Lauren believes would help him "get his self respect back and begin to rebuild himself" (165). Marcus is the first character who has not been "seduced" (Larkin's words) by Earthseed and most particularly by Lauren. Despite his being far more vulnerable than many of the people who came to them on the road to Acorn, Marcus is actively rejecting the attractions of Acorn. Lauren cannot understand this, and in not understanding she can do little to convince her brother. Larkin, who eventually gets to know Marcus better than Lauren ever did, does seem to understand somewhat better.

ˈ   Larkin says that Lauren, her mother, "saw chaos as natural and inevitable and as clay to be shaped and directed." "My uncle Marcus, on the other hand, hated the chaos. It wasn't one of the faces of his god. It was unnatural. It was demonic. He hated what it had done to him, and he needed to prove that he was not what it had forced him to become. . . . His gods were order, stability, safety, control. He was a man with a wound that would not heal until he could be certain that what happened to him could not happen again to anyone, ever" (121). Marcus desired control, over himself and over the world. He does not want power; rather he wants an understanding of the world that gives him certainty. Earthseed provides little certainty except that you can act to make the world what you wish it to be. Christianity, on the other hand, offers an already existing framework within which right and wrong, good and bad are unchanging. In that Christian system Marcus, a good looking man with knowledge of the Bible and charisma, can lead people. Marcus must act in such a way that makes his enslavement make sense. Little in Earthseed can do that for him (this lack of comfort is in fact what many Earthseed adherents do find, if not comforting, then at least sense-making). Finally Marcus sees Lauren's rejection of his Christianity as ultimately a rejection of him and the family in which they were raised.[14] When Marcus leaves he does so as if she has evicted him; he blames her and then says that he forgives her for looking out for her community. "I don't blame you. Really. I shouldn't have tried my hand here. I'll make a place for myself somewhere else" (173).

While it is easy to understand Marcus's motivation for leaving Acorn it is harder to understand why he chose not to tell Lauren that he had found Larkin after she was stolen away from Acorn during its destruction and transition into an internment camp for non-Christians and troublemakers. Marcus does not do Larkin/Ashe Vere any favors either, although she does not interpret his failure to remove her from the loveless and sexually abusive foster family she has been given to as his fault. The one thing over which Marcus did have control, seemingly, was the information that he could give to both Lauren and Larkin. And so he tells Larkin that Lauren is dead (never telling her her own mother's name) and he tells Lauren that he has no information about Larkin. By withholding information Marcus can, in his own head, control the situation.

Once Larkin figures out (in her 30s) that the woman who has been so successful with Earthseed is in fact her mother, she confronts Marcus and goes to meet Lauren. But even then Larkin chooses Marcus over Lauren as the only family she has ever known. This intra-family drama is one of the most difficult parts of the *Parable* story to read. It has no happy resolution; no one is ever punished for behaving badly; Lauren is denied the knowledge that her child is alive and the opportunity to raise that child in love. Larkin says to her mother that Marcus was the first person that she felt loved by. "I guess I never loved anyone until he loved me." Lauren replies, "your father and I both loved you . . . we loved you more than you can imagine. . . . I tried so hard for so long to find you." But this is not sufficient for Larkin. "I didn't know what to say to that. I shrugged uncomfortably. She hadn't found me. And Uncle Marcus had. I wondered just how hard she'd really looked" (441). Larkin will not fully admit to herself that her mother's not finding her is connected to Marcus' withholding of that information from Lauren. Like Marcus, who desires a control he cannot have, Larkin desires a mother who does not exist, a mother who would not have been driven by Earthseed to people the stars. Both Marcus and Larkin seek control over Lauren—both want her to be what she never has been, accommodating wholly to the wishes of others. As a reader of the book it is hard to sympathize with Larkin's own argument (in this her attempted control of the text itself fails). The reader knows the raw pain Lauren has over Larkin's loss. The reader also has the somewhat petulant musing of Larkin herself saying that even if her mother had found her Earthseed would still have been her first and better loved child. This drama illustrates how there can be no divide between public and private. Larkin/Ashe Vere thinks that Lauren chose Earthseed (public) over finding her (private) but for Lauren there was no such distinction.

Lauren chose to continue her commitment to Earthseed while still look-ing for her daughter. Larkin here has an expectation (common to many children) that parents simply live for and through their children. Lauren rec-ognizes, in a way far more painful than most parents have to experience, the extent to which she cannot control either the information she so desperately desires about her daughter or, later, the attitude her own child has about her. This connects the theme of control to the theme of security. If we as humans seek control over our lives (and the lives of those we love) and if we understand that the social contract is somehow offering up the opportunity to wield that control, then our security desire also extends beyond not simply one body and property but to other bodies about whom we care.

Lauren knows that in their minds she has failed both Marcus and Larkin, and she knows that little can be done to solve that. While watching the first liftoff of an Earthseed spaceship with Harry and other Earthseed adherents related to the survivors of Acorn, Lauren notes, "My Larkin would not come. I begged her, but she refused. She's caring for Marcus. He's just getting over another heart trans-plant. How completely, how thoroughly he has stolen my child. I have never even tried to forgive him" (446). This journal entry comes 24 years after Larkin finds her mother. Larkin, who controls the story, includes few journal entries after that finding and the reader jumps those 24 years in a few pages.

And so Lauren ultimately focuses on what is in her own control and with the help of the many allies that she and Len find on the road, Earthseed begins to spread and ultimately flourish in a new way. Larkin's description of the Earthseed and its many communities in the decades after Acorn's de-struction explains Lauren's new method of letting Earthseed spread without her direct influence.

Earthseed was an unusual cult. It financed scientific exploration and inquiry, and technological creativity. It set up grade schools and eventually colleges, and offered full scholarships to poor but gifted students. The students who accepted had to agree to spend seven years teaching, practicing medicine, or otherwise using their skills to improve life in the many Earthseed communi-ties. Ultimately the intent was to help the communities to launch themselves toward the stars and to live on the distant worlds they found circling those stars. (415-16)

Earthseed is out to help itself. The newly trained doctors and teachers are to move to Earthseed communities, surrounded by people who share the new doctors' and teachers' belief systems. They are not to radically shift all of American (or world) society towards colonization of space. Instead they will work towards the stars despite the problems they find at home. When Earthseed adherents look to the future they are not looking to earth, and thus non-Earthseed participants see the efforts and resources as being wasted on "nonsense," according to Larkin (416).

While we see little of the rise of Earthseed after Acorn's destruction and we learn little about how others beyond Marcus and Larkin view it, what is clear is that Lauren is moving forward with Earthseed. In doing so she is moving forward with a kind of social contract that will be open to those willing to adhere to its parameters. Yet Lauren is happy to have Earthseed simply co-exist among those who refuse to enter that contract. Earthseed is contracting to create a community, a kind of civil society. And yet its understanding of civil is radically different: both because it exists within and alongside a state whose re-emergence we barely see and because it is a civil society that will leave earth and seek to flourish elsewhere. This concrete disembarkation from earth means that Earthseed seeks to bypass politics as we understand it, states as we understand them and national security as a model of communal security.

The *Parable* series follows the scripts of the earlier postapocalyptic accounts: start with someone that you get to know, end that person's world as they know it, connect that person up with others and have them struggle to come together and realize that they are better off working together than they are battling apart. The first *Parable* book could be read as just a better version of that very trajectory. But with the addition of *Parable of the Talents* there is the complicating feature of further destruction and the realization that coming together against the outside world is not going to produce the security one desires. Further by looking at Earthseed and Acorn's destruction through the gaze of Larkin/Ashe Vere, we see a different perspective both on the vision of security that Lauren has and on the experience of that security by her daughter.

Destiny as Radical Hope

Lauren uses Earthseed to connect the loss of an idea of the future ("vision") to the rule of emotion. And "when emotion rules alone/ destruction . . . destruction (239).

The connection between vision, direction and purpose illustrates a spectrum of necessary components for producing a changed world. The danger, the insecurity, is that when vision, direction and purpose are not harnessed or worse are wholly abandoned then the negative counterpart, emotion, takes over. This reference to emotion is an interesting modern move. The social contract thinkers all abide by the classic reason/emotion binary. The reference to emotion here as the potential source of "destruction . . . destruction" reveals Butler as a deeply modern thinker. This is why Butler is the right author to compare to the novels previously discussed. Like those novels, the *Parable* series is concerned with why and how people should come and live together under some sort of governing structure. And yet the *Parable* series is not a paean to reason. The emotion/reason binary is complicated here.

First, the danger is when "emotion rules alone" without the guiding power of vision, direction and purpose—all characteristics that are connected to reason, but that need emotion as well to focus and shape those energies. Second, it is not clear that reason is the counterpart to emotion here. Vision, direction and purpose are all posed against emotion alone. But vision, direction and purpose are not simply manifestations of rationality. This is clear in Lauren's discussion with Bankole about moving to Halstead—Bankole uses reason to outline the advantages that Halstead has over Acorn, and he is rationally correct in his assessment. But Lauren's retort uses both reason and emotion to clarify that security means thinking about the future and not simply the present.

The very idea of the Destiny shows the ways in which Butler understands security to mean something more than a cessation of bodily harm. "The Destiny of Earthseed is to take root among the stars" (446). The vision, direction and purpose of Earthseed is to eventually produce the colonization of space. How is this related to security? Because it helps produce the kind of people who will understand what kinds of conditions are needed in order to succeed at such an impossible task. In challenging the religious idea of heaven, Earthseed is out to produce an alternative where one's effort fully matters.

There is security in the Destiny. It may not be very comforting, but the Destiny provides security in the one issue that all of postapocalyptic fiction explores: the very idea of a future. For the reader of postapocalyptic fiction the fear it motivates is not so much a simple fear of death, rather the fear is in the fragility of humanity. Each of the novels discussed in this book raises the possibility that humans as a species could simply die out. *On the Beach* does this most obviously by having the main characters all die within the text itself. Likewise *The Road* does it by making clear that there simply are no means to survive in a world absent any living entity other than a few surviving humans. *Lucifer's Hammer, Alas, Babylon* and *Malevil* (beyond a few pensive journal entries by Thomas) do not dwell on the death of humanity, but each book has its moment of considering the overall impact of the post-apocalyptic event. In *Alas, Babylon* one of the children matter-of-factly notes "if I grow up" (225) and Randy recognizes this as a potential new reality in a post nuclear world.

The Destiny provides a future. First presented a year after the opening of Lauren's journal, she presents the Destiny as "the birthday gift that came into my mind as I woke up—just two lines." Lauren understands the enormity of what this would mean "right now, it's also impossible." And she concludes this initial realization of the Destiny "I don't know how it will happen or when it will happen. There's so much to do before it can even begin. I guess that's to be expected. There's always a lot to do before you get to go to heaven" (Sower, 75). So from the start Lauren sees the Destiny as a heaven stand in. Also the realization of the Destiny is clearly a comfort to her, although she will learn that others will not find the idea of preparing to colonize space as particularly comforting. She presents it as a "birthday gift" and it is a gift that Lauren wants to both savor and explore more fully. She continues throughout both novels explaining and justifying the Destiny because it is the part of Earthseed (next to the idea that God is change) that people balk at, reject and even ridicule.

The connection between the Destiny and security is hinted at above: "there's so much to do before it can even begin." This sentiment—this requirement—for human effort is a relief in a world where it seems that nothing can be done to improve anyone's situation. Bigger walls, more guards, better drills are not going to save Lauren's Robledo neighborhood. Likewise having better walls (in their isolation), more guards and better drills does not help Acorn. But Earthseed does help the people who lived in Acorn to survive after their destruction, enslavement and degradation over the two years that Christian American troops occupied what was Acorn and turned it into a re-education camp. Lauren explains what the advantages of the Destiny are to many of the potential Earthseed adherents. As the Destiny was discussed earlier in relation to fear, here too we can see that the justification for the Destiny is a justification based on attaining security:

> The Destiny is important for the lessons it forces us to learn while we're here on Earth, for the people it encourages us to become. It's important for the unity and purpose that it gives us here on Earth. And in the future, it offers us a kind of species adulthood and species immortality when we scatter to the stars. (170-1)

The Destiny provides the vision, direction and purpose noted in the quote beginning this section. The Destiny gives a goal that requires people to work together; it requires the changes that Lauren, and more importantly Lauren's followers, put into place in the *Parable of the Talents*. The Destiny does not make individual humans invulnerable. But the Destiny does provide humanity itself with more security than it currently has.

Before Acorn's destruction, Lauren is not wholly focused on the Destiny. Her focus is perhaps too narrow and her thinking too blinded by their isolation and better drills. When she repeatedly replies to Bankole's desire to move to a small town where he could be town doctor and Lauren could be a teacher and they could avoid the attention that Earthseed, "that cult," is getting from the new Christian fundamentalist president, Lauren returns to the security that Earthseed and the Destiny provides, a security wholly absent in these small towns. "None of them is trying to build anything to replace what we've lost or to boost us to something better" (PT, 158). Bankole wants Lauren and their baby to be safe; but Lauren does not see that version of safety as security. Bankole tells her that she would have no problem doing the teaching that Halstead needs.

> "You should be able to do it in your sleep after what you've had to put up with in Acorn."
> "In my sleep," I said. "That sounds like one definition of life in hell."
> He took his hands off my stomach.
> "This place [Halstead] is wonderful," I said. "And I love you for trying to provide it for the baby and me. But there's nothing here but existence. I can't give up Acorn and Earthseed to come here and install a dab of education into kids who don't really need me."
> "Your child will need you."
> "I know." (154)

Bankole is providing what the characters of all of the previous novels, excepting perhaps *Into the Forest*, would have jumped at: A town, isolated and potentially safe from attack. A house and a job. A means to provide for her family in the most straightforward ways. But Lauren is not looking for this kind of safety. And Lauren does not see this as a form of security. She criticizes such towns for not going beyond mere existence. As with her home neighborhood in Robledo, Halstead is biding its time until "things" get better. Lauren recognizes first that she has no desire to wait. She wants to act, knowing that the opportunity to promote and shape change is present when so much is in disarray. Further the very idea of biding her time challenges the very philosophy that Earthseed promotes.

The *Parable* series explores the difference between the soluble insecurity of fear and the insoluble insecurity of loss. Lauren's Robledo neighborhood was insecure because the adult inhabitants kept thinking that if they hunkered down out of the gaze of those willing to use violence then the world would become a better place. That insecurity stemmed from a failure of vision, direction and purpose, a failure that was both rational and emotional. Acorn struggles with not failing in this way. They have the vision and the purpose. But they also exist within conditions that are, if not wholly out of their control, are not wholly within their control. The election of President Jarrett has freed the violent urges of Jarrett's crusaders and has provided a justificatory legitimacy to their actions. Acorn is defeated both by a greater power, one that could overrun their carefully planted thornbush fence and system of alarms and emergency drills and by a time of chaos that justified such a use of force as the only way to achieve security. Acorn was attacked as "that cult" and its inhabitants were collared, enslaved, and raped, beaten and killed.

Acorn is attacked by people who have a "vision, direction and purpose." Jarrett's crusaders see themselves as cleansing Acorn and its inhabitants of their sin. This "destruction . . . destruction" is not the result of mere emotion; it is a calculated attack that results in the kidnapping of all of the children of Acorn. Most of these children will be forever lost in the system of Christian America's foster homes. Larkin won't find her mother until she is 32, a lifetime after Acorn's destruction. The radical insecurity that Jarrett's crusaders bring to Lauren, Bankole (who is killed in the initial attack) and Larkin illustrates that security for Earthseed and its followers will have to mean something more than their just having vision.

Jarrett's crusaders seek to do more than simply punish Lauren and her followers for the sin of their "cult." The crusaders are out to degrade and destroy any vestige of hope that the followers of Acorn has that their worldview could ever flourish. By stealing all of the children, changing their names and placing those children up for adoption in Christian American homes, Jarrett's crusaders have taken away one of the most successful attributes of Earthseed—its focus on children. When Lauren and the surviving members of Acorn escape from "camp Christian" after a mudslide disables the slave collars that they have all been wearing, they gather around the hidden caches of supplies in the hills and distribute foot prints and birth certificates of the stolen children. But only after Justin Gilchrist (the 3 year old boy rescued from the highway ten years earlier) finds Lauren, himself after escaping from the Christian American home to which he had been sent, does Lauren learn that the children's names have been changed. After escaping from physical degradation the survivors of Acorn are faced with the insecurity of their lost children.

This kind of insecurity has not been addressed in earlier novels even though postapocalyptic fiction clearly involves scenarios where families are threatened and potentially separated. *The Road* can be read as a meditation on the insecurity of parenting under dire circumstances. But I have argued that its circumstances are so hopeless that shifting from the insecurity of a wholly dead world inhabited by organized and well fed cannibals to the security of a newly discovered cache of canned foods is unlikely at best. *Parable of the Talents* explores a different kind of insecurity of parenting. Here we see that security might well mean living with one kind of insecurity while struggling to focus on another. Larkin describes Earthseed as Lauren's real child and first child. She believes that her mother did not search long enough to find her and in the end, she rejects her mother in favor of Marcus, who betrayed Lauren by finding Larkin when she was three and never telling Lauren of his discovery. This betrayal illustrates another form of insecurity that is wholly real but not necessarily soluble. We can find alternative sources of fuel, or even set up a network of schools that could lead to the potential colonizing of space, but we cannot guarantee that brothers will not betray sisters or that individuals will not be convinced to follow tyrannical leaders out of "fear and depression/ . . . need and greed" (*Sower*, 91). Even the readers are betrayed in their desire to see the lost children of Acorn found. Other than Justin and Larkin, who importantly find Lauren themselves, no other sign of any of the other children of Acorn is found. Neither the reader nor Lauren nor any of the other parents ever discover what happened to their kidnapped children.

Earthseed cannot solve fear, but it can solve the shame of being afraid. Earthseed cannot make someone secure, but it can provide a purpose larger than your own individual life that can expand your understanding of security. "Earthseed was always true. I've made it real, given it substance. Not that I ever had a choice in the matter. If you want a thing—truly want it, want it so badly that you need it as you need air to breathe, then unless you die, you will have it. Why not? It has you. There is no escape. What a cruel and terrible thing escape would be if escape were possible" (444-5). Lauren's understanding of escape here and the role that Earthseed has played in her life recalls the stoic understanding of control discussed above. Lauren wanted to find Larkin, but finding her daughter is not the kind of "thing" mentioned above that "unless you die, you will have it." This is what Larkin cannot understand (and likely will not understand if she remains childless and largely alone, other than Marcus). Larkin and Marcus clearly see the trip to the stars as the escape—an escape from the problems of earth and a refusal to spend the time and energy on those problems. Beyond that they see the journey to the stars as an affront. For Marcus, Earthseed has always been an affront to their upbringing and to Christianity. For Larkin, Earthseed is an affront to her very existence. She will never be able to think of her mother as her mother; instead Lauren will always be Earthseed's founder, and Earthseed will be her "first child." Psychologically Marcus and Larkin seek to control Lauren in order to gain their own security—without that control they can only reject her.

Earthseed counsels that we should not seek the kind of control that Marcus and Larkin want over Lauren. Yet if Earthseed is the answer to the social contract—if it is what we are to contract for—then the novel again challenges our expectations by refusing to let us see Earthseed getting to the point where the Destiny might be something reasonable to affirm. We see Lauren and the others attacked in Acorn, enslaved and degraded. We see them leave Acorn/Camp Christian. And we see Lauren and Len on their first journey north gathering converts to Earthseed and looking for clues about Larkin. But we never see the moment where the contract is affirmed. We never see the moment when Earthseed communities—a civil society embedded in the larger fabric of disarray—establish themselves.

What we do see at the ending of *Parable of the Talents* is the spaceships leaving earth. The very first step of the destiny is achieved. It is a satisfying moment even while Lauren disdains the ship's name: Christopher Columbus, "I object to the name. This ship is not about a shortcut to riches and empire. It's not about snatching up slaves and gold and presenting them to some European monarch" (445). But she also notes, "one must know which battles to fight" (445). These ships are leaving only because of the efforts of thousands of Earthseed converts, most of whom we do not know. And we know (both as readers of Butler and because Lauren reminds us) that all will not be well among the stars.

Butler challenges our expectations. She does this on purpose and she does it subversively. On purpose because the reader must then fill in the blanks, the reader must decide how Earthseed would succeed and why. Subversively because Asha Vere/Larkin knows how this has happened. She has denied to the reader precisely the information that the reader of postapocalyptic fiction wants: The climax where all can step back and say "this is what we have created, now we are home again."

For Butler we cannot go home again and attempts to simply remake "home" from the ashes of a world now gone will simply recreate the conditions that destroyed both Robledo and Acorn. "We'll not go home again" means both that we cannot go home again and that we should not go home again—we have chosen not to go home and if we plan to go anywhere it will be someplace other than where we have been.

Notes

1. Jonathan Lear, *Radical Hope* (Cambridge Massachusetts: Harvard University Press, 2006): 103.

2. Lear's book presents the Crow nation at the time of their demise. He argues that Plenty Coups, the leader of the Crow presented a narrative for Crow survival. This argument for survival represents "radical hope."As a child, Plenty Coups had a dream that the Crow elders interpreted as indicating the death of the buffalo and the incursion of white people and their cattle into the lands of the Crow. This dream heralded a recognition that the traditional Crow way of life as a warrior was coming to an end. In a world without buffalo, a world imbued with a different set of rules, there was going to be no way to be Crow as they understood it. And so, in response to Plenty Coups dream, the Crow were told "to think for himself, to listen, to learn to avoid disaster by the experiences of others. He was advised to develop his body but not to forget his mind. The meaning of this dream is plain to me. I see its warning. The tribes who have fought the white man have all been beaten, wiped out. By listening as the Chickadee listens we may escape this and keep our lands" (Lear 72). Counseling a shift to the ways of the Chickadee provided a potential new way of living. This way of living has nothing to do with the planting of coup sticks and the ethos of courage that had identified the Crow. The chickadee listens and "in all his listening he tends to his own business" (70). Once Plenty Coups became chief he advocated living in the way of the chickadee, listening for a moment when the Crow could emerge in a new way of life. It is important to see that the chickadee is not simply a model of living while biding one's time. Rather, the chickadee is the method by which one attains radical hope. Through fear of the destruction of his way of living, Plenty Coups was able to advocate a method of stepping back and rethinking their way of life in these new conditions.

3. Patricia Melzer addresses these multiple narrative voices in her essay "'All that You Touch You Change': Utopian Desire and the Concept of Change in Octavia Butler's Parable *of the Sower* and *Parable of the Talents*," *Femspec* 3, issue 2, (June 2002).

4. Octavia Butler, *Parable of the Talents* (New York: Warner Books, 1998): 393. All passages are from *Parable of the Talents*, unless otherwise noted.

5. I thank Jamie Huff for working through the idea of this constrained choice. A constrained choice does not deny the agency of the chooser, although it fully recognizes the extremity of the conditions under which the chooser is choosing.

6. This ending is reminiscent of Candide's ending calling for everyone to return to the garden in order to "work without arguing." *Parable of the Sower* is in many ways the anti-Candide.

7. For example: Russell Hoban's *Riddley Walker*, Walter Miller's *A Canticle for Leibowitz*, P.C. Jersild's *After the Flood*, Jim Crace's *The Pesthouse*.

8. Martha Nussbaum, *Women and Human Development* (Cambridge and New York: Cambridge University Press, 2000): 5 and Nussbaum, *Frontiers of Justice* (Cambridge, Massachusetts: Harvard University Press, 2006): 70.

9. Here the *Parable* series acknowledges the complexity of security noted by Cynthia Enloe: "Security turns out to be a broad, many-layered goal. It can no longer be imagined as simply synonymous with militarized security. Security, many women activists working to end armed conflict in various countries have concluded, has to be seen more realistically and more broadly, and that means it has to be seen as more complicated" (Enloe, 132)

10. We will never know what Butler had in store for the Earthseed colonists after they left Earth. But any reader of Butler would recognize that the trip to the stars will not be easy and that both the unintended consequences of their actions and the unknown will produce conditions that we cannot yet imagine. I read Mary Doria Russell's *Children of God* and *The Sparrow* as Butlerian accounts in their own exploration of the unintended consequences that are produced when human ignorance is let loose on another planet.

11. As Lillith in *Dawn*, the first novel of the Xenogenesis series, controls some of her initial job by carefully choosing who to release from sleep first.

12. For example, "Bloodchild," "Speech Sounds" and "Amnesty," all collected in the *Bloodchild* volume (2005), all concern the idea of submission.

13. Epictetus, *Enchiridon* in *Internet Classics Archives*, translated by Elizabeth Carter, Ch. 1. <http://classics.mit.edu/Epictetus/epicench.html> (March 7, 2010).

14. If the character of Lauren Oya Olamina is to be a model for anything it is this: she lives her life without thinking that the choices of others are somehow always reflections on herself. She is dismayed by what Marcus and Larkin have done. But she does not obsessively expect that others will live their lives in such a way that she will be able to feel good about herself.

~

Epilogue

Postapocalyptic accounts are clearly popular. I started this project in the spring of 2007. Since that time we have seen Disney enter the postapocalyptic genre with *Wall-E* (2008). The animated film 9 and the film adaptation of *The Road* appeared in 2009, and 2010 opened with *The Book of Eli*. Recent popular novels have included Stephen Baxter's *Flood* (2009) and William Forstchen's *One Second After* (2009),[1] which Warner Brothers has optioned for a movie. *Publisher's Weekly*[2] recently noted a rise in what it called dystopian young adult fiction, citing several postapocalyptic novels: Michael Grant's *Gone*, Susan Beth Pfeffer's *Life as We Knew It*, Suzanne Collins' *Hunger Games*.[3] NBC plans a mid-season show entitled *Day One*, which will follow a group of survivors from a single apartment building in California. This list, which is already selective, does not yet include a burgeoning trend in postapocalyptic video games.[4]

If there is anything that links all these disparate works together, it is sheer violence, the massive destructiveness of the apocalyptic event. What I have not really confronted in this book is the very idea that we *would be* attracted to stories that demand the destruction of the majority of the population in order to begin again. There is something morally repulsive about these stories, where the lesson of the simple life of satisfying hard work takes a nuclear cataclysm to learn. The stories are often strange fantasies of destruction and domesticity, of massive violence and then the satisfaction of building a new world. Yet it is hard for me, at the end of this project, to simply dismiss the genre as the potentially reactionary, surely violent, morally suspect genre that it is. This difficulty in dismissing the genre out of hand is rooted in two impulses. First, I am a fan of the genre and I would like that fandom to be rooted in something other than my own potentially morally suspect characteristics. Second, I am convinced that approaching the genre for what it is can help us clarify our own personal and political desires.

Is there something irresponsible and grotesque about analyzing postapocalyptic accounts in depth? The world already has more than its share of problems. The imagining of how things could become desperately worse is surely little solace to those who have already had their worlds shattered through war, disease, famine or natural disaster. What sort of impulse compels so many readers to consume these narratives of devastation? Is there an ethics of the postapocalypse? I would argue that the specific works I have analyzed in this book, those postapocalyptic novels that take up the question of how to begin again, are precisely those that give the space for an ethical perspective on the (fictional, it is important to recognize) violence of the apocalyptic event. Rather than simply dwelling on and inevitably glorying in the facts of destruction, these novels raise important questions about our expectations for a flourishing community—and thus, ultimately, about our own contributions to the violence that can bring about our destruction. So even when these novels fail spectacularly in their answers to *how* a community can flourish, that they even raise the question moves the conversation forward.

These novels should be the subject of analysis because they reflect the most basic question of political philosophy: how can a group of people, with disparate aims and interests, live together peacefully? The mechanism for asking this question is artificial, fictitious and violent, but each of these novels (even those that reject any potential answer) confronts the question itself. The novels that answer this question offer a surprisingly limited range of political possibilities. It is as if our cultural imagination is stuck in a loop of what we have already said and done. This is why Octavia Butler's work is so important. She rethinks not only how we might live together peacefully, but also who gets to decide what that peaceful living together might look like.

What is problematic in these novels, particularly the ones in chapters 1-4, is not just the gratuity of their violence. They are problematic in the very way in which they confront the social contract. *Lucifer's Hammer* is problematic on many levels. Simply dismissing it as a particularly violent example of the postapocalyptic genre misses that its deepest problems lie in its use of the Hobbesian social contract to justify the eradication of the cannibals. The novel's rejection of the possibility of starting over alongside cannibals, who just happen to be black, turns genocide into a "rational" move to protect the new community Senator Jellison is leading. The novel does not just destroy every African-American character: it does so through a script that presents that destruction to the reader as perfectly sensible.

Reading these problematic texts through the lens of a critical social contract reveals just where these stories can go wrong. *Alas, Babylon* does not just illustrate a Lockean mindset; the novel also portrays this mindset as perfectly consistent with racial and gender hierarchies. One can argue that the women and African-Americans of the story (and the poor white residents of Pistolville) never consent to the contract that is created in Fort Repose. But the more important point is that in the novel, their lack of consent is never seen as problematic. It is perfectly consistent with the logic of the story that the children, the women, the Henrys and the residents of Pistolville do not need to be asked. Their subordination has been evident throughout the text, which simply presents the legitimacy of Randy Bragg's rule as perfectly normal.[5]

Octavia Butler's *Parable* series models the radical hope necessary to find a new way of living together. Essential to this hope is a recognition of what has gone wrong. This means not simply facing up to the harms of the apocalyptic event. It also means facing up to the harms of the ways of living together that exacerbated that event. The apocalyptic events of the *Parable* series are not all human-made, but they are all made worse by humans. They are all made worse by hierarchies, by bigotry, by discrimination, by oppression. The radical hope that Lauren exhibits is one based in an uncertainty about how we can overcome this oppression. But part of her hope is that she has faced up to many modes of that oppression, even though it is not clear that the Earthseed community may not simply produce new forms of oppression in space.

Lauren's hope is different in kind from the optimism of the main characters of the novels discussed in the earlier chapters. In those novels we saw main characters, like Randy Bragg, who found new meaning and purpose to their lives after the apocalyptic event. Randy Bragg is not concerned with uncertainty because he believes that a solution will be found to the myriad problems facing his Fort Repose community, whether that solution is finding a salt lick or defeating the highwaymen. Likewise the end of *Lucifer's Hammer* makes clear that the future is certain: electricity has been saved, the enemy has been defeated (and as in *Alas, Babylon*, the survivors will prove to be better and stronger than any who survived with the direct assistance of the U.S. government). These novels use the social contract as a mechanism to show the legitimacy of the communities created after the end. The *Parable* series retains a focus on a key feature of the social contract, the importance of consent and participation, while injecting a measure of uncertainty about both the outcome of that contract and the universality of its appeal.

Notes

1. *The Flood*, which has received a lot of positive buzz in science fiction circles, spans a 50 year period of radical sea rise, ending with humans migrating to space and the rest living on boats. It is an oddly apolitical text. There are few overt discussions about how to live together as most people who survive do so by allying with the wealthy who have foreseen disaster and bought land in the highest mountains. *One Second After* is a classic Hobbesian postapocalyptic account following an EMP pulse that wipes out all electrical circuits. This novel follows a small college town and their need to protect themselves from city refugees.

2. The article describes the attraction of such novels as both political and sociological: "After 9/11, it seemed people started thinking about the destruction of the world," says Karen Grove, who edited Susan Beth Pfeffer's *This World We Live In*, the April 2010 release that will end the trilogy that started in 2006 with *Life As We Knew It*. "Then we got hit with New Orleans and earthquakes." Uncertainty plays a role, too. "There's so much mystery about what the future will hold," says Lauri Hornik, president and publisher of Dial Books for Young Readers and Dutton Children's Books (quoted by Karen Springen in *Publishers Weekly*, February 15, 2010).

3. *Gone* involves the disappearance of all adults and is more *Lord of the Flies* than classic postapocalyptic. *Life as We Knew It* is the first in a trilogy outlining life after the moon is hit by an asteroid, moving it closer to earth and wreaking havoc on earth. *Hunger Games* takes place hundreds of years after an apocalyptic series of events and details a dystopian and fractured United States. These young adult novels are an interesting aspect to the postapocalyptic genre. Focusing on teenage protagonists, the novels move away from a focus on building political communities to simply building a small scale communal system for day to day survival. Carrie Ryan's *The Forest of Hands and Teeth* is on the *New York Times* Bestseller list.

4. One website for videogames lists 94 games with a postapocalyptic concept. http://www.giantbomb.com/postapocalypse/92-600/ (retrieved March 5, 2010)

5. In teaching this novel, both to first year students and to senior political science majors, I was surprised to see the degree to which they did not even notice that the story ends up with Randy in charge, the women in their place, the Henrys ignored and the residents of Pistolville essentially erased. That Randy is in charge is simply presented in the text as the most obvious answer. And the subordination of other characters is hardly worth noting because it is in no way presented as a problem—the women seem to consent, by their very willingness to follow Randy. Likewise the Henrys seem to consent by their very contributions to the community.

Bibliography

28 Days Later. Director Danny Boyle. Distributed by Fox Searchlight Pictures. Released November 1, 2002.

2012. Director Roland Emmerlich. Distributed by Columbia Pictures. Released November 13, 2009.

Abbot, Carl. "The Light on the Horizon, Imagining the Death of American Cities." *Journal of Urban History* 32, no. 2 (January 2006): 175–99.

Atwood, Margaret. *Oryx and Crake*. New York: Nan A. Talese, 2003.

———. *The Year of the Flood*. New York: Nan A. Talese, 2009.

Baxter, Stephen, *Flood*. New York: Penguin Group, 2009.

Beck, Stefan. "A Trackless Waste." *New Criterion* 25, no. 2 (October 2006): 78–79.

Beidler, Philip. "Remembering *On the Beach*." *War, Literature and the Arts, an International Journal of the Humanities* 21 (2009): 370–382.

Berger, James. *After the End: Representations of the Post-apocalypse*. Minneapolis: University of Minnesota Press, 1999.

Booker, M. Keith. *Monster, Mushroom Clouds, and the Cold War: American Science Fiction and the Roots of Postmodernism, 1946–1964*. Westport, CT: Greenwood Press, 2001.

Breslin, John B. "From These Ashes." *America* 196, no. 3 (January 2007): 27–28.

Brin, David. *The Postman*. Toronto, New York: Bantam Books, 1985.

Brinkley, William. *The Last Ship*. New York: Ballantine Books, 1989.

Butler, Octavia E. "Amnesty." Pp. 147–86 in *Bloodchild*. New York: Seven Stories Press, 2005.

———. "Speech Sounds." Pp. 87–110 in *Bloodchild*. New York: Seven Stories Press, 2005.

———. "The Book of Martha." Pp. 187–213 in *Bloodchild*. New York: Seven Stories Press, 2005.

——. *Dawn*, vol. 1 of *Xenogenesis*. New York: Aspect/Warner Books, 1987.

——. *Fledgling*. New York: Grand Central Publishing, 2007.

——. *Parable of the Sower*. New York: Aspect/Warner Books, 1993.

——. *Parable of the Talents*. New York: Aspect/Warner Books, 1998.

Callenbach, Ernest. *Ecotopia*. New York: Bantam Doubleday, 1977.

Chabon, Michael. "After the Apocalypse," *New York Review of Books*, February 15, 2007, 54.

Christopher, John. *Wrinkle in the Skin*. Brooklyn, New York: Brownstone Books, 2000.

Collins, Patricia Hill. *Black Feminist Thought: Knowledge, Consciousness, and the Politics of Empowerment*. New York: Routledge, 1991.

Collins, Suzanne. *The Hunger Games*.Scholastic Inc. New York: 2008

Connors, Philip. "Crenellated Heat," *London Review of Books* 29, issue 2, January 25, 2007, 15–16.

Crace, Jim. *The Pesthouse*. New York: Random House, 2008.

Curtis, Claire. "Theorizing Fear: Octavia Butler and the Realist Utopia." *Utopian Studies* 19, no. 3 (2008): 411–431.

——. "Ambiguous Choices: Skepticism as a Grounding for Utopia." Pp. 265–82 in *The New Utopian Politics of Ursula K. Le Guin's* The Dispossessed, edited by Laurence Davis and Peter Stillman. Lanham, MD: Lexington Books, 2005.

Davis, Mike. "Culture Wars: Why L.A. is Synonym for Disaster," *LA Times*, August 16, 1998, 1 (H).

Day After, The. ABC Television Network. Producer William Hughes. First Aired November 20, 1983.

Day After Tomorrow, The. Director Roland Emmerlich. Distributed by Twentieth Century Fox. Released May 28, 2004.

Enloe, Cynthia. *Globalization and Militarization: Feminists Make the Link*. Lanham, MD: Rowman & Littlefield, 2007.

Estabrook, Robert H. "After Armageddon," *New Republic*, August 12, 1957, 20.

Foertsch, Jacqueline. "'Extraordinarily Convenient Neighbors': African-American Characters in White-authored Post-atomic Novels." *Journal of Modern Literature* 30, no. 4 (Summer 2007): 122–38.

Forstchen, William R. *One Second After*. New York: Forge Books, 2009.

Francis, Conseula, ed. *Conversations with Octavia Butler*. Jackson: University Press of Mississippi, 2010.

Frank, Pat. *Alas, Babylon*. Philadelphia: Harper Perennial Modern Classics, 2005.

Grant, Michael. *Gone*. New York: Harper Collins, 2009.

Hegland, Jean. *Into the Forest*. New York: Bantam Books, 1996.

Herbert, Frank. *The White Plague*. New York: Bantam Books, 1982.

Hoban, Russell. *Riddley Walker*. Bloomington: Indiana University Press, 1998.

Hobbes, Thomas. *Leviathan*. Indianapolis/Cambridge: Hackett Publishing, 1994.

Jacobs, Robert A. "'There are No Civilians; We are All at War': Nuclear War Shelter and Survival Narratives during the Early Cold War." *The Journal of American Culture* 30, no. 4, (December 2007): 401–16.

James, P.D. *The Children of Men*. New York: Alfred A. Knopf, 1993.

Jericho. CBS Paramount Network Television. Executive producers Jon Turteltaub, Stephen Chbosky, and Carol Barbee. Broadcast on CBS from Sept. 20, 2006 to March 25, 2008.

Jersild, P.C. *After the Flood.* New York: Morrow, 1986.

Keren, Michael. "The Original Position in Jose Saramago's *Blindness.*" *Review of Politics* 69, no. 3 (Summer 2007): 447–63.

King, Stephen. *The Stand.* New York: Penguin Group, 1991.

Kunstler, James Howard. *The World Made by Hand.* New York: Atlantic Monthly Press, 2008.

Kuznick, Peter J. "Prophets of Doom or Voices of Sanity? The Evolving Discourse of Annihilation in the First Decade and a Half of the Nuclear Age." *Journal of Genocide Research* 9, no. 3 (September 2007): 411–41.

LaHaye, Tim and Jerry Jenkins. *Left Behind: A Novel of the Earth's Last Days.* Tyndale House: Carol Stream, Illinois (1996).

Lear, Jonathan. *Radical Hope: Ethics in the Face of Cultural Devastation.* Cambridge, MA: Harvard University Press, 2006.

Locke, John. *Second Treatise on Government.* Indianapolis, Indiana: Hackett Publishing, 1980.

Macomber, Shawn. "Life after Death, Cormac McCarthy's Post-apocalypse Western." *Weekly Standard* 12, issue 20 (February 2007).

Mad Max. Director George Miller. Distributed by Village Roadshow Pictures. Released April 12, 1979.

Mad Max 2: The Road Warrior. Director George Miller. Distributed by Warner Bros. Released December 24, 1981.

Mad Max Beyond Thunderdome. Directors George Miller and George Ogilvie. Distributed by Warner Bros. Released July 10, 1985.

Mannix, Patrick. *The Rhetoric of Anti-nuclear Fiction.* Lewisburg, PA: Bucknell University Press, 1992.

McCarthy, Cormac. *The Road.* New York: Random House, 2006.

Melzer, Patricia. "'All that you touch you change': Utopian Desire and the Concept of Change in Octavia Butler's *Parable of the Sower* and *Parable of the Talents.*" *Femspec* 3, no. 3 (June 2002): 31–52.

Merle, Robert. *Malevil.* New York: Warner Books, 1975.

Miller, Walter. *A Canticle for Leibowitz.* New York: Bantam Books, 1976.

Mills, Charles W. *The Racial Contract.* Ithaca: Cornell University Press, 1997.

Mills, Charles W. and Carole Pateman. *Contract and Domination.* Cambridge: Polity, 2007.

Mitchell, Richard G. *Dancing at Armageddon: Survivalism and Chaos in Modern Times.* Chicago: University of Chicago Press, 2002.

Morton, Oliver. "In Retrospect: *Lucifer's Hammer.*" *Nature* 453, no. 7199 (June 2008): 1184.

Moylan, Tom. *Scraps of the Untainted Sky: Science Fiction, Utopia, Dystopia.* Boulder, CO: Westview Press, 2000.

Niven, Larry and Jerry Pournelle. *Lucifer's Hammer.* New York: Random House, 1985.

Nussbaum, Martha Craven. *Women and Human Development: The Capabilities Approach*. Cambridge: Cambridge University Press, 2000.

———. *Frontiers of Justice: Disability, Nationality, Species Membership*. Cambridge, MA: Belknap Press of Harvard University Press, 2006.

Outterson, Sarah. "Diversity, Change, Violence: Octavia Butler's Pedagogical Philosophy." *Utopian Studies* 19, no. 3 (2008): 433–56.

Pateman, Carole. *The Sexual Contract*. Stanford: Stanford University Press, 1988.

Pfeffer, Susan Beth. *Life as We Knew It*. Boston: Houghton Mifflin Harcourt, 2008.

Piercy, Marge. *Woman on the Edge of Time*. New York: Fawcett Crest, 1983.

———. *He, She, It*. New York: Alfred A. Knopf, 1991.

Porter, Jeffrey. "Narrating the End: Fables of Survival in the Nuclear Age." *Journal of American Culture* 16 (Winter 1993): 41–47.

Rawles, John Wesley. *Berkeley, CA: Patriot*. Ulysses Press, 2009.

———. *How to Survive the End of the World as We Know It*. New York: Penguin Group, 2009

Rawls, John. *Theory of Justice*. Cambridge, MA: Belknap Press of Harvard University Press, 1971.

———. *Political Liberalism*. New York: Columbia University Press, 1993.

———. *Justice as Fairness: A Restatement*. Cambridge, MA: Belknap Press of Harvard University, 2001.

Richards, Leigh. *Califia's Daughters*. New York: Bantam Books, 2004.

Road, The. Director John Hillcoat. Distributed by Dimension Films. Released November 25, 2009.

Rosen, Elizabeth. *Apocalyptic Transformation: Apocalypse and the Postmodern Imagination*. Lanham, MD: Lexington Books, 2008.

Rousseau, Jean Jacques. *Emile*. New York: Basic Books, 1979.

———. *The Social Contract and Discourses*. London: Everyman's Classics, 1973.

Russell, Mary Doria. *The Children of God*. New York: Villard, 1998.

———. *The Sparrow*. New York: Villard, 1996.

Shute, Nevil. *On the Beach*. New York: Ballantine Books, 1974.

Sponsler, Claire. "Beyond the Ruins: The Geopolitics of Urban Decay and Cybernetic Play." *Science Fiction Studies* 20, no. 2 (July 1993): 251–65.

Stillman, Peter. "Dystopian Critiques, Utopian Possibilities and Human Purposes in Octavia Butler's *Parables*." *Utopian Studies* 14, no. 1 (2003): 15–35.

Terminator, The. Director James Cameron. Distributed by Orion Pictures. Released October 26, 1984.

Wagar, Warren W. *Terminal Visions: The Literature of Last Things*. Bloomington: Indiana University Press, 1982.

Weisman, Alan. *The World Without Us*. New York: Thomas Dunne Books/St. Martin's Press, 2007.

Wilhelm, Kate. *Where Late the Sweet Birds Sang*. New York: Orb Books, 1998.

Williams, Walter J. *The Rift*. New York: Eos/Harper Collins, 2005.

Wood, James. "Getting to the End." *New Republic* 236, issue 4813, May 21, 2007, 44–48.

Index

~

About the Author

Claire P. Curtis works on utopian and dystopian fiction and its significance for liberal political theory. She has published essays on Octavia Butler, Marge Piercy, and Ursula Le Guin. She has taught at Vanderbilt University and Reed College; she is currently associate professor of political science at the College of Charleston in Charleston, S.C.